J.G. REESE

Flamebound

A Thrones of the Veil Novel

First published by J.G. Reese 2025

This novel is entirely a work of fiction. The names, characters, and incidents portrayed in it are the work of the author's imagination. Any resemblance to actual persons, living or dead, events, or localities is entirely coincidental.

J.G. Reese asserts the moral right to be identified as the author of this work.

First edition

ISBN: 979-8-9934331-1-0

Editing by Gabrielle Gentilucci

This book was professionally typeset on Reedsy.
Find out more at reedsy.com

For my sister, you were there when this story was nothing, just an idea born during a hurricane. You are also the reason it found light. This book exists because you believed that I could.

Blood remembers what the soul for-
gets.
In the weaving of the Sanguis bond,
there is no beginning and no end—
only the endless return to the one
who calls you.

- Ancient Veythari Verse

Authors Note

Please be aware that his book contains mature themes and moments of graphic content. While I hope readers can immerse themselves in the story as it unfolds, I want to gently note that this book explores sensitive subjects, including death, immense grief, suicide (with descriptive detail), and periods of extensive violence.

In addition, this story includes explicit sexual content and mature romantic themes intended for adult readers.

Please take care while reading.

Solvane
Human Lands
Nocthallow
Vampire Lands
The Spire
Eryndalis
Veythari Lands
The Embers
THE LANDS OF THE VEIL

Prologue

ZYRENNA

Alira's scream ripped me from sleep.

I was on my feet before the echo of my name faded against the walls; the lavender oil Father used to burn still clung faintly in the cottage air. Moonlight spilled across the floorboards, pale and silver, the kind of light that made the world look softer than it was.

Her voice came again—sharper, frayed at the edges—carrying through the quiet. I crossed the narrow hall in three strides and found her tangled in her blankets, shoulders jerking, fingers clawing at sheets she couldn't seem to escape.

"Alira," I said, crouching at her bedside. My voice softened into something steady. "Breathe. You're safe. It's me."

Her eyes flew open, wet and glassy, hair plastered against her forehead in messy waves. She wasn't small anymore—she'd outgrown half her dresses this winter—but in the throes of a nightmare she looked younger, like the girl I'd once carried on my hip. Her breath came fast, chest rising in uneven bursts.

"I saw her again," she whispered.

I sat on the edge of the bed and pulled her against me. She fit awkwardly now, long limbs and sharp elbows that didn't tuck neatly into my arms the way they once had, but I held her anyway. "I know," I murmured into her hair. "I know."

There was always a stillness after nightmares, when your body hasn't yet caught up with your mind. Beyond the window, the sky stretched clear and starlit, the kind of night that felt too gentle for the memories we carried.

Alira swallowed hard, her voice steadier but low. "It was the Crimson House."

I stroked her hair, forcing my own voice to stay calm. "It's only a dream."

But it wasn't, and both of us knew it never had been.

We were there the day Mother walked into those marble halls.

The Crimson House on Cindral Street gleamed like a sanctuary, its domed roof throwing colored light across the square, its attendants moving with ritual precision. Everything about it was crafted to reassure. To promise safety.

Mother had smiled when she told us to wait outside with Father. "I'll be out soon," she said, trying to sound braver than she felt.

We listened for the door. We listened for the bells.

But when the bells tolled and the doors opened, it wasn't her who stepped out.

A vampire emerged, leather gloves and a black hood obscuring his face. His voice was smooth as he offered practiced words—a miscalculation, he claimed, followed by a hollow apology. The attendants froze, still as stone.

Father made a sound I'd never forget. A sound I didn't think a human could make. I didn't look at him. I stared ahead, rigid, my mind already stitching together the truth before anyone said it aloud.

Three days later, we laid her to rest beneath the vineyard. Father knelt, planting rosemary by her stone—her favorite scent—soon replaced by lavender, to mask the grief that clung like smoke. He tried to be strong for us; he tried to be everything.

But I could see how the pain consumed him, and when winter came, the nightmares took him first.

CHAPTER ONE

ZYRENNA

Winter glassed over Solvane that year—the year everything fractured. Frost clung to the vineyard, turning the dead vines brittle and white, the cottages covered with snow and silence. Even the air felt thinner, every breath stinging my chest.

One night, nearly two years before, I watched Father walk out to the barn. By morning, the lantern inside was dark, and a note waited for me on the workbench when I went to find him. The ink had blurred where a stray tear must have fallen across the page.

I am sorry. I cannot hold it.

There is a kind of rage that does not burn hot. It settles cold instead, creeping through marrow, impossible to thaw. That rage took root in me the moment I folded the note.

It is the kind of rage that forms when the person meant to protect you instead abandons you. When the hands that should have built a wall around you let it all collapse instead. Fathers are supposed to bear the weight, to keep the storm from breaking their daughters. Mine chose to step into it and leave us behind in the wreckage.

The world calls it grief, but mine never softened. They say it fades into memory, into what we hope becomes eventual

4

acceptance. This wasn't that. This was something more, something that made the breath burn in my lungs and made my skin feel too tight around my body. This was the kind of rage that remakes you, that drives your hands to finish what was left behind, that binds you to wounds you never chose.

I carried the note to the vineyard that day, where rosemary grew at the base of the olive trees, and pressed it into the earth next to my mother's stone. The soil was hard from frost, my hands raw and red by the time I covered it again, but I did not stop. I wanted something—anything—to feel the weight I felt. I wanted the earth itself to know.

I promised then what Father could not: I would hold it. For Alira, and for what remained of us.

***

"Zyrenna?"

Her voice tore me from the memory.

Alira was still curled beneath her blanket, shoulders tense, eyes wide and glassy in the dark. Fourteen now, she was stuck between child and woman, her frame too tall for last year's clothes, yet her face held a softness grief had not yet stolen.

"You're crying," she said.

I touched my cheek, surprised to feel it wet. I didn't cry, not where anyone could see. The humiliation hit instantly. My stomach knotted, the sting of weakness hitting like an old wound torn open again. I wiped my face quickly and forced a shaky smile. "Am I? How rude of it to escape."

Her lips twitched with reluctance. "That's stupid."

But it made her laugh just a little, even if it was broken, even though it trembled. I tucked the blanket under her chin, and smoothed back her hair. My own hair fell forward, jet-black until the moon caught it and the strands flashed with a sheen like spilled starlight. Mother used to call it my night veil, as if the sky kept a hold on me. Something that always made me stand out from other mortal humans, but something I learned to appreciate about myself nonetheless.

Alira's gaze softened, the fear in her eyes dimming but not dissolving.

"Thank you," she said below a whisper. "Thank you for staying."

"There is nowhere I'll go that you can't follow me," I promised.

Her gaze lingered before she let out a shaky breath. I stayed sitting beside her, brushing her hair until her breaths steadied. The cottage creaked around us with the sighs of winter. The silence settled thick, but my mind refused to rest, drifting back to Father's note, to both their graves, to the vow that seared through me since.

The part of me that owed that vow to Alira wasn't born simply of blood. I had been loved before—truly—by both of my parents. But even when they were alive, Alira had always been mine in a way no one else was; she was my girl long before she was all I had left. Now she was the only piece of that life still breathing, the only love I had that had not been twisted by power or buried under loss. Everything else had changed shape or been taken; she alone remained unchanged. Protecting her was not a duty. It was the only way to keep the part of me alive that had not already gone to ruin.

* * *

Real sleep never came back to me—not since that winter. Not the kind that leaves you whole in the morning.

On my desk, half-buried beneath loose parchment, lay the contract I had once seen Mother holding.

The parchment was stiff when I pulled it free, the seal of the Crimson House stamped in deep red wax. A chalice and a seven-pointed star, their holy mark of balance.

The script was mercilessly clear:

Vein offering, voluntary. Payment upon completion. Age verified: twenty-four. First offering: scheduled at the first bell, Monday.

The words blurred as I stared at them.

Most humans gave by bloodbag—permitted at eighteen—safer, more sterile, and provided enough coin for bread, though bread didn't stretch far anymore. Not with colder days pressing through the shutters. Not with the vineyard Father left behind failing. Not with debts piled higher than the firewood stacked against the wall. The roof was splitting plank by plank, and I would not be the reason Alira went hungry while I gambled on safety.

Direct vein offerings paid more.

And I needed more.

The law said no human could be offered from the vein until twenty, a safeguard etched after the Blood War. I was twenty-four now, well past the threshold. It was legal on paper, yet most people avoided it if they could. Only the desperate or the reckless bared their skin. I was desperate enough. Direct vein offerings sustained us with enough wealth to breathe another week.

It is only the wealthy families—those with influence old enough to matter—who are granted the indulgence of drinking from the direct human wrist.

A privilege they called it. A blessing. Ironically, though, it was also the thing that killed my mother.

I pressed the contract flat on the desk and signed where my name was meant to live. **Zyrenna Vaeoria**. When the ink dried black, I let myself shake. Just once.

The wind shifted, and the candle on my desk flared, the flame stretched long as though bending toward an unseen breath. A scent rose in its wake; ancient and new at once. The hair on my arms lifted, and for a heartbeat it felt as if the night itself tilted toward me, listening.

The Veil.

Some called it God, while others simply called it the shadow of one. I didn't know what it was, only that it was said the Veil's presence wound through the world like unseen roots beneath stone, threading into everything. Stories claimed it spoke in silences—in shivers beneath the skin, in the pressure behind the ribs, in the certain knowledge that you were being noticed.

I could never dictate if it was real—the Veil, the watching—only that, sometimes, the world felt too aware.

My parents had always believed in it. My mother prayed to it every dawn; my father swore its presence kept the sun rising and the rivers full. Faith in the Veil was the marrow of our house, a trust threaded through our blood.

And yet, somewhere between the loss and injustice, that faith had begun to rot.

My pulse hammered in my throat. Instinct screamed at me to bow, to flee, to fall to my knees toward whatever it was that lingered in the air. I did none of those things. I stayed very still, forcing my voice low and steady.

"Watch all you want," I whispered to the stillness. "But you will not touch her. You will not take anything else from me."

The candle steadied. The whisper vanished, leaving the air with the heavy emptiness I often felt here now.

I folded the contract, its edges stiff beneath my fingers, and set it back on the desk. The seal caught in the candlelight; a reminder of who we had all become powerless to. The vow burned through me again, relentless as ever.

In a few hours, the bells of the Crimson House would toll.

And I would bare my skin to them—to the vampires who destroyed my family.

Not for devotion, and certainly not for peace.

For Alira. For the roof above us. For survival. For the promise I refused to let die.

CHAPTER TWO

ZYRENNA

I woke unrested—as I had every morning, tossing and turning through the night—minutes before the bells sang.

For a breath, I lay still, watching the way dawn seeped through the shutters. The light spilled soft across the wooden floor, painting it with threads of pink and violet, the colors so delicate it almost felt cruel. I let myself pretend, just for an instant, that morning could be ordinary; that it was just another day in Solvane. But memory waits like a patient predator, and it never failed to catch me.

Today would not let me forget.

I rose, pulling the faded ash-gray dress from the chair at the foot of my bed. The fabric was worn soft from years of use, but it moved easily over my skin. Comfortable, familiar. I freed my hair from its knot, letting it spill down my back in a dark cascade. It framed my face, soft where everything else in me felt honed.

In the mirror, I caught my own reflection: hair dark as ink until the light lit it into silver sparks. Eyes too pale for Solvane—eyes more silver than blue, looking like coins struck from moonlight.

Alira used to tease me for them. We were always together—

two girls trailing our father through the vineyard at first light, our fingers stained with grapes as we tried to keep up. Most children did the same if their parents were fortunate enough to earn outside the Houses, for work came before schooling for all of us. Mother taught us letters and scripture at the table, but it was the vines that shaped our days.

Alira laughed through the work. I was always my mother's daughter—quiet, and orderly. She was the steady one in our house, and I loved the calm discipline that settled around her because of it. So I carried that sense of control from the time I was old enough to understand what it did for us.

But after everything broke, control stopped being a choice. It became survival—not about keeping a home serene, only about staying upright in the ruins. That lesson has lived in me ever since—a resilience I was forced into.

The contract slid into the bag at my hip, its seal heavy as though it carried a weight far beyond coin. I tied the clasp shut, then moved—movement was easier than breathing. Stopping meant thinking. I closed the door behind me, the latch clicking loudly enough to feel like a warning.

* * *

The first ring shook the air as I crossed the square.

The sound rolled through the streets, vibrating against pale white cobblestones, settling into the hollow of my chest. My boots struck against the stone, each step echoing louder than it should, as though the whole city leaned in to listen.

Mornings in Solvane were always my favorite, though it never kept an honest season here. Some weeks the air would be soft, warmth would curl through the valley, shutters would yawn open, the scent of bread and fruit carrying down the streets. Then, without warning, the wind could shift—and by the next sunrise, there could be frost biting at the vines, snow pooling in the gutters. When snow did come, it lingered for weeks. No one in Solvane questioned it; the land had always worn its seasons of its own accord.

The vineyard depended on mercy—mercy of the Veil, if one believed in such things—and mercy rarely lasts. A few weeks of winter was my father's worst nightmare. When the frost held, and the vines and coin would dry up, it meant Mother was forced to make more trips to the Houses. Father never went. He only tried once; an old strain on his heart dropped him mid-trial, and the House marked him unfit for life. None of us ever understood why. Which is why he worked himself to the bone to keep the vineyards alive—to spare my mother even a fraction of the hell those trips put her through.

Somehow, hardship never dulled Solvane's beauty—it only made it sharper by contrast. Beautiful things always seemed more dangerous when paired with hunger.

There was no denying it; this week, the air felt caught between moods—warmth still clinging to the valley while a much cooler chill threaded through it. Children darted down the lanes, shrieking with laughter as they chased each other, voices scattering like birds. The laughs disappeared not a minute past when the sun went down. That was a non-negotiable here—night belonged to the vampires.

But then again, so did dawn. So did daylight. So did every fucking thing that was supposed to be ours.

Morning light gilded every rooftop, turning the patched shutters and beams into something almost holy.

Not today.

Today those sounds and scents were knives, cutting deeper with every step. The baker setting out loaves caught sight of my cloak. His eyes flicked to the bag at my hip before he turned quickly, pretending to fuss with his bread. Two older women whispered on the corner, voices pitched low but not low enough to keep me from hearing the pity in them. Their gazes slid across me like hands.

Personally, I hated pity.

Pity meant people had already picked out an ending for you—already imagined the way your story would unfold. And I refused to let anyone script my fate before I even stepped through those damn doors.

But part of me understood it. No one ever said it aloud, but everyone knew what it meant to walk toward the Crimson House at first bell. The first and last bell were the only hours reserved for direct vein offerings; all others belonged to bloodbags. Even that was something the Houses measured and controlled.

It rose at the end of the lane like something too beautiful to be trusted. The familiar domed roof caught the dawn, its stained-glass scattering blues and greens across the square, painting the stones in fractured light. From the outside, the Crimson House could almost be mistaken for a sanctuary, with white marble pillars and archways carved with patterns. A facade of purity, of safety, but everyone knew better. Only predators bothered to decorate their traps.

On the way, I passed the war memorial—white stone, smooth as bone, etched with names of the dead. The Blood War still cast its shadow, though a century had passed. Children left flowers at its base, told by parents to honor what they could not understand.

I remembered standing there once with Father, his hand heavy on my shoulder as he whispered the names of men carved into stone. His voice had broken on one of them. I had stared at the letters, trying to imagine the faces they belonged to, but ghosts don't wear faces.

They only weigh on the living.

History clung to us still.

It was said so much blood was spilled during the Blood War that the earth itself threatened to empty. Villages burned. Cities crumbled. Hunger gnawed until even vampires, so certain of their immortality, began to dwindle. A single vampire outweighed a dozen men, but there were always more men, and so the scales tipped back and forth until neither side could hold them.

When extinction loomed, desperation carved the world anew. As a result, the Treaty of Seven Thrones was born—a pact meant to confine chaos, to keep balance. Seven seats carved into law: three for vampires, two for humans, one for the dwindling Veythari, and one left empty for the Veil. The Council ruled from the Spire, the center of all lands, while Crimson Houses were raised in every human settlement like monuments. Places where humans could bleed under contract instead of blade, where vampires were meant to feed with restraint instead of slaughter. In return, vampires swore to police their own kind, to ensure the old bloodbath never returned, with the Spire watching to make certain no vampire "stepped" out of line in Solvane. And for our cooperation, we were paid coin for feeding them ever so graciously. Amazing deal, really. Who wouldn't want to bleed for pocket change?

Compliance was enforced the same way everything else was—on paper. Every household was required to produce at least one donor each month to keep their protection under the Treaty. In truth, one offering a month barely bought bread, which meant most families bled every week just to stay alive. Only those with another source of income could afford to stretch the time between visits. If too many months passed without an adult stepping forward, the obligation shifted to the eldest of age in the line. Refusal was not tolerated. Families who failed their quota were marked non-compliant, stripped of protection, and left to whatever fate found them outside the law.

They called it salvation—some even called it balance. But to me, the Treaty was nothing but a piece of paper meant to keep us from all dying out at once. They are predators, and we will only ever be prey in the eyes of monsters.

* * *

The closer I got to the House, the heavier my body felt.

I clenched my hands together at my waist to still the tremor in them. Each step up the marble stairs felt like lowering myself into a grave. My heart thudded once in protest, then twice in reminder: this was for Alira. Everything was for her.

The doors opened wide as I reached them, groaning open to reveal a hall bathed in crimson light. Sun through stained-glass poured over the floor like spilled rubies. The air was colder here, edged with the metallic tang of old blood scrubbed but never gone.

A Crimson House attendant stood at the threshold, red robe pooling around his ankles, hood shadowing his face.

"Contract?" His voice was smooth, rehearsed.

My fingers locked tighter around the parchment as I handed

it over. His gaze flicked to my name, and he nodded once before stepping aside.

"The attendant inside will assist you," he said, already turning away as the final bell rang for the hour.

Inside, benches lined the walls. A few humans sat waiting, each clutching contracts like lifelines. A woman twisted her wedding band round and round her finger, lips moving in silent prayer. A young man, barely of age, no more than twenty, stared at the floor as if looking up would break him. His hands shook around the parchment in his lap. All attendants who worked at the Houses were vampires; they drifted like ghosts, gliding across stone, robes whispering with each step.

At the center of the hall, the dais rose, the place where offerings were made.

And beside it, an attendant waited next to two men.

The one on the left tilted his head as I entered, hunger etched hard in his expression. His eyes clung to my throat like teeth already buried there. He shifted slightly, as though scenting the air. My stomach knotted, but I refused to flinch—I lifted my chin instead. My mother's ghost walked beside me, and Alira's future anchored me forward. I would not cower.

The man on the right stole the air from the room.

Strands of dark hair fell over his brow, softening nothing about him. His skin was bronzed, not like most vampires. Ink climbed the column of his throat in dark, razor-clean lines, disappearing beneath a cloak the color of a starless night. The cloak itself was cut to show status—lined in silver, and fastened with a clasp.

His eyes—green, searing—locked on me in an instant. He didn't blink. A smirk touched his mouth—lazy, confident, the kind that could undo a person if they let it. The kind of expression that said he already knew the effect he had on anyone foolish enough to look too long.

Heat climbed up the back of my neck, but in an instant I forced my gaze away, willing my steps forward.

Father's apology echoed in my ears; Mother's rosemary filled my nose. Carrying both with me, I walked toward the dais.

And still, when I dared another glance, his eyes were on me, measuring and weighing. As though deciding whether I was prey, or something that might bite back.

CHAPTER THREE

RHAELIN

Crimson Houses always attempted to smell clean.

They flood the halls with incense and boiled citrus, scour the marble until it gleams, and pretend polished stone can drown what's soaked into it. But no matter how many candles they burn, I smell the truth. Blood never truly fades—not for vampires. It clings in the cracks, in the grain of the benches, in the breath of attendants who've learned to keep their faces still.

I stood at the dais, hands clasped behind my back, while an attendant recited the report. Sweat darkened the collar of his robe, and the paper trembled in his grip. A pattern I've begun to recognize every time I ask for the books. Guilt has a scent; fear carries further.

"Councilor Rhaelin Morrain," he said, voice fluttering. "The fatalities are... regrettable, but rare."

"They are not regrettable." I let the words fall flat and cold. Even the candles seemed to lower their flames. "They are violations. Call them what they are."

He swallowed, eyes moving down the column of ink where three names had been marked—three losses this season alone. The attendants never note the sound a father makes when he learns a door will never open again, nor the emptiness that follows—the way a mother folds in on herself, trying to fill the space her child once held.

"We've increased supervision," he whispered. "Retraining has begun. It was—"

"What it was," I cut in, "was fucking preventable."

He bowed his head. Silence—wise, for once.

The House doors opened on a draft. Despite a century of discipline, my attention turned before thought could catch it.

A woman stepped in.

Plain cloak. Simple dress. The kind worn by those who hoped the world might overlook them. But the room shifted around her as though it inhaled. Light fractured through the stained-glass overhead, scattering blues and greens across the marble; when it struck her hair, raven strands flashed silver, starlight catching fire. She lifted her head—and met my gaze.

Silver-blue eyes—rare, unforgettable. Eyes I hadn't seen in decades.

For a heartbeat, the whole House leaned toward her. Attendants stilled. Humans looked up. A part of me despised them for seeing her at all.

Something violent and quiet stirred—an instinct I'd buried straining toward the surface. Hunger I'd kept muzzled for a century snarled awake simply because she looked at me without fear. No—more than without fear. With heat. With disdain. With a steadiness most humans lose the moment they smell iron in the air.

Footsteps approached on my left, but I didn't turn.

A small, edged smile curled at my mouth before I could stop it—the kind that warns more than it welcomes.

She tore her gaze away first.

"Name," the attendant beside me asked, though his voice carried little authority now.

She handed over the contract without hesitation.

"Zyrenna Vaeoria," he murmured. "First offering."

Zuh-ren-nuh.

The syllables slid into me like a blade being sheathed.

"First offerings are my favorite," drawled a voice to my left.

Varik.

He stepped forward from where he'd been lingering—a shadow made of arrogance and rings he never earned. His dirty-blonde hair fell to his shoulders, catching the House's crimson light. A predator who savored fear more than the feast itself; Houses attract his kind like rot attracts flies. Fortunately, they are also the kind I most enjoy fucking with.

He didn't look at me. He never does at first.

Men like Varik believe a room belongs to them simply because someone once told them it did.

He took Zyrenna's contract from the attendant without asking, scanning it as though the letters were his by right.

"A first offering," he said, loud enough for her to hear. His fangs clicked faintly when he smiled. "Fortune favors me."

My jaw tightened.

The attendant recoiled half a step, paper raised like a shield. Whispers rippled across the benches.

Zyrenna did not move.

Varik paced closer, savoring how humans shrank back to give him space.

"You're prettier than most," he crooned. "Don't worry, little lamb. I'm very gentle."

Her face tilted; silver eyes sparkling.

"Drop the theatrics," she said. "You talk too much for

someone who wants to be thought of as dangerous."

Something old in me shifted. That dark pull, yes—but something else. She had fire.

Varik's smile thinned. His hand reached for her wrist.

I moved before thought.

"Enough."

The word cracked against the marble.

Varik froze mid-reach. Slowly, impossibly slowly, he turned toward me.

"Councilor?" he questioned, disbelief stretched thin across the syllables.

The room braced. Humans went still. Even the incense-heavy air tightened. Zyrenna's gaze flicked from him to me—recognition widening her eyes as she understood exactly who had intervened.

One of the Seven.

I stepped down from the dais, each footfall an echo that filled the chamber.

"She is not yours."

"By contract, she is," Varik replied. His tone brightened with false innocence. "Unless you intend to void the Treaty today."

The Treaty of Seven Thrones.

Men like Varik leaned on its letters when they believed it protected them—and ignored its weight when it required restraint.

I reached him and took the contract from his hand without touching him.

"She is reassigned," I said.

A vein jumped in his jaw.

"To whom?" he asked, the words almost obscene.

"Anyone but you."

Color rose under his skin—an ugly flush.

"Is this your district now?" he murmured. "News must travel slowly from the Spire."

I let the nearest attendant see me smile, because he would understand it as a promise rather than a threat.

"The law is the same in every district," I said. "She is reassigned."

Varik's gaze cut to Zyrenna, then back to me, calculation replacing contempt.

"You forget yourself. We are not in Council chambers."

I let my eyes wander deliberately across the benches—humans clutching contracts, shoulders tight, shame pinching their mouths. A woman pressing her thumb so hard into her seal that wax smeared. A young man's knee bouncing, tendon standing out like a cord.

Then, without looking at him, I murmured,

"I'm going to give you one chance to repeat that."

Silence knifed through the room.

Slowly, I turned to face him—quiet, composed.

Varik didn't answer.

I closed the distance between us, until he could feel the weight of what he'd awakened.

"No?" I asked. "Lost your courage?"

He didn't move. Didn't speak.

Only clasped his hands behind his back, knuckles whitening.

He twitched toward her.

I didn't lift my voice.

"Varik."

His name became a warning, a promise, a final mercy.

A nail hammered through arrogance.

The attendant found his courage on the back of mine.

"Per the Councilor's authority," he announced, far louder than intended, "this offering is reassigned. Effective immediately."

Varik's nostrils flared; I saw the flick of fang before he forced it back. His hands dropped to his sides—the picture of obedience, if one didn't inspect the cracks too closely.

Zyrenna cut him with a look. Unflinching. Unmoved. Eyes like a weapon that knew its edge.

Facing her, I let myself take her in fully. Her hair flowed to her waist—moonlight tangled in darkness. I had never seen anything like it before her. Her scent—Veil above—her scent was wrong in a way that set every instinct on edge. Dark, faintly sweet, lavender caught in smoke.

I caged the hunger with both hands and pressed my will against its bars until it knelt.

"Leave," I told Varik without breaking her gaze. "Now."

"Is that an order, Councilor?" His voice dipped.

"It's a warning," I said. "If you truly think your father's Council seat makes you untouchable, I urge you to test it. I would love to show you exactly how short his shadow truly is."

His lip curled, a parody of a smile. For a second, I saw the boy he had been before he learned that cruelty is the only language some men know to speak.

Then he bowed because pride always wanted an audience.

"As you wish," he said lightly. He flicked his gaze across Zyrenna, lingering longer than necessary, then turned.

He didn't risk a glance in my direction. He knew better.

The door slammed behind him.

Silence held—until I stepped.

"Proceed," I told the attendant, my tone gentle, as though the room had not balanced on the edge of a blade seconds before. "Call the name."

The House took its first breath in a minute.

"Zyrenna Vaeoria," he announced.

She stepped forward.

And there it was again—that subtle tilt in the air, the world bending minutely toward her as though something unseen took notice.

"Offer your wrist," the attendant said.

"No," I said, shaking my head.

The attendant blinked. Zyrenna did not. She only shifted her weight, as if bracing for whatever came next.

I looked at her and willed my voice to behave.

"First offerings are not taken from the wrist in a House with three fresh marks."

The attendant swallowed. "The… procedure—"

"The procedure keeps *you* safe, not them." I drew a breath. "Get the chalice."

The chalice emerged from a locked cabinet—dull silver, old enough to have outlived empires. It meant the cut would be shallow, the blood collected rather than taken by fang. Safer, but never safe. There is no safe way to make a body into currency.

Zyrenna's gaze flicked to my face as the cup arrived.

"Do you always inspect the Houses yourself?" she asked. Her voice had no tremor. Her courage wasn't loud—it was the kind that refused to step backward.

"Only the ones that forget what they are for," I said.

"And what's that?"

"Balance," I answered, lifting my gaze to the attendant. "Not appetite."

Her mouth softened at one corner, as though tempted to smile and deciding against it.

"Some appetite is the point, isn't it?" she murmured.

The sound in my chest might have been a laugh if I remembered how. "The appetite isn't the danger," I said. "It's the ones who pretend it's a right. Offer your palm."

She did. Her hand was small in the air between us, the inner skin more pale than the rest of her. A shudder passed through her—not fear, but anger. She hated being here. Hated being touched. Hated this entire system. I felt that hatred like heat as if it were my own.

A second attendant, steadier than the first, set the blade to her skin. I watched everything: the angle, the tension of her hand, the exact distance between wrist and chalice.

The blade flashed.

A bead of blood welled, then another, forming a vivid line that slid into the chalice.

And then—

The scent hit me.

Lavender. Smoke. Metal. Cold. Something impossibly sweet beneath it all.

Old discipline roared upright in me like a wall. I didn't breathe, didn't blink.

The thing inside me went silent, as though listening.

The blood darkened the bottom of the cup. The attendants exhaled as though they'd been waiting for permission. Zyrenna held my gaze through the entire process—never looking away, never flinching from the weight of what I was.

"Enough," I said, far more quietly than I meant to.

Her cut was small but bright. She pressed cloth to it herself, ignoring the gloved hand the attendant offered. Another choice that told me everything about her.

"As per your request," the attendant said, lifting the chalice, "the House submits the first offering to the Council." He hesitated. "To you, Councilor."

The room shifted—just slightly—as if waiting for my reaction.

I knew the routine.

First offerings always went to a Council member or the family of one. A sip for payment, the rest sent to the Spire, a note added to the books, and I left with my discipline intact. I never fed directly from the Houses—only bloodbags. Always bloodbags.

But my hesitation wasn't in the ritual.

It was in the danger.

Her blood smelled wrong—pressing claws against every instinct I'd spent a century mastering.

If I slipped—even a fraction—there would be no stopping myself.

And admitting that—admitting the hunger had a voice, that this girl's scent had sliced through a century of silence, that something in her blood defied law and logic—that was the real issue.

Zyrenna lifted her chin, a small defiant rise. Most would miss it.

But I saw pain in it. Fury. Something that dared me to look away first.

So I took the chalice.

It was heavy; older than most things. In its curved surface, my reflection stared back—bright eyes, a hard mouth, a man

I had learned to fear and learned to leash.

I brought the cup to my mouth.

The first touch of her on my tongue wasn't taste but temperature. It was winter—frostbite—something that brought on a painful cold burn. Then metal bloomed, and underneath it something that made the world tilt. The thing inside me stopped howling. It went silent, still.

I took one sip. Only one. Then set the cup back into the attendant's trembling hands.

"Seal the reports," I said. My voice sounded distant, as though the stone walls were speaking for me. "Send the sample to the Spire. Under my seal."

The attendant bowed, relief flooding his scent so abruptly I nearly laughed.

Zyrenna did not look away.

Not even now.

She continued pressing the cloth to her cut. She did not thank me, which was good, I wouldn't have accepted it.

I turned before the room could ask anything else of me.

At the door, the air should have felt clean.

Instead, for the first time in a very long time, I felt watched.

Not by the House.

Not by the humans.

But by the thing that coils under the bones of the world and listens when blood moves.

Candles guttered and then slowed, as though something unseen had passed between the flames.

The Veil has many ways of making itself known—ways I knew too well.

None of them right or wrong. But all of them intentional.

I did not bow. Not in over a hundred years.

But I felt it tilt toward me, cold and patient, as if marking the moment.

I knew—with a certainty I despised—that whatever road had opened in that room, I stepped onto it the moment I said "Enough."

Outside, the bells began their next hour.

The city continued pretending that marble could be holy.

And my cravings—obedient and well-trained—sat very, very still.

CHAPTER FOUR

ZYRENNA

The doors swallowed him first.

They closed with a soft finality—no slam, no echo—just the click of marble kissing itself back into place. Red light bled through the stained glass at my back. I stood there for a beat, stuck between inside and out, a hand pressed flat against my ribs as if I could trap the strange pull still tugging me toward the exit he'd taken.

Against my better judgment, I followed that pull, running toward the doors and pushing through them.

The morning was colder than it looked. The air smelled of turning leaves and smoke. My boots clicked against the cobblestones. Across the street, a baker shoved his doors open, warm air spilling out. A woman tugged her child closer. Somewhere, a cart wheel squealed like a mouse.

Rhaelin was already half a lane away, the dark sweep of his cloak moving as if even the city made room for him.

"Lord Rhaelin!"

The name left me before I decided to second-guess myself. It rose hard in my throat, cut the air, and landed between us.

He stopped and turned, green eyes catching the early light.

I walked toward him—because stopping would have felt like

surrender. My cloak snapped once in the wind before settling. People pretended to be very interested in their shutters and loaves as I passed. They weren't deaf; they were careful.

"I didn't need you," I said when I reached him. My hands stayed inside my cloak so he wouldn't see the tremor. "In there."

His expression didn't shift, but the attention behind it honed like steel.

"You're unhurt," he said, tone even. "That was the point."

"I would have survived without a performance."

A muscle flickered once along his jaw.

"You would have survived less comfortably."

"Respectfully, sir, that wasn't your decision to make."

His eyes cut to mine.

"Don't call me *sir*," he said—quiet but firm. "It's just Rhaelin."

The correction caught me off guard.

He continued, "And no. It was my responsibility to intervene. The House had three fresh deaths this season. I don't let men like Varik collect first offerings when the ink on the last apology hasn't dried."

"Right, and do they send flowers with those apologies?" I asked. "Or is the condolence card just a standard template?"

His head tilted slowly, something unreadable shifting behind his eyes—a stare that pinned more than it probed.

"You should be more careful expressing opinions like that, little flame," he said, voice almost amused. "Say it to the wrong Councilor, and you'd be dead by morning."

The nickname tugged at me—annoying, but not unwelcome.

"Must be quite a sensitive system if questions count as treason."

A chuckle escaped him—soft, controlled. I almost doubted I'd heard it.

"You'd be right."

The brief smile that followed—canines flashing—was criminally unfair. It startled me more than his warning.

He glanced at the House, then back to me.

"You left without payment."

"Keep it."

"It's not mine to keep," he said.

"I'm not taking it." It came out sharper than intended. I took a breath.

"I don't want whatever list that puts me on. Favors are chains, Councilor. I don't plan on owing you any."

Something subtle moved in his gaze—respect or curiosity or some calculation that irritated me simply because he was doing it.

"I don't do favors," he said. "As I told you, I was doing my job."

"Were you?"

Something shifted around us. The square didn't quiet, but the air steadied. I expected him to close the distance between us, to loom the way men like him always did—but he didn't.

He held where he was. Exactly two paces away. The distance of someone who understood fear and chose not to wear it.

"I'll have the House send it," he said. "You can throw it in the river if it offends you. But you will have it."

"I said—"

"You bled in good faith, Zyrenna," he said, low enough not to carry. "And payment is law."

The word *law* hit somewhere beneath my ribs.

I hated that roofs leak and bread costs coin and winter steals firewood faster than hope.

I hated that he might be right.

"You walk through this city and expect purity," I said. "I hate to be the one to break it to you—but you won't find it here."

"I expect it to be lawful," he answered.

"Is that what you call it?" I asked. "You seem smarter than that, Councilor."

"It's what the people who survive it call it," he said. "The ones who'd rather live under rules than die under chaos. And again—it's just Rhaelin."

"Does it feel like a choice to you, *just* Rhaelin?"

He studied me for a second too long.

"No."

That surprised me. Worse, it made some traitorous part of me want to keep talking. I ignored it.

He kept staring—not like Varik, but as if taking measurements.

"Do you have anyone to bring you home?" he asked.

"I didn't exactly stagger out of here," I said.

"I know." Calm, but edged with something like frustration. "That doesn't answer the question."

"My sister is home," I answered. "She doesn't need to see me shepherded through the streets like a lamb."

"No," he agreed. "She doesn't."

Silence threaded between us. I didn't realize I'd stepped closer until the space between us thinned—enough that I could see a small scar near his jaw, a white crescent.

"I don't want you near me," I said. "Whatever you think you read in this morning—you're wrong."

He tipped his head.

"About?"

"I'm not a puzzle," I continued. "I'm not a project for a bored Councilor who needs to feel like a savior. I went there because survival doesn't stop. We aren't all afforded the luxury of coin."

A pulse beat sharply beneath my ribs. His eyes flicked—not to my throat or my mouth, but to the place my hand pressed against my coat.

He noticed.

I let my hand fall.

"Understood," he said, after a small silence. He said it matter-of-fact. Not pleased, not displeased, just noted.

"You can reach me," he added. "If there are issues with payment, contact the House. They'll put you through."

"Naturally," I countered. "Best to keep distance between the prestigious and the disposable, right?"

The words were out before I could leash them. I didn't know why I kept throwing sparks at him like I wanted to watch something burn. I was smarter than this. But with him, it kept slipping past my teeth, reckless, as if my mouth hadn't gotten the memo that I needed to survive today.

I didn't wait for his answer. I turned, cloak snapping in the cold air, leaving him with his courtesy and his chains.

I felt his eyes on my back as I walked away.

The bells rang, marking the next hour.

I kept my pace and did not look back.

CHAPTER FIVE

RHAELIN

The city woke around her while I walked its shadow.

Disposable, she had called herself—as if she were anything close. I nearly laughed at the audacity. A girl who could upend a room with a single sentence and she thought she was nothing.

Zyrenna Vaeoria kept her cloak close and her hood low, moving with the certainty of someone who knew the streets by memory rather than map. She chose alleys that cut faster, lanes where shutters stayed open, corners where eyes did not linger.

I followed her.

Not out of doubt or guilt. And certainly not out of shame.

I followed her because Varik looked at her a moment too long.

Because three deaths stained the House books.

Because every instinct I had turned toward her like metal to a magnet.

Duty gave me the excuse. A Councilor oversees the Houses. A first offering after a season of deaths was reason enough to watch.

I kept the distance exact—far enough her ears wouldn't

catch my steps, close enough no one else would try theirs. Every shift of her shoulders, every turn of her head, tugged at something under my ribs. A faint pull at first... then tightening, aligning.

When she stopped at a small square to buy an orange, warmth spilling from the bakery behind her, the pull went taut. Ridiculous. I shut it down with practiced discipline, but the tether didn't loosen. It hummed, patient as breath.

Her lane lay near brittle winter vineyards. She paused at her door, scanning the street with instincts enhanced by experience, not fear. Only when she stepped inside—and the door closed with the softness of wood worn thin from years—did I stop.

Only then did I turn away.

* * *

The courier was late. I knew it from the frantic pace: too quick, too eager. Barely twenty-two, leather satchel strapped across his chest, Crimson House wax sealing the flap. He carried it like it scalded his hands.

I stepped into his path.

He skidded. "Councilor Morrain—sir—I was told—"

"I know what you were told."

My voice cut clean. "Give it to me."

His throat bobbed. He unfastened the strap with shaking hands. I took the satchel and drew out the vial. Inside, her blood glimmered faintly in the glass.

"This will not reach the Spire," I said.

A beat of terrified silence.

"You'll return to the House and tell them you were relieved

by authority. If anyone asks, you were rerouted to the east district. You didn't see me. You don't know who took the vial."

I placed coin in his palm—enough for two weeks.

"Yes, Councilor."

He wasn't lying. I saw the relief roll through him.

Once he vanished down the lane, I broke the cap.

Her scent rose instantly. It filled my senses with a sweetness I couldn't put a name to. I tried to ignore the desire that landed with it.

I didn't drink it.

Instead, I poured the blood into the rocks at my feet, covering the soil with my heel until no trace remained. The empty tube I kept.

The Spire would not have her.

* * *

The Spire greeted me with its usual hush. Stewards bowed without meeting my eyes. Doors closed carefully after me, as if afraid to echo.

In the archives, shelves climbed into darkness. The air held ink and leather and the weight of old truths. There are books you are meant to read, and books you find only if you knew exactly where to look.

I went to those.

I already knew what her blood meant. I knew it the moment it touched my tongue. The way every other urge in me fell silent. The way centuries of control collapsed into a single point of focus.

I didn't come seeking discovery.

I came hoping I was wrong.

The first scroll's ribbon crumbled under my fingers. The title had been scraped away long ago, but the opening line remained:

On Sanguis bonds and the measures taken.

Measures—

The word they used when they wanted to hide what they did.

The list beneath was short: a handful of names, many dates. Beside each name, the same notation: *silenced.*

Sometimes softened to *resolved by consensus.* Sometimes *incident closed.*

Every phrase meant the same.

Not cured, not freed; executed.

My hands curled tight.

The memory surfaced—the last Sanguis bond I witnessed. The night the Council dressed murder as mercy.

A man and woman, kneeling apart in a sealed chamber. I saw it the moment I entered—how their eyes followed each other even through the chains. How their breathing synced without effort. The Council called it corruption, a sickness. A threat to the city.

We told ourselves it was necessary.

At least that was what I told myself when I went home sick that night. I knew better now; the rest of the council members forgot by morning. I told myself in the beginning that if left alive, it would unmake the city.

The woman—the vampire—was killed first. The man followed an hour later. They sealed the record in wax, filed it deep where no one would read it again.

They called it a solution.

I obeyed. I had no choice then.

But I did not forget.

I closed the scroll and opened another: *The Veil and Threads of Blood.*

The bond is not a blessing.

It is a chain.

It gives hunger a single answer.

I set it aside. The vial in my pocket pressed against my side like a heartbeat.

Zyrenna Vaeoria.

Human. Mortal. To the Council now, a liability. To men like Varik, an opportunity. To me—

The pull answered before I finished the thought.

—to me she was both my survival and the thing that would break me.

I opened the oldest book—the one with signatures that mattered. The one the Seven pretended didn't exist. Entry after entry matched the rooms that haunted my sleep.

There was no pretending I imagined anything.

I pressed both hands to the table until the wood creaked.

There is no cure.

There never was. I knew exactly what the Council would do if they learned Zyrenna carried a Sanguis bond.

It would not happen again.

Not while I still drew breath.

CHAPTER SIX

ZYRENNA

The cottage felt smaller when I stepped inside, like the walls had leaned in while I was gone.

I lifted my cloak from my shoulders, hung it on its hook, and closed the door with a soft thud that felt too final for a morning like this. My fingers lingered on the fabric longer than they needed to. Maybe because my nerves hadn't quite calmed yet. Maybe because part of me was still standing in that crimson-lit hall with a vampire's stare pinned to my spine.

I walked through the narrow hallway and into the kitchen.

The hall smelled of lavender and old wood. A scent that had always felt safe and familiar for me.

Alira looked up from the table, a tangle of thread caught around her fingers. Her blue eyes found mine, relief blooming across her face before she hid it—too fast, too practiced. She did that when she thought I needed her to be strong for me, as if she wasn't allowed to need anything herself.

"You're back," she said.

"I'm back," I responded. My voice sounded like mine, but my body did not.

Something buzzed under my skin—not fear, not relief, but

a current, bright and restless, as though the morning had hooked a wire through my ribs and walked away without severing it.

I set water to boil, hoping heat would steady me. It didn't… obviously.

I chopped onions too fast, too fine, until they blurred and a sting rose behind my eyes. The cottage filled with familiar scents—steam, herbs, smoke drifting from a neighbor's chimney. None of them touched whatever was wrong.

Alira appeared beside me, placing her bundle of yarn down.

"I can do that."

"I've got it."

The words came out harsher than I meant. I softened it. "You set the bowls."

She didn't argue.

The kettle's chatter scraped at my nerves. I poured water over barley and herbs, steam fogging the glass above the sink. I washed my hands twice, then again, until the skin along my knuckles flushed pink.

The scent of the House clung anyway. Incense. Metal. Him.

We ate at the table, bowls warming our palms. Alira talked about small things. Mostly about the vineyard, and our neighbor Ferran, who said meat would be scarce next week. I nodded where I was supposed to and laughed where I could. But the hum beneath my ribs only grew louder.

She reached for the salt and stopped mid-movement.

"Your hands are shaking."

I curled them around the bowl. "Just hungry."

"Zyrenna…"

Her voice pulled my gaze up. Her eyes always aged when she worried. I hated it. "It's nothing."

"Did something happen at the House?"

"It's over." I didn't let the word wobble. "It's done."

"That's not the same thing," she whispered.

I forced myself to breathe evenly. "I'm fine," I said—and because *fine* is a word that breaks if you look at it wrong, I added, "Truly."

She held my stare, searching for cracks, then let go.

Containment—I'd lived my life by that rule. Built walls stone by stone, over the years. Crying was something I did alone, if at all. Because if I started, I wasn't sure I'd stop.

But there were days the silence turned in on me.

Days when my own doubt ate through the edges of that wall, whispering that I was doing it all wrong. I wondered if my restraint hurt her—if Alira ever looked at me and thought her pain was unreasonable because I never showed her mine.

I loved her more fiercely than anything that had survived this city. But loving her didn't mean I knew how to raise her. No one prepares you for that—how to become someone else's anchor the same day you lose your own.

When we finished, she took the bowls to the sink. I wiped the table, the cloth catching on the groove Father carved years ago with his knife. My heart stumbled once before I gathered myself.

Alira yawned.

"I'm gonna go wash up."

"Thank the Veil. I didn't want to be the one to say—"

"Shut up, I don't stink," she shot back.

We both laughed, and as she turned down the hall, I blew her a kiss. She rolled her eyes, but I caught the smile.

The cottage quieted again. I tidied things that didn't need tidying—plates already straight, cloth already folded, chairs already aligned. The hum waited, patient as a held breath.

I braced my hands on the counter and bowed my head.

"Stop," I whispered, not sure which part of me I was speaking to. "Go the *fuck* away."

But it didn't.

I blew out the candle above the sink and lit the one by the window instead. The dim light of Solvane peeked in through the glass. I tried to read, but the words drifted. I tried to sew, but the needle bit my skin. I tried to pretend the feeling in me was only my body's way of shaking off the memory of the day.

But the memory of him kept surfacing where I didn't want it, the way he stepped between me and Varik like a wall. The calm in his voice that made people listen. The look in his eyes when I told him I didn't want his help. There was no surprise, no offense, only a kind of acceptance so clear it made me angrier than an apology would have.

Because if I let myself see him as a person, I might forget he is just a predator with a crown.

Every aspect of it infuriated me.

He wasn't a savior. He was order in a city that dressed punishment as peace. He was the hand that wrote laws and the blade that enforced them. If I kept thinking of him as a person, I would forget that the House exists because men like him decided it should. His green eyes cut through me like they had a right to. He hadn't saved me. He'd stolen the choice from me, flipping the narrative like he was a hero offering me one. He left me powerless in a place I had walked into determined to prove I was anything but.

That was the heart of it, wasn't it?

I had walked into the House with my chin lifted, contract

clutched in my hand, ready to face whatever bloodthirsty prick waited. I wanted to prove to myself, and to the ghost of my mother that I wasn't afraid. That I could bleed on my own terms.

But terms don't belong to us, not really. That's a falsity. Everyone in Solvane knows it, though no one speaks it aloud, that the Council's laws were never meant to keep us safe. They were written to keep us docile, to dress up our submission into something useful through law. People smile, they bow, they mutter their thanks, but behind closed doors every family curses the Seven for the contracts that chain us and the Houses that drink us dry. It is the city's quietest truth: survival here means swallowing rage until it rots your bones.

Suddenly, my hand moved to my sternum without permission. The hum answered, as if whatever pull I'd tried to leave behind in that colorful hall had stayed with me.

I pressed harder, like pressure could quiet it. But, if anything, it grew clearer.

"I am fine," I told the empty window.

"I am whole."

I told myself it was nerves. That my body was shaking off the memory of the House. That it was the kind of tremor that comes after you've survived something you weren't sure you would. Like waking from a nightmare while the fear still lingers behind your teeth.

"Tomorrow," I said softly, a promise to no one. "Tomorrow I will be fine."

But the truth sat in my chest like a stone:

I was running out of lies to tell myself.

CHAPTER SEVEN

RHAELIN

I sat at the Spire table for the weekly Council meeting, listening as they discussed numbers, quotas, compliance— all spoken in calm voices by people who had long forgotten what any of those words cost outside these walls.

The Veil's throne sat untouched at the head of the table, as it always did—vacant, and yet the most present thing in the room. The empty space carried more authority than the six beings seated around it combined.

The chamber carried a darkness to it, the kind that everything good and warm knew to hide from.

Kalor droned first, paging through reports with irritation disguised as boredom.

"Marks are up this season," he said, as if he were commenting on weather. "People stop resisting once they see what happens to those who do."

Seraphine didn't bother looking up. "Fear keeps order. It always has."

Merek scribbled numbers, pretending he mattered. Orien watched quietly, her stillness more dangerous than any raised voice. She was the only one whose silence meant anything.

I let them talk.

People reveal more when they believe no one is listening. I learn the most when I make them forget I'm in the room.

Cassira finally snapped. "You sit there like this is good news. Wipe the smugness off your faces. Three deaths in one quarter draws attention—the wrong kind. Mortals talk when they get scared. When they talk, they stop sending their families to the Houses. Then what? You planning to drink air when the doors stop opening?"

Cassira of Solvane—the human lands—was the only one here with a working mind, the only one not blinded by wealth, though she never used that mind for anything good. Human or not, she was more dangerous than most of the immortals at this table—and just as calculating as Orien.

Kalor gave a laugh without humor. "You act as if they have a choice. If they stop sending them, it's treason."

Seraphine waved a dismissive hand. "Relax, Cassira. A few coffins doesn't undo an entire system."

Merek nodded eagerly, like a dog hoping for scraps.

Cassira's jaw ticked from irritation. "Systems crumble from the edges first. But by all means—keep thinking the ground can't shift under you."

She was right. In all honesty, this place was run by imbeciles dressed as visionaries. But she was no less ruthless than the rest of them. Just more observant.

I had been quiet long enough. There are moments when silence teaches nothing.

My voice cut through their conversation without raising a single decibel.

"You're not as untouchable as you think."

Silence shuttered the room.

I lifted my gaze from the table as Seraphine's fingers

stilled. Merek's pen froze mid-stroke. Even Kalor sat back, narrowing his eyes. Cassira glanced at me—not in challenge, but acknowledgment. She had been waiting for someone else to name the truth.

"It's a bad look," I continued, "to pretend nothing stands above you. The Veil is the god of balance. Do you think He will sit idle while you send your sons and daughters into the Houses and let them undo what keeps this city standing?"

The air thickened.

"You've all seen what happens when you make the mistake of thinking your will outranks the Veil."

And slowly, I saw as the reminder ran through all of them.

Their screams filled my ears again, as if I were back in that moment—the sound people make when they finally understand they are not at the top of the hierarchy.

The Veil had never been seen physically by the Council before that day. Until then, it existed only in whispers, in sensation—felt in the marrow, not seen with the eye.

But that day, it manifested. Not as rumor or breath, but in form—flickering too quickly for any gaze to hold. Its face never settled; its eyes changed as though every gaze that had ever looked upon it had been poured into one.

People argue whether the Veil is real—some serve it with fanatic certainty, especially the Veythari, and others dismiss it as faith and folklore. The Council never had that luxury. We have felt its presence in this room more than once; there is no mistaking the weight of it.

But that day was the first—and only—time we saw what stood behind the feeling.

We had all circled around the table that day, glasses raised for a toast. I lifted mine only halfway before it happened.

The candles around the chamber had burst, wax hitting stone with a splatter, and the pressure in the air had shifted until breathing felt like dragging weight through water. Then, the Veil was simply there. Not the whisper in the marrow we were used to, but in His physical shape.

They dropped before the Veil even spoke.

Kalor hit the floor first, choking. Seraphine followed with a sound I had never heard from her—raw, scraped out of her throat. Merek folded in on himself and sobbed without air. Cassira braced on her hands, shaking. Glass shattered and only Orien and I sat untouched, unaffected. Only she and I remained upright.

The Veil turned its head toward the wine I still held in my hand. I lifted it, smelled the bitter edge beneath it, and understood the plan with perfect clarity—they'd meant to poison me.

They'd meant to kill me before I took my official seat on the Council after the Blood Trials.

The only reason I hadn't caught it myself that day was because of the hollowness I'd been carrying—an emptiness so loud it drowned out every warning.

So, in a way, the Veil saved my life that day.

It didn't need to justify itself. It only had to appear—and in doing so, it made their guilt public before it ever silenced their screams.

Its voice filled the chamber—not loud, but ancient in a way that left no air around it. The kind of voice that did not ask to be believed.

It addressed them first.

It named their treason, as if the act itself had already entered the record of the world. It stripped them bare in their own chamber. Insulted—offended—that they believed their will meant anything here. That they would try to kill me—the victor of the Blood Trials, a seat earned in blood—and pretend bloodlines made them greater than the one who earned it.

The Veil made its will felt.

Their bodies answered before their minds did—spines bowing, hands clawing at their throats, teeth bared in sound they could not control. Cassira shaking against the floorboards, Kalor gasping like a netted animal, Seraphine's scream tearing itself out of her as if dragged from the root.

No one in that room doubted what held them down.

No one outranked the Veil.

Not a House, not a Council, not bloodline, not coin, not crown. When it chooses to act, it does not negotiate. It simply enforces.

When the Veil turned His attention on me, I felt His judgment like a hand around the bones of my skull. It commanded balance. Ordered me not to kill them. Warned me that their punishment would not come from my hand.

Not because they deserved mercy—but because balance demanded restraint.

It was not sparing them. Nor was it sparing me.

Their treachery had already been recorded; killing them would not correct what had been broken. The Veil enforces balance, not vengeance.

I obeyed because the will of the Veil is not an invitation—it is the law that predates every law we've written.

But walking out of that chamber, two things were already written into fate:

One: I would kill them eventually.

Two: The only reason they remained alive was because

something older than all of us told me to wait.

The memory dissolved, and the chamber returned.

Looking back at Kalor, his jaw worked. He had the impulse control of a child—one of the many downsides of being a vampire—and unlike most immortals, he didn't bother to pretend otherwise.

I let the silence stretch until it pulled taut.

Then I stood. The scrape of my chair against obsidian rang through the room.

"This meeting is finished," I said. "Audits by the end of next week. If another mark appears after that, I will assume you cannot control your own bloodlines and proceed accordingly."

Kalor opened his mouth—then closed it.

Seraphine's bored mask faltered and slid back into place.

Cassira folded her hands on top of the table.

I didn't bother granting them a second look as I left.

The corridor beyond the chamber was dark and cold. Down the hundreds of steps within the center tower, guards stood in strict formation as they always did, spears polished, eyes forward—order on the surface to disguise rot underneath.

Outside, the cities waited—unaware of how close their fate truly sat in the hands of fools. They believed the Spire unshakable, believed the Council eternal. Let them.

Delusion makes collapse come cleaner.

CHAPTER EIGHT

ZYRENNA

A week passed before I finally admitted that whatever I was feeling wasn't leaving.

What began as quiet ripples now pressed like a pulse that didn't belong to me. It stole breath at random, tightening in moments I couldn't predict. Sometimes it flared with no cause; other times it settled over me in a calm so foreign it chilled my skin. It moved through me like a second heartbeat—one slightly out of rhythm with my own.

One night, lying in bed, a surge of something electric hit me so completely it shocked me upright. It lingered there for moments too long.

The longer it went on, the harder it was to excuse. It wasn't anything I could claim as mine. It filled me, claimed space inside of me, blurred the edge where I ended. It crawled through me like an infection, threading itself deeper every time I tried to ignore it.

Something was wrong. Terribly wrong. It was unrelenting— almost as if it were searching for something within me or calling out to a part of me I had not yet discovered.

And honestly, I didn't want to.

* * *

The vineyard behind our cottage was dying.

Leaves curled inward, crisping at the edges. Rows that once smelled of sun-warm grapes now carried only the faint bitterness of rot. I crouched in the brittle vines with a knife and a basket, sorting what might survive from what was already lost.

Alira sat on the stone wall, legs swinging. She watched me with that too-grown look she didn't realize she had.

"You're different," she said.

"I'm tired," I replied, not looking up.

"You've always been tired."

Her legs kept swinging, but her gaze didn't. "You don't look at me when I talk anymore. Like your head's somewhere else."

My stomach dropped. The knife slipped, snagging a stem.

"I've just got a lot going on, too much on my mind. Nothing you need to worry about."

"You *only* say that," she countered, "when there's something I should worry about."

"Alira—"

"I'm not a child."

"You are," I said softly. "And that's not an insult. It's the only good thing about being your age."

Her mouth twitched like she wanted to argue but decided against it. She jumped off the wall, and walked toward me.

"Great. So I've got, what, a few years before I end up bitter and hating the world like you?"

"Cruel." I threw her a look, but I couldn't stop the small smile that pulled at my mouth.

"True." She bent, picked up the knife, and pressed it into

my hand. "Go inside, I'll finish."

A protest rose in me—but the tug under my ribs surged, undeniable. It stole the strength from whatever I meant to say. I pressed a kiss to her forehead before turning toward the cottage.

I didn't breathe until the latch fell into place behind me.

* * *

Later, in the square, whispers had followed me.

Markets were smaller this time of year—baskets of onions, barrels of apples, coils of smoked sausage, steaming kettles selling broth for coin. This weather still gave enough to live on, kinder than snow, generous enough to keep the markets filled.

And today, voices carried my name.

"That's her. The girl from the House."

"Apparently, Lord Morrain walked her out himself."

"She's either blessed or cursed."

"Blessed," another hissed. "He's the pretty one."

"Cursed," said an older woman. "No one leaves with the Seven's eyes on them."

I slowed just enough for them to hear me.

"Careful," I said. "The House isn't the only place that listens."

Silence rippled behind me, their whispers gone until I was out of earshot.

Ferran, our neighbor, waved me over from behind his mini shop, where he was peeling oranges with a knife a bit too dull.

"Didn't think you'd be walking the markets so soon," he said.

"Why?" I asked. "Because half the city's older women

have nothing better to do than whisper about whatever's still breathing?"

Ferran laughed a genuine laugh, the sound filling my ears. "You've got that right. If gossip ever died out, half this city would forget how to breathe."

"Well, good thing there's never a shortage of shit around here," I muttered with a wink.

He slid me a slice of orange. "On the house. Don't tell."

I smiled, peeled a piece off and popped it into my mouth. For one breath the hum inside me went silent, as if something elsewhere paused. But it quickly returned.

"You need sleep," Ferran said. "Or chaos. One of the two."

"Sleep," I said. "Chaos finds me either way."

Ferran huffed a laugh. "You sound like your mother when you say things like that. She'd tell me chaos was just another word for being alive—right before she'd yell at your father to pour her more wine."

His knife paused over the peel, the humor in his face softening. "World's been too still since the two of them left."

Ferran's wife had passed years ago after being sick for many years. After she was gone, my parents would invite him over for dinner whenever they could. They'd grown close over time. My father traded bottles from the vineyard; Ferran always offered what little he had from the shop in return. It wasn't much, but he'd never let our table go without something fresh, even when we knew money was thin.

My throat tightened, but I forced a small smile. "Yeah," I said. "The world didn't know what to do with itself once they stopped arguing."

He laughed softly, and for a heartbeat I knew he'd fallen into his own head. "Argue they did," he said. "But those two loved each other more than sense. Couldn't stay mad long enough to finish a fight—probably why there were so many."

The words landed where I had no armor. People rarely spoke of my parents anymore; grief made everyone quiet with time, and quiet made it easier to pretend the loss had dulled. It hadn't though—it only learned to sit deeper.

His voice had pulled it all back up, just enough to make my chest feel tight. I felt the threat of tears, and I refused to let him see.

I nodded with a smile and a small laugh. "Yeah. They were pretty great."

I took a step back before the ache could climb any higher. "I'll see you, Ferran. If I have any glasses to sell, the first one's yours."

"Don't flatter an old man," he said with a smile.

I turned to leave, but his voice caught me one last time. "Oh, Zyrenna? Watch yourself. Varik—Kalor Draevan's boy—he's been lingering around moments too long lately."

I hesitated. "Let him linger. He'll get bored soon enough," I countered. "Thanks again."

But the words felt thinner once they left my mouth, unease settling through me. Varik's name had always carried weight—his father's even more so. Kalor Draevan was one of the Seven, seated on one of the three vampire thrones alongside Rhaelin in the Spire. He was the kind of man who flaunted power because he needed someone to believe it.

As if summoned by the name, the hair on my arms lifted before my eyes confirmed it.

Rhaelin.

The height, the poise—no one carried power like that. Even from behind there was no mistaking him. He had the kind of presence that didn't need sound to fill a room. The kind Kalor envied.

He stood near a fountain beside a man cloaked in gray. At first, I thought it was human—until the hood shifted, revealing a face pale as stone, faintly luminous even in shadow. The eyes were worse: restless, shifting, colors bleeding and reforming with every blink.

A Veythari.

My breath froze.

Their kind had been ancient before the Spire formed. When the war raged, the Veythari didn't choose sides. They closed their borders and claimed silence as obedience. Some cursed them as cowards. Others whispered it was faith, that they heard the Veil's will more clearly than anyone else.

That faith won them a throne when the Treaty was carved. Not out of loyalty, but because no Council dared exist without the Veil's most devoted to bind it.

They were rare now, a couple hundred at most, and it wasn't often that they would wander. Especially, to Solvane. When one left Eryndralis—the Veythari lands—it was never chance. Seeing one here felt like an eclipse.

Rhaelin touched the Veythari's shoulder—a brief, respectful gesture. The man dipped his head in answer.

A jolt of irritation hit me like a slap. I sucked in a breath, my hands closed in the folds of my cloak. The emotion wasn't mine, I knew that much.

Rhaelin turned his head. His gaze cut through the market—through bodies, through sound, through everything that wasn't me. His eyes were green as cut glass, bright and impossibly sure, and I hated that I felt them before I met them.

And for a heartbeat, I forgot myself.

Forgot Solvane.

Forgot the crowd.

Forgot that this man was one of the Seven—one of the architects of the very system I hated.

All I felt was the pressure of his attention, settling over me like a cloak I hadn't agreed to wear.

I should've looked away. Should've reminded myself of everything he was—what he represented, what he'd done. But my body didn't listen. For a moment, there was only the pulse in my throat and the weight of his gaze holding me there.

Then, somewhere beneath it, I found the voice—the one threaded with fury and rage and everything he'd caused.

And with it came the strength.

I was the one who broke it. I turned away before the voice forgot itself again.

All while the pull followed me the entire way home.

CHAPTER NINE

ZYRENNA

Two more nights passed.

And still it didn't stop.

I walked the road that cut behind our dying vineyard, where the brittle olive trees moved in the wind, and the air carried the familiar smell. I went there because it was ours—my father's hands in the soil, my mother's laughter through the rows. If the world was going to keep clawing at something beneath my ribs, then I wanted to face it somewhere that still belonged to me.

Twilight bled out behind the hills. The last of the light being swallowed by the day.

That's where I saw him.

Rhaelin stood in the road like he'd been carved there and forgotten, cloak dark against the pale ground, hair catching the weak light.

His skin, usually sun-warm bronze, had leached to ash. The unshakeable stillness he wore like armor had thinned, stretched—like something inside him had been scooped out, leaving only the shell in place.

For a heartbeat, I wondered if this was the inevitable end—the past week catching up and declaring me clinically insane.

"Zyrenna," he said. His voice struggled to reach its usual even pitch and missed.

Nope. Guess not.

"Nuh-uh." I stopped where the road bent. "You don't get to come here. You don't get to haunt my fucking road, too."

A wince flickered across his mouth—there and gone. "Believe me," he murmured, voice deep, "I'd rather be anywhere else."

"Then leave."

He stepped forward.

It wasn't the graceful, effortless glide I had seen in the House. This step was careful, almost hesitant—like the ground no longer trusted him to stand.

"What happened to you?" I asked, the words spilling out before pride could stop them.

His eyes locked on mine. "You happened."

A breath of humorless disbelief escaped me. "Flattering."

"It's not," he rasped. Another step. Slower. "I haven't fed since the House."

"Then go back," I snapped. "The line's long, but I'm sure some poor soul—"

"I can't."

"Won't," I bit out.

"Can't." His voice tore on the word. "You feel it, Zyrenna. You feel the pull. Don't lie."

That thing inside me twisted.

"I don't know what you're talking about."

"Don't." His voice cracked like a whip. "Curse me, hate me, spit in my face. But don't fucking lie." His gaze sliced clean through the dark. "You've felt me. My anger. My calm. My hunger. It bleeds into you."

A cold pulse ripped through my chest. "What the fuck is happening?"

He let the silence stretch until it trembled.

Finally: "It's called the Sanguis bond."

The world dipped.

"It's forged when a vampire drinks from a human whose bloodline resonates with theirs. Once bound, the vampire cannot survive on the blood of anyone else. It kills them. And if the human offers their blood to another, the betrayal poisons them."

I forgot how to breathe.

"When you say resonates…you mean, we—what? Share—"

"Not kinship." His mouth hardened. "More like… one vein pulled through two bodies. The bond gives it its own pulse. Every tremor runs both ways." His voice dropped, low and ruin-soft. "Your blood beats in me. My hunger beats in you."

"No." I shook my head. "Bullshit."

The soup I'd eaten at supper threatened to surge back.

"Bullshit doesn't drain the color out of my skin." He lifted a hand, let it fall. "Look at me. Do you think I'd choose this?"

I wanted to deny it, but the truth was written all over him.

"How have I never heard of it?" I whispered.

His jaw flexed. "Because the Council made it so. A bond makes a vampire unstoppable. It doesn't just feed, it claims. The bonded human amplifies, steadies, and anchors the vampire. And in return, the mortal feels the vampire's emotions bleed through them. That kind of power can't be commanded, can't be leashed. So the Council buried it. Declared it myth. And when they found pairs?" His voice dropped lower. "They erase them, every last one."

The road tilted beneath me.

"Erase, Rhaelin?" I snapped. "Are we fucking serious? Is that what we're calling cold-blooded murder now? If we're softening the language, maybe next time we'll call it mercy."

Anger flowed through me. My own this time.

His gaze flicked over me. "You think I don't know what it is?" he said, voice low. "I've witnessed it—watched them call it justice. The name never mattered."

I almost laughed.

"Don't pretend you stand outside it," I hissed. "Your hands aren't clean."

"No," he said quietly. "They're not."

That honesty—unvarnished, unpretty—landed harder than denial.

"What happens if they find out?" I asked.

"They'll kill us both." His answer was flat. "Or worse, they'll use it. The Council has always known what this bond does. How it twists possession into madness. They would cut us open and use it as torture, bleed you to keep me chained, or bleed me to make you beg. The bond is power. And power is only useful to them if they own it."

Air tightened around my lungs.

"Humans and vampires don't—" I tried to speak and the sentence broke.

"We don't," he said, finishing the words for me. "We were never meant to belong to each other. Not in this world." His gaze narrowed. "So when the Council sees me burn down half the world to keep you breathing, they'll know."

I folded my arms tight across my chest, as if it would keep me from shattering.

"Why tell me now?"

"Well, for one, because you deserve to know why your chest

burns at night," he said. "Why my anger rattles you. Why you think you're losing your mind."

His mouth twitched. "You're not. You're *feeling* me."

He paused. Something pained flickered across his face.

"And because," he added softly, "I need to survive."

My chest constricted.

The air left my lungs in a rush, my eyes searing into him. He didn't reach for me, he just stood there.

"Don't look at me like that," he said. "If I could tear this out of myself, I would."

My voice came out raw. "So what then? I roll out a rug and you drink from me like I'm some fucking chalice?"

"Not a chalice, a deal."

My eyes narrowed. "A deal?"

"You feed me. No Houses. No witnesses. In return…" His voice hardened. "I erase your debts. I file a protective order, so your sister's name never reaches the House. Guards on your road. Coin to last the colder months. A roof that holds." His gaze cut through me. "And I keep the Council off our throats."

My jaw dropped. He knew fucking everything.

"Wow, anything else I should know about my own life before we continue?"

"Consider it preparation," he said, all too casually.

"Do you spy on everyone you make deals with, or am I just special?"

"You're not that special," he said, eyes flickering over me with a trace of a grin. "Just the one person keeping me alive from now on, that's all."

I almost laughed. Almost.

"And what do *you* take?" I made my voice ice.

"I keep my life," he answered.

A beat passed.

"Beyond that… blood, silence, exclusivity. Your blood's already bound. If you let another vampire drink, it *will* sicken you. And if I take from anyone else," he met my eyes, "it kills me."

The weight pressed in. "Exclusivity," I echoed. "That a polite way to attempt staking ownership?"

He chuckled low. "No. But if it ever came to possession, I wouldn't need to try. Anyone who touched you would learn very quickly why that wouldn't be a good idea." He paused. "And it will consume you soon enough too."

The words landed like iron. I kept my face neutral, but my pulse didn't get the message.

In that same breath my head started the math: Alira safe, debts erased, guards on the road, coin to last, a roof that wouldn't leak when the first storm hit. It made me furious that my survival could be bartered that way, and it made me angrier still that I was considering it.

"What if I say no?"

He swallowed. "Then I still file the order. Still patch your roof. But I die slow—and you'll feel every hour of it while it's happening."

From the cottage, muffled by distance, came the faint sound of Alira's laugh. Aunt Kaelen's voice answered, warm and sure. The road felt suddenly too narrow for any refusal.

"Terms," I said.

He straightened, relief barely visible. "Name them."

"One: Alira is exempt forever. Not a season, not a year, forever. Put it in writing with a seal the Council can't burn if they wanted to."

"Done."

"Two: Coin upfront. Three months. I won't gamble on your promises."

"Done."

"Three:" My voice shook. "If I say stop—you stop. Always."

Something in his face softened, the hard lines easing but not gone. "Always."

"Four:" I added, before I could lose my nerve. "Not here, not the House—not anywhere anyone can see. You choose a place where no one will see."

"The Spire," he said. "My tower—there's no stewards, no attendants. No one but me."

It should have terrified me, the idea of walking into his domain with no witnesses, no neighbors pretending not to listen through thin walls. Any sane person wouldn't have requested it. But beneath the fear there was a colder truth: he needed me breathing. The bond had seen to that. He couldn't bleed me dry without damning himself in return. That didn't make him safe—but it did mean, for once in my life, I wasn't the only one with something to lose.

Maybe that was why I trusted him with this one thing. Not because he was good, but because survival had finally placed us on the same side of the knife.

I believed him when he promised me privacy. "And if I change my mind—"

"You walk away," he said. "You don't owe me an explanation."

He hesitated, something flickering behind his eyes. "But I'd rather we talk before it comes to that—because ultimately, it ends with my life, and inevitably yours."

I stood very still. The hum under my ribs had tightened,

thinned to a wire. The closer he placed himself, the calmer I became—whether I liked it or not. When his control frayed, my pulse followed. I hated that my body was learning his rhythm.

"Then now," I said, because waiting would kill me faster than his teeth. "This is the only time we do it here."

My throat tightened. "Do it now—before I think of another reason to say no."

I scanned the tree-line, the road, the fields—making sure no one was close enough to see, to hear, to make this worse.

"Look at me, not the trees. I don't let anything get near you."

The words landed before I could make sense of them. As if this—watching the dark for me, keeping the world at a distance—was something he did often.

Not *won't let anything near me*—but *don't*.

Something ongoing. A pattern. As if he had done it before I ever noticed.

I forced myself not to ask—not to react at all.

He moved with careful slowness, showing me his empty hands again like I was the one with the blade.

"Your wrist," he said.

I held out my arm. He took it the way you take something you don't want to frighten. His breath ghosted warm against my skin before his mouth did. The first touch of his lips sent heat skimming through me. The sting when his canines pierced was clean, hot—a bright pain that cracked and then flooded.

It poured through me in a warm, tidal sweep, loosening muscles I hadn't even known were locked. It seeped into places untouched for months, places I'd learned to starve as thoroughly as he had. And yet, beneath that warmth, something ancient in me recoiled—an instinct as old as bone whispering *no, no, no* even as my body answered *yes* to the hunger leaving him.

My fingers closed around his shoulder without permission. Nails bit into leather. The pain flared and then shifted, turning electric, blurring too easily into something dangerously close to want. His hand came to my wrist, tightening once, a warning or a grounding—I couldn't tell—before he forced himself to ease.

He drank like a man who'd taught himself starvation.

Measured. Controlled.

Stopping sooner than instinct demanded.

And then he tore himself away—too fast, too disciplined.

Color bled back into his face slowly, as if someone were lighting a candle from within his skin, coaxing him back into himself. He drew his tongue over the punctures on my wrist; the bleeding stilled instantly, the skin knitting beneath his touch like it had always known how to obey him.

I stared. I hadn't known that was possible.

"It only closes when the one who bit you does it," he murmured, eyes fixed on my wrist like it held his reflection. "If anyone else tries, they'll only make the puncture worse."

A cold thread slid beneath my skin.

"You took less than you did at the House," I said. My voice came out thin, strange—like it didn't trust me anymore.

"I'll never take more than you can spare."

His eyes were bright again.

"I can't afford to."

We stood there breathing the same cold air. My wrist throbbed less. The world had not tilted, and yet nothing stood where it had been a moment before.

"When," I asked, "do you expect me at the Spire?"

"Tonight," he said. "After midnight."

His tone had gone even—surgical, almost.

"We'll set a schedule. Several nights with me, then I'll return you home for the rest of the week. I'll take enough to last three days at a time. Think of it as fasting the rest of the week. It keeps the bond steady… and it keeps you from having to see me more than necessary."

He said it like it was a mercy.

"I'm taking your word that it's private, Rhaelin. I'm not walking into a nest of monsters," I said.

"No," he said softly. "You're walking into one who won't let the others touch you."

"If they come for me," I said, "you will not treat me like a contract."

He leaned in, enough that I could see the small white scar near his jaw. "If they touch you, little flame," he said, very calm, "none of them will see morning."

And *Veil help me*, I believed him.

"Give me the order for Alira before midnight," I said. "And the coin. If anything feels wrong, I don't come."

"You'll have both."

"I won't die like my mother did, not at the hands of your kind. If I say stop—"

"Then it ends," he cut in, and something like pain—real, unguarded—crossed his face.

"Every time."

I opened my mouth to argue again, to test the edge of that vow—but he lifted his hand between us.

His pinky extended.

I blinked at it. "You're not serious."

He didn't move. Didn't blink.

"Well, Zyrenna," he answered, "does it look like a joke? I don't give out my pinky promises to just anyone."

I simply stared. The gesture looking like it meant more to him than any oath he'd taken.

Against my better judgement, I signed, and hooked my pinky around his.

"God," I muttered. "To think one of the most feared leaders in the nation seals deals with a pinky promise. No wonder this place is so fucked."

He only winked, the bastard.

"Thanks, sweetheart," voice full of amusement, "I didn't claw my way to 'most feared' just to disappoint you."

He stepped back first, as if distance would keep us from feeling what we'd already learned the second he drank from me.

"I'll wait at the south steps," he said. "If you don't come, I still file everything. I will still keep the House off your road."

"Don't make this noble," I muttered. "It's not."

"No," he agreed. His eyes darkened.

"I'm hungry."

The corner of my mouth almost lifted. Almost.

"Go."

He inclined his head—polite, formal, as if we were two people with manners instead of a monster and a girl bargaining with her own body. Then he turned into the thin light and walked away, any trace of the staggering gone. The bond paid attention to every step until the bend in the road took him from sight. Even then it didn't release me. It only eased, like something patient that had learned it could wait.

I told myself I could live with this.

I told myself the Spire was just a building.

I told myself I would walk away if anything felt wrong.

But when the bells began counting the slow crawl toward midnight,

I realized I had already started listening for them.

CHAPTER TEN

ZYRENNA

By the time I went to meet Rhaelin, I had reconsidered the deal a few dozen times. Every scenario I played through ended the same: nothing secured the one thing that mattered the way his promise did.

Alira's safety.

She was asleep in Aunt Kaelen's cottage—the house right next to ours. She was my father's younger sister, and the only one left to help with Alira when I couldn't. Alira needed far less than she once did, old enough now to manage the basics, but she still needed someone.

We all did.

Rhaelin waited where the road curled past the vineyard. Streetlamps cast long shadows across the cobblestone; his black cloak moved in the wind like it belonged to the night. His eyes snapped to mine the instant I appeared.

It would've been a lie to pretend he wasn't beautiful. The fade along his temples was blade-clean, a few strands fallen loose across his brow that made the danger in him worse, not better. His face was all edges and angles, every line precise, tattoos peeking out around his neck.

"You're late," he said.

"You're insufferable."

The corner of his mouth tilted. "So goddamn lethal with that tongue."

I wanted to claw the look off his face.

He didn't answer—he simply stepped forward.

Shadows unfurled from his back.

Wings.

They stretched open in one slow, devastating sweep—vast obsidian membranes threaded with faint light, the frame all carved strength. The torchlight behind him bent and vanished into the darkness of them. A faint black shimmer pulsed through their veins as they moved.

I froze. "You—" My voice snapped in half. "What the *fuck* are those?"

His eyes glinted, amused. "I don't know, Zyrenna. Maybe they're just really big arms."

"Dick," I muttered, pulse stumbling. "I've just never seen them up close. Usually vampires in Solvane keep their wings hidden." I huffed a laugh. "Guess it's the one thing they're not trying to measure dick size with."

He leaned in just enough for the air to shift. His voice dropped, "If size were the contest... I wouldn't need wings to win, sweetheart."

My brain shut down faster than I'd like to admit. Heat crawled up my neck; the flicker of triumph in his eyes said he'd noticed.

He laughed—quiet, satisfied—the kind that made it very clear who just won that round.

He stepped closer until only cold air and tension remained between us. "You're not climbing the Spire by stairs. Piss me off enough and I'll change my mind."

Before I could choose between a shove and a retort, he caught me around the waist and pulled me in with solid hands.

The world dropped.

Wind tore past my ears. The road, the vineyard, the olive trees—all of it shrank in a heartbeat. My stomach flipped clean over; my cloak whipped behind us like a flag in a storm. His chest was firm, and I hated myself for noticing. The tether burned between us, an invisible—unrelenting line.

"Relax," he murmured. "You keep fighting the air like that, and I'll start to think you don't trust me."

"Wouldn't be a far-fetched assumption, Councilor," I said.

His laugh was low, real this time, a vibration more than sound due to the wind.

"I intend to change that, Zyrenna."

I hated the way he said my name—like it already belonged to him.

We climbed higher. I'd never been higher than a rooftop; now the entire world peeled open beneath us—ridges of hills, the dark spines of forest, the black mouth of night swallowing everything familiar.

Minutes later, rooftops scattered the dark like broken teeth. A pattern of red lights emerged—one I'd only seen carved into maps.

Nocthallow, the vampire capital.

Colder air swarmed the air now. Streets glowed with endless rows of crimson torches; firelight bled against obsidian buildings that looked carved from shadow. Black banners snapped over every avenue, silver sigils flashing like knives.

A kingdom carved from night.

What stole my attention though, was the stars. They seemed to burn brighter here—bigger—as if I could reach my hand out and grab one.

"Slow down," I said softly.

He did. He slowed until we hovered, suspended in the wind. Neither of us moved. Before I could think better of it, I lifted my arm, palm open to the sky.

The world fell away—the path, the capital, even the sound of our own breathing—until there was nothing but stars and the dark above.

Light met my hand.

For one stunned, impossible second I held one.

The star was warm, weightless, alive against my palm like something the world had forgotten to keep out of reach.

A breath escaped me, full of disbelief.

"How is this possible?" I whispered, eyes still on my hand.

Rhaelin didn't look at the sky. He watched *me*—watched me as my fingers cupped the light. "It isn't the actual sky you're touching," he said. "Each star above throws its echo—a projection—down below. That's why there are more lights here than there should be."

I looked back up. The night was drowning in them—millions—far too many to belong to a single sky.

"And I can just…touch them?" I asked, unable to hide the awe in my voice.

"You can touch the copies," he replied. "Not the source."

"It feels so real," I said.

"Most beautiful things do," he answered.

Silence stretched, filling itself with questions I had never dared speak aloud.

In that second, the light in my palm shifted. What had been a soft glow began to gather—brightening, as if drawing itself back to a single point. Color deepened, then pulled inward until it pulsed out altogether, like a candle pinched between two fingers.

I stared at my empty hand, skin tingling.

Slowly, I looked at him, my brows pulled tight in a silent question.

Rhaelin studied my hand, then my eyes.

"…That's new," he murmured, half to himself.

A few beats passed. "You ready?"

I swallowed, still reeling, but nodded once.

He adjusted his hold, and the wind reclaimed us.

"So is it true?" I said once I found my voice again.

"What?" he said, head tilting.

"That Nocthallow is kept in permanent darkness."

His gaze flicked down, amused. "You've done your home-work. Most mortals don't get that far."

"So it's true."

"It's true." His mouth curved, but his voice edged. "The sun doesn't kill us. It strips us down. Makes us slower. Duller. A vampire in daylight is nothing compared to one in the dark. The Veil made it so."

"So you're a believer."

"It's hard not to be," he said, "when you've sat beside a throne carved for Him."

"Him?" My brow furrowed.

"Yes, Him." His gaze stayed forward, but something in it tightened. "I've been in the Veil's presence before."

That pulled my spine a little straighter. "What? You've seen it? I thought it was only felt in whispers and spirit."

"I lived because of it," he said simply. "But that's a story for another time."

Curiosity ate me alive, but I forced myself still. My eyes

caught on the starlight again. I felt his eyes linger on me a moment too long before he looked ahead.

The wind drowned every other sound. Eventually, we left the capital sprawling under us. He didn't fly straight from Solvane to the Spire, he'd widened the path on purpose. I kept that to myself and filed it next to every other quiet calculation I'd begun to make about him.

"By horse, it's a day to Nocthallow," I managed when I remembered to breathe. "Walking, two or three. And you just—"

"Holy hell," he drawled. "Third time I've left you speechless today, little flame. You're losing your edge."

I rolled my eyes.

"Distance is a human problem," he said, more evenly. "At this height, at this speed, the world below might as well be standing still. That's why the Houses stand in every human town—easier for us, safer for you."

"Safer?" I barked a laugh. "My mother is rolling in her grave right now, Rhaelin."

His jaw tightened. "Fair."

The city fell behind us, and the horizon opened to what lived at its center. The Spire; we were entering the Ring of Thrones.

Six towers rose in a circle around a vast central column that speared through the sky. The three vampire towers stood tallest: obsidian needles carved with old runes, their surfaces so black they swallowed the torchlight whole. The two human towers were pale stone, banners bright even in the near-dark. And the last tower—black glass, humming faintly with light like a candle cupped behind a palm.

"Is that for the Veythari?" I asked.

"Yes," he said. "A dying breed clinging to scraps of power. Their lands are empty more often than not. They once carried strong magic, but it's thinned over centuries. All that's left is what they call truth-sense."

He watched my face. "They claim they can feel a lie in their bones. No one knows for certain if it's real, or if they've just convinced enough people to believe it."

I'd heard of that. Most people just wrote it off as strong faith in the Veil—convincing themselves to believe whatever they needed to be true.

I had read about the Spire in lessons with Mother, in pages that smelled of ink. Words aren't the same as seeing. From above, the seven towers made a circle that felt less like architecture and more like a trap set for the sky.

"What's inside the Spire?" I asked before the thought could turn mean.

"Everything that makes the other towers behave," he answered. "Records. Archives. Safekeeping vaults. Laboratories. A few secrets even the thrones pretend not to know."

We banked toward the third tower, one of the vampire strongholds that ringed the central tower. Rhaelin tilted his wings and dropped. The descent punched the air from my lungs; wind seared my face until my eyes watered. My stomach lurched.

"Careful," he said near my ear, amused but steady. "Wouldn't want you fainting before we've landed."

"I'll faint the day you grow a soul," I shot back, though my grip on him didn't loosen.

His laugh was low, carried off by the wind.

The tower's ledge lay below us, a narrow balcony of dark stone tucked away from the grand stairs below, where I assume guards and courtiers came and went. This place was different—exactly what he said it would be. Hidden, private.

Rhaelin's wings beat once, twice, and then folded in tight as his boots struck the balcony with a sound like stone against stone. He set me down with a care that made my skin crawl. My legs wobbled, traitorous from the flight, but I held myself upright.

His wings dissolved into shadow, vanishing as though they had never existed at all. For a moment the silence of the place pressed in on us, thick as the stone walls themselves.

"Welcome to the Spire, Zyrenna," he murmured. "The center of our world as we know it."

I hated the way my pulse answered him.

And still… when he pushed the doors open,

I followed him inside.

CHAPTER ELEVEN

RHAELIN

The Spire always looked beautiful from the outside. Towers lit with old sigils, bridges strung between each keep. People came here and called it holy. To me, it was a cage dressed up with nicer walls.

Seven Thrones, six fortresses. The Veil doesn't need one; the lands already belong to it. When the Veil wanted to be heard, it was.

No guards waited, no attendants. I had chosen the hour and the door to make that true. The balcony sat in a blind angle between watch routes, no view from the bridges, no way for curious eyes to follow us in. I had promised her privacy. Hell, I even gave her a pinky promise—one of the three I've made in my entire life. The other two were under the threat of violence.

"This way," I said. My voice carried flat and even in the cold. "As agreed," tipping my chin toward the opening.

We moved down a narrow hall, footsteps hitting old stone. The keep was bare, no banners on the inside, no trophies, nothing to soften it. I didn't keep much company here. Even sound seemed reluctant to remain; every step faded too quickly into silence, as if the walls themselves consumed it.

She looked around once and snorted. "No wonder you're always broody. Living in this cave would sour anyone."

"And yet, you walked in willingly," I shot back.

"Don't mistake necessity for choice."

The bond tugged hard at that, her irritation sliding through me, a hot thread of resentment trying to drag mine with it. I exhaled through the pull until it eased, unwilling to let her mood dictate mine.

I led her through the inner hall to a smaller chamber, my room. The walls were plain stone, built for strength, not beauty. A fire that always burned low, protected by Veythari magic. A map hung on the far wall, edges frayed from handling, pins marking borders that always changed. A cabinet of glass held swords and blades, weapons scarred from use. No ceremonial edges, no polished hilts—tools of survival, that's all.

"This doesn't look like a home," she said quietly. "It looks like a war waiting to happen."

"That's all the Spire is," I said. "A war paused long enough for everyone to pretend we've found peace."

Her gaze flicked back to me, edges glinting like steel. "That doesn't sound like something a Councilor should admit."

For a moment, I nearly gave her the truth: that peace was the greatest lie this place had ever told. Instead, I smoothed my voice flat. "A Councilor's opinion doesn't matter. Only their ability to stay silent."

She frowned, but she didn't press.

I crossed to the cabinet, pulled the stopper from a glass decanter. The sharp burn of whiskey filled the air, grounding me in a way nothing else did. I poured a glass, took an unhurried sip, letting it coat my tongue until it chased some of the cold from my chest.

"Drink?" I asked over my shoulder.

She didn't answer right away.

She just stood there, caught between caution and curiosity, the firelight turning her hesitation into something that scraped at me.

Then she nodded, small and decisive.

I poured another glass and held it out. She crossed the room slowly, each step measured. When her fingers brushed mine to take it, the bond jolted through me like lightning.

Fucking hell, Rhaelin. Pull it together. One brief touch from her and you short-circuit like a twelve-year-old discovering what his hand is for.

She felt it too, I saw it in the swallow at her throat before she looked away.

She chose the couch by the fire, sinking into the cushions with the kind of deliberate grace that said she refused to show nerves. I sat opposite in the tall chair angled toward the flames, glass in hand. For a long stretch, the only sound was the crack of wood and the faint clink of ice when I shifted my drink. Silence pressed heavily, but neither of us reached to break it.

She stared at me. Not like humans usually did—afraid, hesitant, unable to hold my gaze for more than a breath. Instead, she met it. Fierce, and silver bright. The kind of eyes that didn't just look at you—they *undressed* your thoughts, searched the spaces you didn't want touched. I'd seen a thousand shades of beauty, but nothing like that stare. It wasn't attraction; it was gravity.

The connection made it more intense. Every flicker of her attention slid under my skin like a blade. Most men would've looked away—she was counting on it.

But she didn't know me yet.

She didn't know how much I fucking loved it—how I'd hold her stare until she forgot how to breathe.

I shifted my weight, slow enough for her to notice, letting the space between us tighten. My hand drifted to place my glass on the edge of the table beside me, just enough to look casual, though every instinct wanted to close the distance.

Then I tilted my head, studying her with all of me.

"You make hatred look incredibly tempting, Zyrenna."

Her hair had come loose, black as midnight, but the firelight caught threads of what looked like shimmering silver that moved like living starlight. Her skin held a faint gold warmth, out of place in the cold iron of this keep. She wasn't fragile like most humans, but lean strength wrapped her in quiet defiance. And her mouth, a gentle curve masking something deadly, capable of cutting me deeper than steel with a single word.

For a heartbeat, she didn't move. The pulse in her throat stuttered, her mouth parting like she meant to bite back. I felt it through the tether before I saw it: that flicker of heat, quick and unwilling.

Then she looked away, as if that could hide it. The corner of my mouth tugged higher.

We sat in silence for a long time afterwards, but it was welcomed. We didn't try to fill the space with noise; sometimes silence said more.

"Tell me about your mother," I stated.

Her eyes flickered—just for a moment. Her breath hitched, anger rising like a shield, but the pain beneath it leaked through the cracks.

She shot me a look that said *don't you dare.*

But the more I sat, unmoving, the more I saw her easing. Sometimes stillness is its own kind of permission.

She hesitated, warring with herself, then—slowly—she gave in.

"My mother," she said finally, with a low huff. "Not much to tell. She went into a Crimson House to keep her family fed—and never walked out. They called it a miscalculation. That's what they always call it."

The word cut straight through me. I had heard it too many times, that same excuse repeated. Always the same, always a lie.

Zyrenna's gaze stayed on the fire.

"There's more," I said, quieter this time. "You don't carry that kind of grief for just one person."

Her jaw flexed, her eyes now testing me.

A short, humorless laugh slipped out. "You've got some balls…"

I didn't look away. She wasn't wrong—it was invasive.

But I couldn't find it in myself to care.

If she gave me even a piece of herself, it would be worth the cost.

And the fact that she wasn't walking away meant she was already halfway to giving it.

"My father tried to hold it together after that. For us, for me and my sister, Alira. But one night he went to the barn and never came back." She swallowed hard. "I found him the next morning."

The tether yanked, her fury slamming into me.

She wasn't finished. Her fingers whitened around the glass as she drew back a long sip. "And before that"—she paused, searching for air—"my closest friend. I never really let people in, not fully. But she… she was different. I trusted her. She was the only person outside of my family who truly knew me. And then—" her voice faltered, thin, "one day she was there, the next she was gone. No body, no answers. Just her absence."

She stared hard at the fire, words trembling. "I think I knew. Even before anyone admitted it, I knew she wasn't coming back."

Her voice dropped, brittle.

"If not for Alira, I don't think I'd still be here. She was all I had left. Feeding her, getting her to smile—it reminded me there was still something worth staying alive for."

A bitter laugh escaped.

"That's the difference, I guess. I knew I had someone to live for. My father just pretended he didn't."

The bond surged with her confession, emotions so heavy my fingers dug into the glass just to keep it from spilling.

"You were too damn young for that kind of burden," I said.

Her eyes darted to mine, wide, startled. "How—"

"I can feel it," I admitted. "Not the details. Just the weight. How old you were when your life stopped belonging to you."

Her lips parted, but no sound followed.

I should have looked away, should have buried it under the mask I always wore. Instead, I let my gaze linger on the silver fire in her eyes, on the resilience carved into someone too young to carry it.

"I'm sorry, Zyrenna," I continued. "About all of it."

Her laugh came bitter, trembling at the edges. "Then stop adding to it."

The words cut deeper than they should have. The resentment that followed branded me, the same mark she carved into every Councilor, every vampire who had ever bled her kind dry.

"I am not like them," I said, harsher than I intended. My grip on the glass tightened until the whiskey shivered inside it. "The others inherited their seats, their coin, their power. Nothing was handed to me. Don't assume you know the cost I've paid, or the pain that forged it. I've respected your pain. Give me the same, Zyrenna."

Her eyes flickered. The retort I expected never came.

"I didn't mean…" Her voice thinned. She drew a breath. "How did you get your seat here then?"

I looked into the fire, then back at her. "The Blood Trials."

Confusion crossed her face. "And I'm supposed to know what that is?"

For a breath, the words nearly spilled—the weeks of carnage, the faces that haunted my sleep, the endless nights soaked in blood so I could stand here now. I saw flashes: blades clashing in the dark, screams swallowed by fire, my own hands raw from tearing through flesh just to keep breathing.

But I locked it down, forced the mask back into place. My voice came out flat. "Enough questions, sweetheart. You've reached your limit for today."

Her head snapped up. "My limit?" The spark in her eyes caught fast. "You ask someone to tear open the worst things that ever happened to them, and then you shut down the second it's your turn?"

The air between us thickened, the tether humming like a drawn wire.

I didn't move. Didn't answer. Because she was right.

"Next time you want honesty," she said, voice shaking, "don't make someone dig through their pain just to keep you company. Fucking selfish prick."

She didn't stay another second. She turned and crossed into the adjoining chamber.

The door clicked shut, but the tether throbbed between us still—her anger, her grief, her defiance—all bleeding through. I stared into the fire until my glass felt heavy in my hand, and only then let myself breathe.

Sleep would not come easily tonight. Not with her so close.

Not with her words still echoing like truth I refused to face.

CHAPTER TWELVE

ZYRENNA

The adjoining chamber was as bare as the rest of the keep: stone, a narrow slit of a window, a table with a basin of water. A folded blanket, a single candle. No tapestry to catch sound.

Depressing.

At this point, even a shitty rug would've been a kindness.

I sat on the edge of the bed and stared at my hands until the candle guttered.

I regretted telling him anything at all—regretted letting him see even a piece of it. The loss, the weakness, the part of me I'd spent years keeping buried. He didn't deserve to know that piece, and there was no reason I could justify for why I gave it to him.

But the quiet he left me with had its own cruelty. And maybe that was what pulled the memory loose.

I was small again, knees pulled to my chest, the night heavy with the smell of rain and earth from the vineyard. My mother sat beside me on the edge of my bed, humming something wordless. Her fingers moved through my hair, carefully tracing it back behind my ear again and again until the rhythm softened the crying out of me.

I can't remember what I was sad about now.

Only that she stayed. That she didn't tell me to stop. That she let me break and never once made me feel weak for it.

When I finally looked up, she smiled—tired but bright. "You don't have to be brave every second, Zy," she said. "Even the strongest things rest."

She brushed her thumb over my cheek, catching the last tear before it fell. "One day," she whispered, "you'll understand that softness isn't the opposite of strength. It's the part that keeps it alive."

I used to believe I'd always have that—her hands, her voice, the safety of being small enough to be comforted.

Now all I have is the echo of it and the silence that came after.

The candle trembled beside me. I blinked, and only then realized my face was wet. The tears had come without warning, without permission.

But I didn't stop them. There was no one here to see, no one to protect from the breaking. So I let it happen—quiet, unpretty, human.

It hit me then, in the stillness, how warped I'd truly become. Not in a dramatic, tragic way—just… altered. Somewhere along the way, anger had stopped being a reaction and started being my baseline. My first language. The emotion I reached for before I even knew I was reaching.

I don't know when that shift happened. Maybe after my mother. Maybe after my father. Maybe after losing people I wasn't supposed to lose. But it changed something fundamental in me. Turned softness into a liability. Turned hope into something I didn't have the energy to entertain.

And the worst part was I'd gotten good at pretending it didn't bother me.

I wiped my face with the heel of my palm, not because it made anything better, but because I needed the motion. Needed to feel like I still had control over something, even if it was just that.

A knock came, low but firm. Once, then again.

"Zyrenna," his voice carried through the door. "Open it."

I scrubbed a hand over my face, anger replacing what the tears had emptied. "Go to hell, Rhaelin."

Silence, except for the faint internal hum of the bond tightening like a warning.

"I could," he said after a beat, voice dropping lower. "Or you could open the door and save us both the trouble."

My throat burned. "You don't know when to quit, do you?"

"No," he said simply. "Not with you."

Something in me cracked then—exhaustion, maybe, or the stubborn need to prove he couldn't see through me. I stood and yanked the door open.

He was leaning one shoulder against the frame, half-shadowed by the hall light. His expression softened the moment he saw me, and I hated how quickly he noticed. His gaze lingered on my face—the red still on my cheeks, my eyes—and I saw the flicker of it: pity.

"Don't," I said, my voice all edge. "Don't ever fucking look at me like that."

He didn't ask what I meant. He already knew.

"Can I come in?"

I hesitated, every instinct screaming to shut the door in his face, but I stepped back anyway. He crossed the threshold without a word.

He glanced once around the room, then sat on the edge of the bed, leaving just enough space for me to join him. He didn't look up when he spoke.

"Sit," he said softly—not an order, but something closer to a request.

I took the space next to him against my better judgment.

"I'm not here to fight," he said. The candlelight caught the edges of his face.

"I'm sorry for shutting down," he said.

"You gave me something you didn't have to—something that doesn't come easily to you. I know what that costs."

He paused, the muscle in his jaw working. "But I'm not sorry for asking."

"No?" I huffed in disbelief.

His voice roughened. "No. I will always push you, Zyrenna. I will always try to know you—even when it's the last thing you want. Because if I stop trying, if I stop *seeing* you, then this," his hand lifted slightly between us, hovering over the space that thrummed with the bond, "becomes nothing but a chain. And I won't let it be that."

The words hit like an open hand.

"You should go," was all I could manage.

He didn't move, didn't even blink. The silence stretched until I felt it in my teeth.

"Zyrenna," he said finally, my name a low command that didn't need volume to carry weight. "Don't shut me out after that."

My blood boiled at the audacity.

"No?" I let out a harsh laugh, bitter at the edges. "Are you fucking serious? I don't get to shut you out?" I stood up. "That's ironic, no?"

He didn't answer. Just watched me with that steady, infuriating calm.

"Alright then," I said, my voice shaking with fury and something far worse. "Tell me, Rhaelin. Who have you lost? Tell me one goddamn thing about you. Your favorite color, the way you take your tea—I don't care. Just stop *fucking* staring at me like I'm some puzzle you're trying to solve."

The silence cracked open between us. And then—

The bond warned me a heartbeat before it hit: the pulsing weight, the shift in pressure, memory that wasn't mine. It slammed into me, grief so heavy it bent me forward, so fierce it hollowed me from the inside. Faces I didn't know. Voices cut off mid-syllable. And one boy—his face so like Rhaelin's my lungs strangled around it.

"Stop," I gasped, fingers whitening around the bedframe.

It vanished. Snapped back behind iron control, retreating so fast it left me dizzy.

When I could breathe again, he was standing in front of me now. Still close enough that I could smell cedar tightening around my throat. His eyes burned down into mine. He wasn't trying to frighten me—I knew that much. It was the opposite. He had let me see what I was asking for.

And for one raw, unguarded second, I understood why he never told me anything. Why he built walls high enough to bury entire histories. Because I had just felt a second of what he carries, and if that is what he lived through behind those walls—

He wasn't protecting himself.

He was protecting me.

My breath still came uneven, my mind aching from the aftershock. "How did you do that?"

His eyes shut for a moment. When he opened them again, they were softer.

"Please, Zyrenna," he said quietly. "I know it's asking for the impossible, but you need to trust me."

He stepped back a fraction, though his voice stayed close.

"I keep that part of me closed for a reason. I will not let my pain crush you the way it's crushed me." He drew a slow breath. "But I promise you this—when you're ready, when you and the bond are strong enough to hold it, I will show you. Because you showed me."

The words settled between us, heavy with truth, and something like fear.

"Who taught you that kind of control?" I asked.

"No one," he said. "It took years."

He looked like he was going to say something else and decided against it. This time, I was grateful for it. I wasn't sure what I would have done with it.

He took a few steps away from me now, heading towards the door. My eyes pinned his back.

"Thank you," I said, barely above a whisper. The words felt strange, fragile, like they didn't belong to me.

He paused—glancing over his shoulder.

"Silver," he said quietly. "And no tea."

The answer hit harder than it should have. Simple. Honest. Exactly what I'd asked for.

"And don't thank me," he said softly. "I wouldn't have had the nerve to walk in here if you hadn't found the courage to lower your own walls first."

I didn't trust myself to respond to that, so I cleared my throat instead. "I'm going to try to sleep."

He nodded. "Let me know if you need anything. I'll see you tomorrow."

I stood up, and just as he reached the door, he said my name in the way that makes me forget the way anyone else says it.

"Zyrenna."

I looked back. He walked over to me and handed me pills that were wrapped in a linen cloth.

"For the nightmares," he said. "Tuck it under your pillow. It doesn't knock you out—just quiets the noise. Only if you want."

I turned the pills in my fingers. "No one says my name like that."

His face was unreadable, just pure intensity searing from his eyes. "Because it isn't theirs to say." A beat passed. "Goodnight, little flame."

Heat climbed under my skin before I could stop it. He turned to leave, and I shut the door before he could see what a single sentence had done.

I took one of the pills—then slid the rest beneath my pillow and tried to let sleep find me. Cedar—and the faint bitter trace of it—drifted up from the linen. I matched my breathing to the scent until darkness took me.

CHAPTER THIRTEEN

ZYRENNA

The first time he fed from me in his tower, it felt like my body forgot which parts belonged to me.

Not from pain, though there was that. His fangs sank fire through my veins, and I lit up like lightning. But worse than the bite was what followed: the pull of his hunger, the iron will holding him back, the way his body went rigid to keep from taking too much. The bond turned everything into a line of fire.

When he lifted his mouth, his lips were stained. His tongue passed over the wounds, sealing them closed so they didn't bleed. He stared at the floor as if it had wronged him, fury carved into his jaw, not at me, but at what we were. We did not speak of it.

The second time was quieter.

He took my wrist without ceremony, without the distance of the first time. His hands were steadier. Mine were not. I sat on the edge of his worktable while he stood, and there was something unbearable about the normalcy of it—the way the candlelight moved, the way he exhaled slowly through his nose like he was calibrating himself. Like he was learning the exact measure of restraint I required.

I watched his face instead of looking away. I don't know why. Maybe because watching felt like refusing to pretend it was nothing. His jaw stayed tight the whole time from the effort of holding back. I could feel something straining him. The bond fed me that much at least: the size of what he was containing.

When he lifted his head, his eyes found mine before he could stop them. Something moved through his expression—gone before I could name it. He sealed the marks, the same as before. His thumb pressed over them briefly, the way you press a letter into warm wax. Like he was intentionally leaving something behind.

Neither of us called it what it was.

* * *

Back in Solvane, Aunt Kaelen distracted Alira, keeping her busy with chores and stories while I slipped in and out with more excuses. Kaelen's stories ran like the tide, never ending. She always gave me the space to come and go without sharing where I'd been.

When Alira asked, I said I'd taken contracts in another district, extra vein offerings to keep us ahead. Half-true. The other half sat in my chest and tugged whenever it wanted.

Alira nodded like she believed me. Sometimes I thought she did. Then other times I watched the fear behind her eyes and wanted to rip the bond from my sternum just to show her it wasn't a rope around my throat.

A rhythm formed whether I wanted it or not: a few nights home, a few nights at his keep. He said it was safer this way. If he took too much at once, it would leave me weak, and flying to me every night wasn't private or convenient. By spacing it out, he could take enough to last until the next time without draining me completely. Rhaelin came and went as he promised. If he approached the vineyard, I felt it before his boots touched the road. He never crossed the fence without my glance saying he could. He could have, but he didn't.

Every time I left again, Alira watched me like she was trying to memorize my shape, just in case. Aunt Kaelen backed me, but the ghost of our mother hung in the silence between us.

* * *

Back at the keep a few weeks later, the bond didn't stay quiet. At first it was flashes, his temper turning on itself and going cool, a rough thread of humor when I snapped at him, satisfaction when a pin moved on the map and stayed. Weeks made it heavier though. I woke in the dark with the shadows of his nightmares pressing on my chest. I learned the rhythm of his focus, the way his mind lined up problems and moved through them until there were fewer; simply through the flooding relief that ran within me. Small things, stupid things, but the bond didn't know the difference.

One night, heat slammed through me without warning.

Not anger—something *else*. Something that crawled up my spine and stole every inch of air from my lungs.

For a full, blinding heartbeat, I thought he wasn't alone.

That someone was in his bed.

That I was being forced to feel every goddamn breath of it.

Rage detonated in me so fast it almost staggered me. I wanted to rip the sensation out of my body like a thorn. I also wanted to storm down the hall and tear his door off the hinges.

So yeah…

Maybe *this* was the possession he warned me about.

The pressure faded. Eventually.

Only to return days later—same burn, same pull low in my stomach that wasn't mine, same vicious punch of jealousy I refused to acknowledge.

Every time it hit, it felt like being split in two: the part of me that knew this was just the bond doing whatever the hell it wanted… and the part of me that hated sharing *anything*.

Especially that.

I told myself I didn't care what he did in his bed. Told myself it wasn't my problem. Told myself it would be so much worse if I actually cared.

Although this tie between us made me want to punch him half the time, a part of me welcomed it.

After years of building walls, the bond shoved me straight through his—even when he refused to tear them down completely. It was the closest thing I'd felt to safety in years, even if it also felt like standing in the middle of a warzone.

But that safety burned with suspicion. He was hiding something. I felt it at night when his anger curdled into something colder. The way he looked at the Spire, at the Thrones, like a predator circling prey.

* * *

Tonight, the keep had gone too quiet. The kind of quiet that made the air feel sentient—listening, waiting.

I found him the way I always did when sleep refused me: bent over the map table, hands braced, fire throwing gold across his back.

As much as it pissed me off to admit, this was my favorite version of him—uncovered, unguarded, the kind that made me forget what he was supposed to be. For a moment, I forgot the titles, the power, the distance. I saw only him.

He didn't turn when I entered; he knew I was there.

"What's wrong, little flame?" he said, the rasp of his voice faded by the hour.

I stayed by the doorway, arms crossed like armor.

"I could ask you the same," I muttered. "Do you ever sleep?"

He lifted his head just enough for his attention to brush over me.

"That's not what you came for."

My pulse kicked. God, I hated him.

"I'm awake because the bond is an asshole," I snapped. "That's all."

He said nothing, but the room shifted—quiet, expectant, like even the dust was waiting for me to keep going.

I looked away, jaw tight. "Earlier—it… surged. Hard."

"When?" The word was mild, but the look wasn't.

"I don't know," I lied. "Two hours ago."

For a single heartbeat, his posture didn't change—but something in him did. A subtle shift. A realization he didn't bother to hide from me.

Then, very quietly, he started laughing. Not loud, not cruel—just a low, disbelieving sound, like a man who'd just put together the last piece of a puzzle and couldn't decide if it was amusing or inevitable.

"What?" I snapped.

"Nothing," he said, though his eyes said everything. "Just… interesting."

I bristled. "Interesting?"

He took a step toward me. "What did it feel like?"

"Heat," I muttered. "Pressure. Something intense. And I thought—"

The words stuck, humiliatingly.

"I thought you weren't alone."

He looked at me like he was trying to confirm something for himself. "You thought someone was with me."

I forced a shrug. "Doesn't really fucking matter, does it?"

He didn't flinch at my harshness. Didn't give me the dignity of looking away.

"It matters," he said quietly. "It matters a great deal."

I scoffed. "Not to me."

A lie. A badly wrapped one. The bond pulsed once—as if it were irritated at my lie. *Traitor.*

That almost-smile ghosted across his mouth, darker than it had any right to be. "Of course," he murmured. "Not to you."

"Don't do that smug shit," I said.

"I'm not being smug," he answered, taking another step. "I'm being observant."

"Wow," I said. "A new skill."

"You sound very certain someone was here," he said.

"I'm not," I bit out. "I just don't care."

"You care enough to lie about caring."

"Fuck. *Off.*"

He stepped in—close enough now that my pulse jumped to match his.

"You're furious, little flame," he said softly. "I can feel it radiating through you."

"I'm furious because you're infuriating."

"No." He shook his head once. "You're furious because you

keep pretending possession doesn't own you now. And the bond is done pretending with you."

"Don't flatter yourself," I snapped.

"I'm not flattering myself," he murmured. "I'm stating a fact."

"You don't get to decide what I feel."

"I don't," he agreed, stepping closer. "But luckily, the bond tells me anyway."

I swallowed, hating the way heat curled low in my stomach. "Then the bond is defective."

His mouth twitched—the beginnings of a smirk. "If the tether were defective," he added, "you wouldn't be standing here trembling every time I take a single step toward you."

"I'm not trembling."

"Liar." His voice dipped, velvet over a blade.

I didn't realize I'd backed up until the table pressed into my hips. Rhaelin followed, caging me in without a single touch. Both his hands came down on the stone beside me, one on each side, braced near my hips. Not touching. Just there. Choosing not to.

His face hovered inches from mine, his breath warm against my cheek.

"I thought I told you not to lie to me," he murmured, low enough that it hummed in my bones.

The bond coiled tight in my ribs.

"Back up," I said.

"No."

"Why do you even care what I think?" I demanded. "You don't answer questions you actually owe me, but you're suddenly pressed about this?"

"Because this," he said, eyes dragging over my face, "is about you. Not me."

I hated the way my chest tightened at that.

"I felt something I didn't ask for," I said. "I woke up choking on want I didn't create. I assumed the obvious."

"You assumed the worst," he corrected.

"Same thing."

He exhaled slowly, the sound brushing my lips. "Zyrenna, listen to me. There is no one else. Not now. Not since you walked into that House and decided so."

Heat shot through me. "I didn't ask."

"No," he agreed. "You'd sooner swallow glass than ask. But you felt something and turned it into a weapon. You don't get to do that and keep pretending you don't care about the answer."

"Then say it plainly," I forced out.

Satisfaction ran through him at those words, instantly regretting that I spoke them.

"Plainly," he said. "There is no other woman. I haven't taken anyone into my bed. The heat you felt wasn't someone else. It was me."

The room tilted around us.

"Are you—" I whispered.

"Must I spell it out for you, little flame?" he murmured. "You're an intelligent woman."

My breath left me in a sharp exhale. My god.

What a fucking idiot, was all I could say to myself.

"So I'm supposed to what?" I snapped. "Pretend that's normal? Pretend it's fine that your midnight hormone surge decides to hit *me* like I asked to be part of your personal crisis?"

He laughed at that—actually laughed.

"No, sweetheart," he said. "Please don't be mistaken. I am

not a man in a crisis."

My heart stuttered.

"I know exactly what I'm doing," he said. "What I'm feeling. And why the bond reacts the way it does."

"Oh, perfect," I shot back. "So you're self-aware and still forcing me to feel it."

The anger twisting in my chest was rising. And it wasn't just coming from my end.

I continued, "So what's the plan then, Rhaelin? I live with it?" I said. "Your hunger. Your rage. Your nightmares tearing me up while I sleep. And I pretend it isn't breaking me?"

His jaw locked; he had to unclench it to speak. "You think I wanted this? You think I enjoy a tether that shoves my life into someone else?" The next words were low. "If I could cut it out of us both, I would."

"Liar." My palm hit his chest before my brain caught up. Warmth under the shirt, muscle unyielding, none of it helping. "You don't get to play victim, Rhaelin. You stand at the top while I bury my family piece by piece."

His hand slammed the table next to us, stone rattling under the force. He didn't scare me—he wasn't trying to. Shadows surged at his shoulders, wings threatening to unfurl. "If you knew what it cost to stand in this chamber," he said, voice gone raw, "you'd choke on the words before you spoke them."

"My mother bled out on marble while your kind called it regrettable," I spat. "My father..." my throat tightened, but I forced it out, "I carried his bloodied body because he couldn't live with the pain of her absence. I cleaned what was left. You feel that though, don't you? Every time *my* chest caves in, every time *I* wake up choking on their ghosts? You know it, Rhaelin. And yet you sit here and pretend you're fucking shackled. You're not shackled, you're one of the goddamn chains!"

The bond cracked wide open, grief and rage colliding, bouncing between us until I thought it might tear my ribs apart.

His wings flared. The air thickened, pressure rolling off him in waves.

He leaned in, his chest rose and fell too fast, his jaw locked like he was one breath from breaking. "For the last time," he said, "do not mistake me for them."

I met his eyes, both burning now. "Then stop pretending you're *fucking* powerless," I said. "You *are* the power."

For a moment, silence. His wings curved forward, shadows wrapping us in a cage no one could break through.

"I am not your enemy, Zyrenna," he said at last, voice breaking. "But if you keep trying to make me one, I will burn us both for it."

My lips trembled, but I forced the words through anyway. *"Then burn us."*

His eyes narrowed, glass cooling too fast. Something behind his face broke; he didn't let it show more than a second.

"The bond doesn't end," he said, evenly. "Not with distance. Not with hatred. Not with time." A breath. "It ends only in death."

The words landed and the pull confirmed it. Not a threat, a fact. It felt like a stone set in place.

"We live with it," he said. "Or we don't."

He watched me intently. The pressure dropped by degrees. Wings gone. He pushed off the table and gave me my space back slowly.

I said nothing.

"When the bond surges, it means my focus scatters. I've learned that your emotions cut through it. I just need to feel them."

"Alright," I stated, frustration coiling through me. I began to turn away deciding I was done with this conversation for the night.

"Absolutely not. Come here," he said. "You don't get to accuse me of another woman who doesn't exist like we haven't both been cutting each other open."

Rage colliding through me. "Yes, Rhaelin. I do."

I closed the distance in two steps. "Because I'm the one keeping us both alive. I'm the one lying to my sister. I'm *not* the one who walked into the House waiting to be fed."

"Neither did I," he snapped.

"But you choose what to hide."

"I choose what keeps you breathing."

It felt like electricity from both our stubbornness was running through me.

"Tell me why you get angry when I look at you," I said, sick of the guessing.

His brows shifted. "You think it's anger?"

"It burns."

"So does restraint," he said. A slow roll of his shoulders, the fabric pulled tight. "Mine. From you."

The room narrowed. His honesty completely threw me off. "Then the heat—"

"Is you," he said. "It's because of you."

I held still. The bond didn't, it was climbing upwards like it had decided for both of us.

"Then stop looking at me," I said.

"No can do."

We stood there, breath for breath.

"You can't keep asking me to carry it all and pretend it isn't there," I said.

"I'm not asking you to pretend." His jaw flexed. "I'm holding it in place."

"It doesn't feel held."

"It is," he said. "If it wasn't, Zyrenna... we wouldn't be talking right now."

Something in me ruptured—quietly, invisibly, but enough that I felt the shift in my bones.

I couldn't look at him. Not when the truth hovered so close I could taste it.

Not when the air between us felt too thin to breathe.

If I stayed another minute, I was going to say something reckless. Something real. Something he wouldn't let me take back.

And I couldn't survive that—another unraveling in front of him.

My mouth went dry. The room tilted a fraction; I set my palm on the table, then took it back like it burned.

I turned before he could say anything else.

The hall was cooler. Stone took the heat out of my skin. I focused on simple things: cloak, door, air. Don't look back. If he gave me one more truth, I would end up in his hands and hate myself for it tomorrow.

At the threshold I found my voice. "Take me home," I said, not loud.

Silence, then footsteps.

I didn't wait for an answer. I stepped onto the balcony until he met me there.

CHAPTER FOURTEEN

ZYRENNA

I stayed home for four days.

Four days of pretending the bond wasn't tugging at me. Four days of sweeping the path between the vineyard rows as if work could muffle what lived within me. Aunt Kaelen kept Alira busy with baking and small lessons. Her voice stayed even, her hands never shook. She braided dough into ropes and my sister did the same.

But Alira noticed. Of course she did.

She sat across from me one evening at the kitchen table, dark hair falling into her blue eyes, picking the crust from a heel of bread between us. The kitchen smelled like yeast and apple. We'd left the window cracked just slightly for air.

"Tell me what's been going on," she said finally. "Every time you come back, you look more tired. Like something's eating at you."

My throat tightened. I forced a smile that felt like a bruise. "I've just been working more. Extra vein contracts in the other districts. It's nothing to worry about."

Her face pinched. "Like Mother?"

The words cut. I reached across the table and took her hand. Her fingers were cold from the draft. "No. Not like Mother."

Her eyes searched mine, too big for her face, too honest for this house. "Then promise me. Promise you'll come back."

I hated the ease of the lie, the way it knew my mouth. "I promise."

She nodded, but the doubt didn't leave. She never said I don't believe you. She never had to. I spent the next hours soaking up everything I could: the way she tilted her head when she laughed; the way she sucked jam from her thumb like a child even though she hated being called one; the way she leaned against my shoulder when she thought I wasn't paying attention. Peace was a thin blanket these days. When she went upstairs, the house exhaled and the ache in my chest grew at her absence.

I found Kaelen in the kitchen. She was packing the leftovers into jars, tying cloths over the mason jars with practiced knots. She had brought supper as she often did, a duty she claimed the week my mother passed and never surrendered, but food was always scarce no matter the source. She and my mother had been inseparable. Grief had carved her, too. The difference was, Kaelen didn't let it hollow her. She added weight where we needed it. Not for me, but for Alira. They had always been closer.

For me, her presence rubbed raw. Every glance pulled up memories I couldn't smother without feeling the burn. Even so, respect ran thick through us. She respected that I would bleed and fight and break if it meant Alira lived. I respected that she stood where my father had fallen and didn't call herself a hero for it.

And lately—because I don't have many people left—I've been trying to meet her halfway. Trying to make the pieces between us mean something instead of letting them rot.

It isn't easy. But then again, I guess nothing worth keeping ever is.

"Listen, Zyrenna," Kaelen said, lowering her voice. She tied the last cloth and tucked the jar into her basket. "I don't know where you've been disappearing to, and I won't ask. We are all owed a measure of privacy."

Her pause stretched.

"But Alira notices. She's young, not blind. She looks for you every time the door opens. She worries when you don't come back by dawn."

"I always come back," I said, too fast.

"Do you?" Her eyes pinned me. Not cruel, not accusing, just true. "Because if one day you don't walk through that door, she will not survive the pain. She has always loved you more than anyone; you have always been her solace."

The words landed like stones on my chest. I didn't ask her to soften them. I wouldn't have let her.

"I'll try like hell to keep that girl above water if it comes to that," Kaelen went on, voice roughening. "But there's only so much death a person can take before it hollows them entirely. I've seen it. I've lived it. And Alira… she's too young."

I swallowed, and the ache grew.

Kaelen lifted the basket to her hip. "So promise me. Whatever it is you're doing, I'll keep telling her your story, the one about extra contracts, extra vein offerings. I'll keep the lie alive if it lets her sleep. But understand…" her eyes shone, though her voice didn't break, "I love you both. And if pain comes for her the way it came for your father, there will be nothing even I can do to drag her back. You may be protecting her now, but if you're gone, no one will protect her from herself."

Silence weighed the kitchen down. My hands curled on the table's edge until my knuckles hurt.

"Promise me," she said again.

I nodded. It was more than a promise. It was a thank you I couldn't say aloud.

She left with the soft click of the back door and the rustle of the olive leaves beyond the yard. I stood in the empty kitchen and listened to the house remembering other sounds: my mother's low song when she measured flour; my father's boots dragging after dusk; Alira's toddler-steps on the stairs. The past has a way of hanging up its coat and staying.

* * *

That night I shut my bedroom window. Tonight, I wasn't ready. Not after the fight that left everything in me scraped raw with Rhaelin, not after Kaelen's words, not after the way Alira had said promise like it was a thing you could hold. I chose time. So I didn't go to the olive path. He could survive a night without me.

I lay down without lighting the candle. The room knew my shape in the dark. The bed knew where I curled when the bad dreams came. I let the nightmares take the first move.

Sleep dragged me under fast and hard, the way a tide drags a body off shore. It didn't start with pictures. A door that wouldn't open because my hands wouldn't work. When one horror ended, another began. Each time I reached the end of one scene, another took its place. Faces blurred. My mother's scarf hung on the peg by the stairs where it always had and always would. My father's voice said my name from the courtyard and then went quiet.

Then the dream tilted.

I was twenty-four, not the child I'd been then, but standing in the same moment all the same. I woke in my old room, the air heavy with winter, and walked to the kitchen the way I always had—expecting to find him at the table, half-asleep with his hands around a mug. He stopped going to bed once mother died.

But he wasn't there.

Something inside me went still. Part of me already knew what that meant.

I went outside, toward the shed where he kept the tools for the vineyard. Frost cracked under my boots as I ran, breath tearing at my throat. Every step felt like confirmation of a truth I hadn't yet seen but had been carrying for years.

The door resisted when I tried it—jammed, as though he'd tried to block it, to spare us the sight. I forced it open anyway.

And there he was.

The memory hit with perfect, merciless clarity: granite biting into my knees… blood too hot on my hands… the thin, precise line across his throat where he'd cut the world out of himself.

I remembered the sound I made—raw, broken—remembered the way my body folded in on itself as if the grief were physical enough to drag me to the ground.

I remembered falling.

And in the dream, I fell again.

When I jerked awake, the moon hadn't moved much. The room held a thin kind of light. My mouth tasted like metal, and for a second I didn't know where I was. Then the ache in my back from this bed and this house told me. The bond told me the rest.

It was burning hotter.

I sat up—mind slow, skin prickling. The air changed before the sound did. The shadows shifted like they'd made room for someone. My body knew first, the prick up the spine, the stuttered heart, before my eyes confirmed what they already believed.

He was already inside.

"Zyrenna." His voice came rough, restrained.

I spun, fury climbing my throat. "You can't just—"

"I know."

He didn't lift his hands, didn't reach for me. He kept them at his sides like he was restraining a storm.

"I'm sorry. You weren't coming back."

He stepped closer. The tether throbbed, so much so that it nudged my balance. His eyes caught the moonlight and went feral green. He stopped a pace away, giving me space and stealing half of it at the same time.

I wrapped my arms tight across my chest. "I wasn't ready. You don't get to decide when I am."

Something rippled across his face. Pain. He buried it almost as soon as it showed.

"I understand," he said quietly. "And it *is* your choice."

The weight in his voice wasn't authority—it was guilt. "I'm sorry it has to be this way. If I could leave you with them, I would."

My throat tightened, though I refused to show it.

"It isn't about what either of us wants." His gaze held mine, unwavering. "I need you."

The words froze me clean.

Need is a strange blade. It cuts two directions at once. Warmth crawled under my skin, the kind that tells you someone just changed the rules in a room you thought you understood.

"And I'm afraid," he added, voice dropping to something that brushed my bones, "it will be that way until your last breath."

Something inside me jolted—rage, fear, want—I couldn't tell them apart anymore.

He moved one step closer. The air thinned. The bond tightened… and steadied, like it approved of something I absolutely did not.

"Vulnerability is something I trained my whole life to avoid," he said. His jaw worked once, muscle tightening as if he hated every word he was forced to speak. "My father taught me weapons, not emotions. He taught me that vulnerability is a weakness. That if something can be used to take pieces of you, you cut it off first."

He swallowed—barely audible.

"I need you to understand."

My voice betrayed me when I spoke. "Understand what?"

His breath left him—like the truth cost more than he'd expected.

"That you are my weakness, Zyrenna." He said it like a confession he'd delayed so long it had begun to rot inside him.

"My vulnerability. If anyone on the Council learns it, it gives them another reason to kill me. Everything I bled for in the Trials—everything I clawed to keep—turns to nothing."

He dragged a breath through his teeth, eyes flicking away, as if the words burned to speak.

"The Veil made me earn my place in the Spire," he said. "But the others didn't choose me. I've lived over a century, and you are the one thing I cannot master. The one thing that breaks my control."

His voice frayed. "And the only thing that's pulled me out of a century of emptiness."

It wasn't the kind of speech men made for anyone. It wasn't pretty, it wasn't careful. It was raw and unmasked and, for once, not about keeping me quiet.

I didn't move. If I moved I wasn't sure which direction I'd go. Anger felt wrong now, like the emotion wasn't mine or his. I thought about Alira asleep upstairs, hands tucked under her cheek, mouth open the way she won't forgive herself for in the morning. I thought about Kaelen tying knots and telling me the truth, because no one else would. I thought of all the things we'd lost, all the things still at risk.

"Then let it down for me," I said. "Be vulnerable. Make me feel like I can be that in return. Show me I can trust you. Prove you're not like the rest, the ones you say you despise as much as I do."

His eyes poured into me.

"Prove my sister's future is safe. Prove I won't leave her broken the way death already left us." I swallowed. "Give me something real. Show me what you're hiding. And then maybe—" my mouth twisted, "—maybe I can stop being such a stubborn, unyielding pain in your ass."

That earned me the smallest, most unwilling smirk.

His fangs caught the moonlight, and one of those infuriating dimples carved into his cheek like it was mocking me for ever thinking I was immune.

It broke something open inside me I did not want broken.

He knew. And I hated that I knew he knew.

His hand lifted, stopping just shy of my wrist. The air

between us turned electric, humming loud enough to feel in my teeth.

"You are astounding, Zyrenna."

Time stilled. Then, quieter—

"Tonight is yours. Stay."

No command, no expectation, just an offering.

For a second, I couldn't move. The word *stay* hung between us. How he said it like he wanted me to have everything I had ever let myself want.

"I'll come for you tomorrow night," he said. "I have something I need to show you."

I nodded once. Relief and ache collided so intensely my knees wanted to bend.

He didn't move closer. "Keep the window latched. I don't want to be able to get in here again."

The house went quiet, listening.

"Thank you," I said.

He inclined his head. No smile, no triumph. Only the line he'd drawn and chosen to honor.

At the window he paused, hand on the latch, head turned over his shoulder.

"Goodnight, Zyrenna."

"Goodnight," I managed. I didn't trust my voice to carry anything else.

I stood up, and locked the window behind him. I got back into bed, closed my eyes—but sleep never found me after that.

Tomorrow, then.

CHAPTER FIFTEEN

ZYRENNA

The night smelled like rain and earth when we left Solvane.

I shut the door behind me and checked the latch twice out of habit. The window stayed closed like I'd promised. The stones along the path still held the day's warmth, guiding me toward the olive trees where he stood waiting.

We didn't speak right away. The bond flowed, strong enough to pull me the last few steps.

He tipped his head, a question and an answer in one.

"I'm okay," I said, even though my feet were already betraying me.

"I know." The smirk was faint; the green in his eyes looked like it had learned fire. Of course he had the kind of smile that could ruin nations. Typical.

Then, before I could think another foolish second about it, the ground dropped away.

* * *

Flying was not graceful.

It wasn't slow, but speed and terror that punched straight

into my chest. Solvane shrank beneath us, suddenly fragile from above. Rooftops turned into pale shells; the river cut silver through the dark; and miles beyond, Nocthallow glimmered like a fistful of coal with embers still trapped inside.

The first gust hit. My body betrayed me, curling closer, fingers curling tighter. For someone supposedly cold-blooded, he radiated heat like a forge. I had never seen wings before his—and I hated that the sight of them stole the air from my lungs.

Veins shimmered beneath the membrane, faint and black, pulsing like a heartbeat.

"Breathe," he said, voice a low rumble through the wind.

"Yeah, no problem," I muttered. "I'll just relax while you kidnap me through the clouds."

A laugh rolled out of him—dark, satisfied.

"If this were kidnapping, little flame, you wouldn't be clawing your nails into my back trying to get closer."

My head snapped up; wind whipped my hair across my face. "Don't flatter yourself. It isn't voluntary."

His mouth tilted, smug and dangerous.

"Not yet."

The bond pulsed, and I wanted to punch him for how easily he twisted me into this, how looking down made me dizzy and looking at him made it worse.

I stared past his shoulder to distract myself. Far off, the Spire rose like a single spine against the horizon. Beautiful from here—too beautiful. But beautiful things often lie.

"Prettier from a distance," he murmured near my ear.

"You're the one sitting in it," I shot back.

"I'm sitting in it so one day I can burn it," he said. No

hesitation, no joking.

We didn't speak after that.

Questions crowded my skull but I kept them locked tight. The land unfurled beneath us until every patch of earth slipped into deeper shadow.

* * *

We landed in a clearing in a thick forest, the kind of dark that eats noise. I had never been this far east before. At first I saw nothing but moss and trunks as we started walking.

Then he stopped beside a broad rock face, nothing special about it except the way he looked at it.

He reached out and swept his hand across the surface, brushing away a thick patch of moss. It peeled back in one smooth drag, damp and green, revealing what had been hidden beneath it.

A carving.

A circle, etched deep into the stone. Lines spiraled inside it like roots or veins, converging at the center where a single drop had been chiseled. A drop of blood.

He pressed his palm to the heart of the carving.

Light rippled out from under his hand—first a dull red, then brighter. A thin line split down the rock, glowing as if something inside had finally taken a breath.

The wall parted without a sound.

My skin prickled. The bond tightened—not in warning, but like it was standing up straighter, recognizing something I didn't have a name for.

"You feel it," he said softly.

I didn't answer, but I did. Whatever lived in that stone was old. Older than the Spire. Older than the Houses. Old enough to feel familiar without ever having touched it.

Magic lived here.

He looked back at me, a rare softness threading through the green of his eyes.

"Welcome to the Embers, little flame."

We stepped into the passage. Torchlight flickered along the walls, catching the same sigil on the rock outside. The tunnel sloped downward, cool air threading under my cloak.

The place felt alive.

Not loud, not chaotic—alive the way a held breath is alive, all tension and intent, waiting for release.

The tunnel opened into halls and rooms carved directly into the rock, lit by burning candles. Still darkness consumed it though. The air carried cedar and leather—the same scent that lived in his keep, only denser here, richer. As if more of him belonged to this stone than to the Spire above.

Along the walls: racks of weapons. Crates stamped with the veined-circle mark. Everything organized with the brutal kind of purpose that made sense for him.

"Keep your hand here," he murmured, brushing my knuckles toward the wall. "It widens, then narrows again. You'll get lost and end up in the storeroom."

"Is that where you're planning to take me?" I asked. "Locked away with grain."

"Worse," he said without breaking stride. "Trapped with dried figs."

"Monstrous."

He didn't announce himself. He moved like the tunnels recognized him.

"This way."

We passed beneath a low archway, and the sound changed—metal striking metal, boots grinding over sand, the thud of bodies hitting the ground and rising again. A training hall opened before us, wide and echoing, its floor carved into several sand-filled rings.

In one ring, a human woman with braided hair and a spear faced a male vampire wielding a staff. You could always tell when someone was vampire—their movements had a precision that bordered on unnatural, an aura that seemed to bend the space around them.

She slipped beneath his first strike; he pivoted, checked her cleanly in the ribs, and they reset without a word—like two halves of the same movement.

No one watched like it was strange.

There had to be a hundred of them—more, maybe—spread across the room. Humans and vampires trained side by side across the hall—calling corrections, passing water skins, laughing between rounds. A boy not much older than Alira gripped a wooden staff with both hands, biting his lip in concentration. Nearby, a gray-haired human blocked three lightning-fast strikes from a quick-footed vampire and wheezed out a laugh like the whole thing was normal.

In Solvane, we tell stories until they calcify into rules: humans bleed, vampires feed; anything else is chaos. But this wasn't chaos. This was order—real order. Not the kind that grinds you down into a number or a quota.

This was... shoulder to shoulder.

My mind couldn't reconcile it. Everything I'd ever been taught cracked down the middle.

People made space as we passed—some with a chin dip, some murmuring *Commander*, a few offering quiet smiles that said *you're back.* He returned each look, not with a Councilor's distance, but with recognition. Names. Faces. History. He belonged here in a way I had never seen anyone belong anywhere.

My stomach dropped. I must've gone pale, because he stepped closer instinctively, not touching, but his hand hovered near the small of my back like a promise he wasn't sure I'd take.

"Now tell me again we're all the same monsters," Rhaelin said, not unkind.

It cut anyway.

Because I couldn't. Not while standing here. Not while watching people bleed and sweat *with* vampires instead of *because of* them. Not while every truth I'd held like a shield was suddenly full of holes.

Conversations thinned as we moved deeper; heads turned, eyes measured. His hand stayed where it was—hovering, steady, not guiding me, but ready if I needed it. He didn't need to touch me for the room to make space.

We took our place in front of the crowd, the air tilting as every gaze shifted toward us.

Rhaelin let the noise die down, then took the room. "I leave for a few weeks and you shitheads still haven't burned the place down. Miracles do happen."

Laughter rippled throughout the hall. A few called quiet welcomes, some lifting their chins in greeting. Someone near the back shouted something about how long it took him to return.

Only then did he shift, the air tightening a fraction.

"This is Zyrenna Vaeoria," he announced. "You speak to her as you would to me. You look at her as you would look at me.

If you cannot manage that level of respect, you do not speak or look at all."

A brief silence followed—not tense, just a single shared beat where the room seemed to *register* the weight of his words. A moment of understanding. A moment that said they knew exactly what it meant for him to speak my name with that kind of authority.

Then the quiet broke.

A few voices rose at once—soft greetings, chin-dips of respect, someone offering a warm "Welcome, Zyrenna," from one of the rings.

Another called out, "Good to have you here," and a small ripple of agreement followed, genuine and unforced.

The room eased back into breath and motion.

But the warmth of it didn't reach me.

Everything felt too bright, too loud, too alive.

My pulse roared in my ears like I'd been dropped underwater.

The floor tipped once; my stomach hollowed. I didn't know where to look—faces, weapons, banners overhead, all blurring into noise. It was too much and not enough and utterly impossible to hold.

And then he stepped into my line of sight.

Close enough that his shoulder blocked the crowd, close enough that only he existed.

"Zyrenna," he murmured. "Here."

My eyes dragged up to his.

"In for four," he said quietly, "out for six."

His voice anchored me; it always did when I least wanted it to. "Stay with me. Not them."

How any of this was real? How any of it was possible?

He breathed once so I could match him. Once. Twice. The sound in my ears softened; the floor steadied. My chest deciding it was okay to loosen.

When I finally glanced past him again, the room had already moved on. Eyes elsewhere. Bows drawn. Staffs lifted. The world didn't care about my near-collapse.

But *he* watched me. Only me.

"You're planning a war," I whispered.

His eyes met mine.

"No, Zyrenna. The Council already started one. We're planning how it ends."

For once, the bond wasn't playing tug-of-war—no push, no pull, no war inside me. It felt like agreement. Like alignment.

"These people," I said quietly. "They're yours?"

"They're under my command," he answered. "Their lives are my responsibility."

He paused, gaze sweeping the fighters across the hall—human and vampire, grit and grace side by side.

"But their lives are their own."

My throat tightened. "How is this even possible? This many people—humans standing equal to vampires. It's unheard of. A single vampire could tear through a dozen humans without pause, Rhaelin."

He gave a single, measured nod.

"It's unheard of because humans never fought beside vampires—only against them."

His voice slipped into something older, something weighted. "They were never given the chance to learn from us... or us from them. They only knew chaos. Scrambling to survive. Always on the defensive, never the offensive."

He watched a human girl drive her spear into her sparring

partners armor, reset, strike again—precision, not fear.

"I've trained almost everyone here," he said. "Those I trained passed their skill on. Humans can fight back, Zyrenna—sometimes better. A vampire's weakness is impulse. We strike too soon, blind with hunger."

His eyes cut to mine. "But mortals? When trained—they can read a field before they step into it. They can wait. That patience puts a blade at our throats. They've always had the ability. They just never believed it, because we carry the fangs."

I stared at him, disbelief tangling with something that felt dangerously like awe. "But how have you managed this?" I asked. "How have you not been caught—with this many people?"

It spilled out of me. None of this felt real.

His jaw tightened.

"After the Blood War," he said, voice dropping low, "people got sloppy. The Spire took years to build after the fighting ended—and while they stacked stone and carved thrones, the fractures beneath them spread."

He looked away from me, toward the hall—toward all the lives he'd gathered under the Council's blind nose.

"The Council was too busy polishing their seats of power to notice," he said. "They paraded the Treaty like salvation while the Crimson Houses kept filling graves. Humans bled dry while the Council turned its face the other way… the way they still do."

"That was when I started," he went on. "Not before the war—I was too young then. But after, when the smoke cleared and the dead were still being buried… that's when I began pulling people into the shadows. One fighter, then two, then a dozen.

Humans who had nothing left to lose. Vampires who couldn't stomach the Council's rot. I trained them, they trained others. Until what you see here was no longer just an idea."

His gaze swept the room—faces, histories, loyalties he'd carved from ruin.

"My seat on the Council made the rest possible," he said. "It gave me access to things. Lists of condemned districts in Solvane. Names. Contract schedules." His jaw cut sharp. "I knew which vampires were dangerous, which ones enjoyed the hunts, which ones the Council planned to unleash next."

He stepped forward, voice lowering.

"And from there, I learned how to pull them out—quietly. How to reroute the contracts. How to make orders disappear before they were ever carried out. How to make it look like those directives never existed at all." A mirthless laugh. "The Council was too stupid—or too proud—to notice."

He drew a quiet breath.

"I watched humans run blind and vampires tear through battle without thought. The Blood War was chaos—whole cities burned for greed and hunger. That's when I realized mortals could fight as well as we do, if they were taught. Better, even."

I looked toward the sparring ring again—the human woman driving her knife clean into a vampire, the others watching, learning. Blood spilled from his chest, but he would heal.

"And they've never noticed?" I asked. "Never suspected any of this?"

"They don't look for strength in the places they've already dismissed," he said simply. "They look down on you—on humans. That arrogance is my shield. As long as they believe you're nothing but prey, they will never see what you're becoming."

The bond flared, like it recognized something I wasn't ready to.

"And what are we becoming?" I asked.

"The thing they should have feared all along."

My throat constricted, but I forced the words through it.

"Then why hasn't anything been done? You have weapons, strategy. You've been building this for decades. It's been over a hundred years, Rhaelin."

He hesitated.

Not a dramatic pause—a painful one.

The kind that tells you the truth is heavier than the silence that holds it.

"The numbers," he said at last. "I've trained just over five hundred men and women I trust. Humans and vampires both. Fighters who bleed for something more than coin. Every one of them could stand against a Council soldier—some against three."

His tone hardened. "But the Council commands thousands. Entire legions sworn to the old bloodlines. For every one of us, there are twenty of them."

He drew in a slow breath. "And then there's the matter of time. Human time. Men and women of your kind dedicated their entire lives to this—training, gathering intel—only to age out before they ever saw it finished. Because the moment was never right. Because survival demanded patience. Because the Council kept tightening its grip."

The pain in his voice was quiet but unmistakable, the kind that didn't fade—only learned how to stay hidden.

"It clearly wasn't for nothing," I said. "If they gave their lives to this—to *you*—they must have seen something."

He held my gaze a moment too long. Long enough that I was the one who looked away first. *God, his stare.*

Silence accompanied us as we walked on. Past drying clothes being hung, to a narrow infirmary—cots, clean linens, a glass cabinet lined with vials. Past a storeroom stacked with bowstrings, packs, flint, and coiled rope.

We turned into a long chamber filled with tables. Maps sprawled across them—borders, patrol paths, notes in the margins: names, times, routes. Not guesses but stolen truth. My stomach tipped. The Council would kill for less than this.

I didn't understand every mark. But I understood the room—people moving like the next second mattered. A narrow-shouldered vampire adjusted a pin by a nail's width. Two teenagers, one human and one not, whispered code phrases until they no longer stumbled. On the far wall, a chalkboard listed names under *Missing*. Some lines were struck through, rewritten beneath *Found*.

"Later," he said, catching my expression. "You'll see more when you need to."

We kept moving until the corridor opened into a wall of steel blades—short knives, curved swords, polished axes. He stopped, looked at me, then at the weapons.

He chose a knife with dark leather wrapped around the hilt. "For you."

I took the knife, heavier than I expected. He watched me find the weight of it, then reached for my hand. His fingers closed lightly around my wrist, adjusting the angle with a touch that made the bond flare like someone striking flint.

"Strength starts at your core, not your shoulder," he said. "The forearm is for precision—control, not power."

"I'll remember." And I meant it.

Footsteps approached. A scarred vampire stopped a pace away, pale-eyed. Up close, the scars cut everywhere—jagged, old, the kind earned from surviving something meant to end you.

"Commander," he said. Then to me: "Vaeoria." Not mocking. Just testing the shape of my name.

"Darius," Rhaelin returned.

"We moved the watchers east of the Spire," Darius reported. "Two rotations. If the Spire has extra eyes in the woods, we'll catch them before they catch us."

"Good," Rhaelin said. "And the records?"

Darius's mouth curved, almost satisfied. "Destroyed. What we couldn't burn, we bled of ink."

I didn't ask what records, I could guess. Contracts or names. Proof that someone was owned on paper.

Darius's gaze flicked to my knife, then to the distance—or lack of it—between me and Rhaelin. "If she trains," he said, "she starts with the planks. Blades later. Balance first."

Rhaelin didn't argue. "You'll set the drills?"

"I will," Darius said, and walked off with a nod that felt like a promise.

We continued.

The next room was smaller, warmer, edges softened by blankets and cups and a kettle cooling on a stone counter. People sat at a long table eating stew. A human woman looked up, grinned—a bright, easy smile. Hair cut to her jaw, dark eyed and amused. A ring on her finger bore the veined-circle sigil.

"Maris!" Rhaelin said—far too enthusiastically for someone who usually threatened people for sport. "Any word from Southmarket?"

Maris didn't even look up at first. "Why are you talking like you've had three cups of coffee and a near-death experience?"

He let out an overly dramatic sigh, the kind that belonged on a stage. He pressed a hand to his heart like he'd been mortally wounded.

"Maris," he said, voice full of tragic grandeur, "must I truly come within inches of death for you to be even *slightly* excited to see me?"

Maris didn't blink. "Apparently."

He exhaled sharply through his nose—offended, theatrical, ridiculous.

"Any word from Southmarket?" he tried again, tone still far too bright.

Finally, unimpressed, "Three crates through the well," she said. "Salt, flour, two sacks of barley. We'll have bread again."

Her gaze slid to me, not unkind, more curious. "So. You're the one everyone's been talking about."

I blinked. "The one?"

"We heard about you before we saw you. Word is you told the noble shithead to 'drop the theatrics' in his own region."

My ears burned. Beside me, Rhaelin's mouth barely moved. The expression wasn't quite a smile—more a *not sorry* carved into his face.

"He was performing," I muttered.

"And you cut the show," she said, approving. "Good. A mouth like that saves time."

Rhaelin gave a low laugh. "If you only knew," he murmured.

I rolled my eyes, which only made his almost-smile sharpen.

"Eat," Maris said, sliding a bowl toward me. "You'll need it."

I took it—because I wasn't stupid enough to refuse stew when someone offered. The first spoonful tasted of rosemary, rich bone broth, and something faintly sweet. I hadn't realized how hungry I was until my hand trembled around the spoon.

The flavor stirred a memory I hadn't touched in years—my grandfather bent over a pot in the kitchen, stirring with the same patience he gave the vines. My father used to say that recipe was the only comfort worth passing down, the one thing that survived debt and war.

For a moment—with each bite—it was like sitting at that table again, before everything fractured.

"Thank you," I said.

"Don't thank *me*," Maris replied, already bent over a report full of supplies. "Thank the whole shift that moved the ingredients through without anyone seeing. You want to stay alive, you learn the routes. You want to keep others alive, you learn them by heart."

"Maris runs supply," Rhaelin said. "When people eat, it's because she made sure they could."

"Flatter me later," Maris said dryly. "We're low on bandages. Someone bled all over three shelves."

Rhaelin's gaze snapped instantly to my wrist.

Of course it did.

Heat climbed my cheeks. I set the bowl aside and lifted my arm in blatant, theatrical exaggeration to prove I was fine.

Looking back at Maris he said, "Do you ever deliver information gently?"

"Once," Maris said. "Didn't care for it."

I laughed mid-bite, almost choking on the stew.

When I finished eating, we moved on in silence, turning down another corridor. The air grew cooler, heavy with the scent of earth and stone.

Along the walls, crimson-orange veins glowed beneath

the rock in rhythmic pulses, like the embers of a dying fire refusing to go out. The stone hummed with it, an undercurrent of power that felt disturbingly alive, as if the whole place had a heartbeat I could almost hear.

"Where does it come from?" I asked quietly. "All this magic down here."

He slowed, brushing his fingertips against the wall as if checking for a pulse. "Not from me," he said. "From a friend. A Veythari named Aurelian—the one you saw me speaking with in Solvane."

Shock hit me. "Veythari know about this place?"

"He's the only one who does," Rhaelin said. "Aurelian is ancient—older than the Spire itself. He never lost his power like most of his kind. When this place was first built, he still carried great strength—enough to twist stone and root. I was fortunate he had anything left to give."

He stopped before a narrow door and pushed it open.

A small room waited beyond—bare but clean. A carpet on the floor. A shelf with a pitcher and two cups. A single hook for a cloak. A bed with blankets folded with almost ceremonial precision.

"This is yours," he said.

"Thank you," I said. "I don't even know what to say."

"You don't have to," he replied. "Training starts tomorrow. Staff, then dagger. You'll learn to move, to break holds. You will not be powerless here."

He hesitated, his gaze steady. "And if you stay—"

A pause.

"It will be because you choose to. You only stay if you want to."

I looked down at the carpet, at the clean lines of the room, at the simple courtesy of a space meant for me. Something in my chest ached in a way I didn't yet have a name for.

No one had made space for me in years—not like this, not without asking something in return. It shouldn't have mattered. It shouldn't have hit anything inside me. But apparently I wasn't as numb as I thought—because it did.

CHAPTER SIXTEEN

ZYRENNA

Rhaelin left me at the door with nothing more than a nod.

"I'll give you the night," he said, his voice low. "Settle in. No one will disturb you."

And then he was gone, boots echoing down the corridor. For the first time since the vineyard, I was alone.

The room felt quiet. Just four stone walls, a bed, and the low hum of rebellion through the walls. It smelled faintly of clean linen and the smoke that lived in the bones of this place. I lowered myself onto the bed, trying to convince myself I could rest here. The quiet pressed at my ears.

I sat, lay back, then sat up again. The bed gave a little under my weight and complained when I moved, a low creak that made the space feel even more bare.

A soft knock broke the quiet, so soft I almost didn't hear it.

My heart climbed into my throat. He'd said no one would come. I stood anyway, fingers finding the latch before my brain did, I opened the door, and went cold.

Torchlight touched a face I knew better than my own. High cheekbones. The faintest scar at her temple from the summer the ladder slipped when we were eleven. Eyes I had spent years memorizing because I never thought I would see them again.

"Solena?" The word scraped out of me like I hadn't used it in years.

Her mouth curved, hesitant but real. "God," she breathed, and a laugh folded into it like she didn't trust it yet. "It's actually you."

The world tilted. For years, I'd told myself she was gone. No body. No goodbye. No answers. Just a hole you learn to walk around so you don't fall in it. I had buried her a hundred times in my chest, every time Alira asked why Solena stopped coming by the vineyard. And now she was here. Breathing.

Air tore through my lungs. I reached out, drew back, then reached again, like my hands didn't belong to me. "No," I whispered. "How...?"

"I'm here," she said, stepping forward.

That was all it took. Whatever I'd braced, whatever I'd trained to hold, dropped.

I grabbed her and held on like I could keep time from moving by digging my nails through her cloak. She was real. Her arms came around me hard. Her breath shook against my hair.

Tears burned and spilled without permission. I suddenly didn't care that I wasn't alone. Years of longing ripped open in a heartbeat. "I thought you were dead," I choked. "Solena, I thought you were dead."

"I know." Her voice cracked. "I know, and I'm so sorry."

She was warm. She was stronger than I remembered, a tightness under her skin that hadn't been there before.

I pulled back far enough to see her face. The years had drawn small lines at the corners of her eyes.

"Rhaelin saved me," she said before I could ask again. "After that… I couldn't go back. Not to Solvane. If anyone had seen me, if anyone had been watching, they would've followed me straight here. Straight to him. To all of this." Her gaze flicked down the hall. "I couldn't risk the movement. I couldn't risk telling you."

"So you just left?" I said, the words cutting sharp, even through the relief flooding my bones. "I searched for you. I waited by the well, night after night, convincing myself you'd come. You were all I had. I told myself you were dead."

Her eyes shone, glassy under the torchlight. "I wanted to go back every day. But down here we have rules. People above ground stay above ground. People below typically stay below. If we cross lines for personal reasons, we get people killed. If I'd gone back, it wouldn't have been just me they took. You, your sister, your father, anyone you stood next to." She drew a breath that sounded like a cut. "I thought staying away was the only way to keep you safe."

The bond pushed at the edge of my awareness, a question without words. Not invasive. Just there, like a hand hovering at my back. He didn't know why my chest felt split or why my breath couldn't find a pace. He only felt the storm and held on, the way he does. I let it flow through me, and for once I didn't push him out. I reached back, just enough. A quiet assurance, the pulse of *I'm okay.*

Solena still had my hands. Her palms rougher than before. "We compartmentalize, Z," she said softly. "You remember how we used to make rules for stupid games so we wouldn't fight? It's like that, just with lives. Above and below don't cross, only certain circumstances. If someone resurfaces after being written off at a House, the Spire's watchers catch it. So we don't surface. We cut the line clean."

"Clean," I repeated, and heard how my voice went dark on it.

She flinched, but didn't let go. "I know what it sounds like," she said. "I hated it. I hate it still. But I would hate getting you killed more."

"I would have hated it less if you'd let me know you were alive," I paused. "Hell, you could've brought us with you. Left us a sign."

"Moving one person is a risk," she said. "Moving a family is a bell going off. We've lost people trying. And, Zyrenna—you wouldn't have left them."

She let that sit, then added, quieter, "I tried once. Do you remember how we used to stack stones by the river?"

My breath hung.

"I paid a boy above ground who is in the Embers to stack three stones on the flat rock at the bend—our mark," she swallowed.

I saw it, clear as the day it happened. Late afternoon, market dust on my shoes, the river running low. Three stones, neat on the flat rock. For one heartbeat my chest cracked open. Then I told myself it was children. I walked past without looking back. At home I shut the pantry door and slid down it, crying into my sleeve at the reminder. I scrubbed the hope out of me and swore I wouldn't ever allow myself to hope again. Not for a second did I let myself think she was alive, because if I was wrong, it would finish me.

Tears burned my eyes now. "I saw the stones, Solena. I just couldn't put it together then."

We stood in it. The hurt, the relief, the old rhythm of being ten and running barefoot through the vines with our skirts hitched and our hands stained purple from stealing figs. I saw us at the table, waiting for my mother to finish cooking, the air thick with hunger and laughter. I sat down on the bed needing to gather myself.

"I'm angry," I said, quieter. "I don't know where to put it. At you for staying gone. At myself for not seeing the signs. At them for making this the way it is… does he know—"

She cut me off, firm but gentle. "No. I don't see how he possibly could. He doesn't speak our names above ground. Be angry. You're allowed. Just don't put it on him for this."

I sat with that, the truth settling heavy. I had never given Rhaelin Solena's name when I told him about my best friend who disappeared. There was extreme comfort in knowing he had no part in withholding this from me. We sat in silence for minutes.

"You will never know how truly sorry I am, Z. I will never forgive myself for the pain I made you carry."

She didn't rush. She didn't dress it up to make it less than what it was.

"I know what that does to a person, especially after your mom. I know the way it rots every corner of your brain. I know you counted bells and watched the roads."

Her voice thinned, then steadied. "Every morning for a year I woke up and faced west, because west was Solvane to me. When I kneaded bread for the hall I counted like we used to count rows in the vineyard so my hands wouldn't shake: twelve turns, fold, then press. When a runner came in from your district, I had to sit down or my knees would go weak. I practiced knocking on your door in my head a thousand times, preparing for the opportunity one day if it ever came."

Her eyes shone, unflinching. "You were my best friend. I chose what kept you breathing. I'm not asking you to forgive me tonight. I'm asking to earn it back inch by inch. But most of all, I just need you to know how fucking sorry I am."

The ache under my ribs shifted; it didn't loosen. Grief, yes. Anger, still. But threaded through, a thin bright line I hadn't let myself feel in years—relief. She was here. She was real. I didn't have to pretend she was a ghost that only visited when the house was too quiet.

"Now probably isn't the best time to tell you this but…" I paused. "My father," I said, and the words felt heavy as a stone in the mouth. "He couldn't handle the world without my mother. Couldn't hold it."

"Zyrenna," she whispered, then again, louder, as if saying my name could undo it. Her shoulders shook. Tears spilled unchecked down her cheeks, catching on her jaw, her mouth trembling with the effort of trying to speak. She pressed a hand against her lips, as though to dam the sobs, but they kept coming.

"I should've been there," she said, voice splintered. She clutched at my hands like she was afraid I'd slip away. "I am so sorry," she said, repeating it a few times.

She leaned into me then, head against my shoulder. I felt her grief as much as I heard it, a trembling that rattled through her bones and into mine. We breathed. The shape of the hurt didn't shrink—it became shareable.

I stared ahead of me. "I need an answer and I don't want it dressed up."

Solena's head lifted off my shoulder, staring at me now. "Ask."

"Can I trust him?" I asked. "He shows me enough to keep me from giving up. Not enough to let me all the way in."

She didn't pretend to think about it for long. "Don't look for the answers in what he says. Watch what he does. He guards his vulnerabilities and his truths like weapons, but I've seen the way he moves for the people he protects. That's where his honesty lives. If he's letting you close, that's no small thing, that's more than any of us down here have ever gotten."

She hesitated, then added quietly, "I was in that room when he introduced you. You didn't see me, but I saw him. The way his presence folded around you, the way he looked at you. If anyone can open him, Zyrenna, it's you."

I digested her words, letting it sink in.

"I'm here because of what he's done, not what he's said. He doesn't make promises he won't bleed for. And he doesn't ask what he won't do himself." Her gaze softened. "You don't have to trust him today, but if you stay, you'll see."

I nodded, her words steadying something in me. For the first time in years, I felt like I had a friend.

She pushed to her feet. "I'm going to let you sleep. It's long past midnight, and I've got things to do before the morning shift. I'll find you tomorrow."

At the door, her hand paused on the handle. She glanced back, her voice low, rough at the edges. "I really am sorry. For the barn, and for everything between then and now. But God, Zyrenna… I'm damned glad you're here," she said as she wiped away the last tear.

When the door closed, the room felt both bigger and more bare. Relief and anger kept trying to sit in the same chair. I paced once. Twice. The knife in my pocket tapped my thigh with each step.

I sat for what felt like hours, trying to calm the storm inside me, but there was no silencing it. Solena was here, she was part of this.

The tether kept humming, like Rhaelin already sensed something shifting in me. Before I could talk myself out of it, I pushed to my feet. My hands still trembled as I left the room, moving down the corridors lit by the veins in the walls. I had to tell him.

When I finally found him, hunched over a table, he looked up immediately, like he'd been waiting.

CHAPTER SEVENTEEN

ZYRENNA

He stood too easily for someone that large, too steady, too certain. Torchlight skated his shoulders and left him unchanged. His eyes fixed on me, not like he was looking at me but through me, measuring the shape of something I couldn't hide if I tried.

"What is it?" he asked, full of concern.

I opened my mouth, then shut it again. The words felt too heavy, too impossible to shape. Finally, I forced them out.

"Solena," I whispered. "She's alive."

For a moment, nothing moved—not his breath, not a muscle in his jaw. Then—

"I'm not sure I understand, little flame."

"No body. No answers..." My throat closed, but the rest broke free anyway. "All this time, I thought she was dead."

I saw his expression start to shift. As if I could see him begin to piece it all together. The bond surged so violently, shock crashing through me that wasn't mine. His hand pressed flat to the table, grounding himself.

"No," he said quietly, disbelief shaking the word apart. "She was the one you meant?"

I nodded.

He exhaled shakily. "Zyrenna, if I had known—"

"It's not your fault," I said, the words coming out quicker and harder than I intended. "You couldn't have known. None of us could've."

Silence pressed between us. My thoughts raced until one slipped out before I could cage it.

"Why show me any of this?" I asked at last. Quiet—because anything louder would've broken me apart. "You could've kept me in your tower. You could've kept me blind."

"Because you asked me to prove something."

His voice didn't waver. His gaze didn't shift. "And because we both know you are worth far more than the Spire."

He stepped closer—not crowding, just near enough that the air thinned, the way it does before a storm.

"I've put you in a position of power," he said, voice low. "I showed you this so you'd see I'm not the selfish, bloodthirsty bastard you've painted me to be. To give you some *fucking hope.* To make you want to live—truly live—not just breathe because the world hasn't killed you yet. To believe in something more than graves and debts."

His jaw locked; the muscle there jumped once, betraying him.

"You could walk into the Council chambers tomorrow and destroy me with what I've given you tonight. Ruin everything I've built."

"But why risk that?" I asked. "What if I say no?"

"You won't," he said simply.

My eyes narrowed. "Confident."

He studied me—too long, too thoroughly.

Then "Alright," he said. "Zyrenna—are you going to run to the Spire and tell them everything you saw tonight?"

Goddamn smart-ass.

"Well… no."

"Right. And how do I know that?"

He leaned closer, breath ghosting my ear. "Because I've never met someone with that much fury in them who wasn't me."

My body shivered.

"You are a flame that could burn the whole damn world, Zyrenna," he murmured. "And I intend to be there when it happens."

Chills ripped down my spine. For a heartbeat, every reason I had to hate him blurred—bent—fractured. Trusting him felt less like surrender and more like gravity, inevitable and already pulling me in.

He stood directly in front of me—close enough that I had to tilt my head back to meet his eyes.

"And don't think for a second I don't feel it," he went on, voice unrelenting.

His hand rose, fingers sliding through my hair from the crown down, tracing the line of my spine, his fingers stopped just above my waist. He knew exactly what it would do to me.

"Every ounce of want in you," he murmured. "The way you want me—the same way I ache for you."

Heat punched through me so hard my knees nearly buckled. The bond crackled bright and merciless. I stayed upright only because falling would've meant admitting everything at once.

"You won't walk away from this," he said, not as a threat, but as a fact. "Not from the power. Not from the revenge you've starved for since the day you lost your mother and your father. And not from me."

His voice dropped, lethal.

"Because I make you feel what you swore you would never feel again."

My pulse roared. The room collapsed to him alone.

His mouth hovered a breath from mine, tone cool and even.

"But I won't take one step further—not until you admit it to yourself. Until you can look me in the eye and say you want this."

His gaze held me pinned in place—green, unblinking, cutting straight through me.

For a terrible, perfect second, I couldn't hear anything except my heartbeat trying to escape my chest. He felt it—of course he did—and amusement flickered down the tether.

Bastard.

He saw enough to know I was at the edge. And the bond—god, the bond—made it unbearable, too much pouring through me to hold alone. He eased back half a step, giving me space without breaking the pull. A small, careful nod followed—the one I'd learned to read.

I see you. I'll hold it.

Then his side of the tether blew wide. His steadiness slammed into my chest, lowering my pulse so suddenly my lungs seized.

"In for four," he murmured. "Out six."

I matched him without choosing to—annoying as hell that it actually worked.

His gaze flicked to my hand fisted around the table's edge, white-knuckled. He reached as if to cover it. Something that should not have been as intimate as it was.

"You can still end it," he said quietly. "Walk away tomorrow. Tell me to close the door. I'll fly you home myself, and I'll make sure no one gets within a mile of your street."

"You think I'll walk?" I asked.

"No," he said. "I think you'll walk forward. Because that's who you are."

He was right, and we both knew it.

"I'll see you in the morning," he said. His hold on me released slowly—so slowly it felt like it cost him something.

My pulse thundered, every beat a protest.

And for the first time tonight, I knew he'd feel it—the heat he'd dragged me through again and again, slipping back across the bond to him.

But this time it would be my own.

CHAPTER EIGHTEEN

RHAELIN

The training hall smelled of iron and sweat. The kind of scent that settled in stone and lingered, no matter how many times the floors were washed. I'd lived in it long enough for it to feel like home though.

But today, when Zyrenna walked into the ring, it didn't feel like mine at all.

It felt like hers.

Maris had found her leathers: dark, close-fitted, stitched for movement, nothing ornamental—temporary until she earned her permanent set. Her hair was pulled back tight from her face, the ponytail stopping just above her waist. The kind of style meant for battle, meant to keep nothing between her and whatever she chose to destroy. She stood too straight for a novice. Fury makes that posture. She carried it like steel.

Fucking beautiful.

Darius stood across the sand, staff in hand. He waited for my signal, patient as ever. The room's rhythm shifted. Strikes softened, then slowed. Heads turned. No one crowded close. They only watched.

"She'll start with balance," Darius said evenly, his gaze placed on me.

"Don't talk to him," Zyrenna cut in. "I'm the one you're training. Look at me."

I laughed a low laugh, the kind that said this girl was ruthless. Darius blinked, caught off guard, and for once had nothing to say.

When he found his voice again, it carried a different weight. "Very well, Vaeoria."

Her silver-blue eyes cut to mine, all ice and warning. She liked me near, but not too near; it made her lose control. Something I understood well.

In that look, I couldn't help but feel it. The echo of last night still burning in my veins, her satisfaction flooding me as if it were my own. It was heat under my skin, a hunger coiled low in my body, so intense I could taste it. If I let myself linger on it, this training session wouldn't last more than a minute. I forced the thought back, burying it where it belonged. She needed balance, not my hands shaking with want. Still, when I reached for her hand, she didn't step away.

"Here," I said, guiding her grip to the staff. "Thumbs down, not out. You want control, not clumsy swings."

The second my fingers skimmed her wrist, her breath caught. Something only I would have noticed. Want roared through me so fast I nearly dropped the fucking staff. Keeping my hands to myself was becoming the hardest discipline I'd faced in a century.

Not yet. Not until she admitted what I already felt screaming through her blood.

Darius circled. "Step," he said. "Pivot. Strike. Keep your hips low."

She moved. Not graceful but fast. I prefer fast; you can teach precision.

"She's quick," Darius said after her third strike. His approval was rare. He carried himself the way the war had left him: quiet and scarred. He and I had bled across the same fields and survived the same nights. There were only a few men whose judgment still meant anything to me. Darius remained one of them.

"She's furious," I corrected. "Fury fades. Discipline doesn't."

Her eyes flashed. "I can hear you, dick."

"Good," I said. "Prove me wrong."

Darius let out a short, amused breath. "Furious indeed."

Her first mistake was all heel. She planted too hard, hips behind her stance, and the staff dragged her off center. I tapped the end of the staff, not hard, and she stumbled half a step.

"Again," Darius said. "Eyes forward. Don't watch your hands."

She tried to watch her hands anyway. Everyone does. I slid two fingers under her elbow and set it one finger's width closer to her ribs.

"Get low," I told her, voice low so it didn't live outside the ring. "Focus on driving through your core."

"Link your breath to movement," I added as she became breathless. "Inhale during defensive stances to regain your control, then exhale when you strike to generate more force."

We worked the planks next—two narrow boards laid out inches above ground. She looked at them like they insulted her intelligence.

This she was good at. Balance came to her as easy as taking a breath. We drilled. Step, pivot, strike. Reset. Step, pivot, strike. Reset. Hips under you. Eyes forward. The hours bent around repetition. She sweat through her leathers, hair sticking to her temples, cheeks flushed. Twice she bit back a retort and swallowed it, tiny victories you only see when you live inside a person's control the way I now do.

She made her way back to the floor while Darius barked orders. She shot him a look that would have gotten most men killed. He answered it with a slow, deliberate wink—the kind that said *you'll have to do better than that to rattle me.* She tried not to grin and failed. It knocked something open in her stance. But Veil, was it worth it.

"Again," I said.

She came at me then—hesitant at first, then braver—staff angling for my shoulder. I blocked without effort. Not to show her I could. To show her where the opening would have been. Her hips lagged. I tapped her shin with mine. She hissed, corrected.

The next pass she went high, dropped low, and cracked the end of her staff against my thigh hard enough to leave a bruise.

"Better," I said.

"You blinked," she shot back, breathless.

"Maybe," I allowed. Praise sits poorly in my mouth when it isn't earned. This was earned.

Darius left us with drills when the room picked up again.

"Water," Maris called from the doorway, tossing a bottle. Zyrenna caught it without looking and drank like she'd suddenly remembered she had a body.

"You're not hopeless," I told her when she passed it back. "That's the highest praise you'll get today."

She barked a laugh. "You're an arrogant bastard."

"Quick learner," I said—and watched her fight a smile until she lost.

The bond carried her exhaustion straight into my bones—and beneath it, a small, fierce satisfaction that hadn't been there when she'd walked in. Good. I wanted the work to carve something solid for her again. Wanted it to take up space where the grief had been eating her alive.

"Again," I said.

She huffed, wiped her mouth with the back of her hand, and stepped onto the plank.

* * *

By the time Darius called the last set, her shoulders were shaking but she was still setting herself to go again.

"You're done," I said. "We want you to be able to use your arms tomorrow."

Her eyes softened—just a flicker, a surrender she didn't mean to give. "Thank you."

We sat on the edge of the ring for a minute like two people who didn't owe the world anything. Feet buried in the sand. The hall emptying around us.

"Thank you," she said again, not looking at me. "It felt… good."

She searched for the word as if she had to drag it out of a locked room.

"I haven't worked like this since before my mother died. After that, everything got heavy. Time got small. Every piece of me went to Alira."

I let the silence hold it with her—didn't try to fix it, didn't tell her she was strong. She already knew.

"I'm glad it helped," I said. The truth, even if it wasn't enough.

She stretched her neck then—a small unconscious movement. Rolled one shoulder. Enough to tell me that she was tired.

And then I felt it. The pull. Low and specific, the particular hollow that lived in me when I'd gone too long. I hadn't meant to let it show. I'd gotten good at keeping it behind the restraint—she didn't need to manage me on top of everything else she was carrying. But the bond didn't lie, and she had started learning to read it the same way she was learning to read the sand in the ring: by feel, by instinct.

Her eyes came to mine.

She'd already felt it.

I said nothing. But still—she held out her wrist.

No preamble. No question asked and no answer offered. Just her arm extended between us, the inside turned up, the small blue lines of her veins visible in the low light of the hall. The same quiet matter-of-factness she gave everything she'd already decided on.

She'd known before I did.

Something moved through my chest. Old and too large for the moment. I took her wrist. Carefully—more carefully than the hunger asked for. Her pulse jumped when my mouth met her skin, and I felt that too. The warmth of her poured into me like the first real breath after too long underwater. Immediate. Necessary. The particular sweetness of her blood that had stopped surprising me and started feeling like something I had no word for yet.

I pulled back before I wanted to. Sealed the marks. Set her wrist down with more gentleness than the gesture required.

When I looked up, she was watching me with that expression I was learning: the one she wore when she was adjusting some internal calculation. Rewriting some equation she'd convinced herself was settled.

She didn't say anything—neither did I.

She went still. The bond drew tight in the air between us, vibrating with the thing she was about to say.

"I'm grateful you brought me here," she said finally. "Seeing what you've built… it's given me a hope I haven't felt since I was a child."

Her gaze lifted to mine.

"I know you risked your position bringing me here, and I won't ever put this place—or you—in danger. But I can't keep leaving Alira like this, Rhaelin."

My breath stilled.

"The time away is already more than I can stand," she continued. "I promised her I wouldn't go anywhere she couldn't follow. I break that promise every time I walk out the door."

There it was.

The knife I'd been waiting to feel. I took it without flinching.

"She's all I have," she said. Her voice was stronger than any steel on our walls. "Every day I leave, I risk her thinking I won't come back. And if she knew the truth…"

She swallowed. "I can't decide if it would kill her or keep her safe."

I welcomed all the emotions that surged through me from her end.

"If you tell her," I said, slow so I didn't step wrong, "then she knows. She can hate me. She can fear me. But she'll know why you leave. If you want her below, then it happens. She will be safe here."

Her eyes snapped to mine, fierce and afraid all at once.

"How can I guarantee nothing will happen to her?" she asked.

"I wouldn't have brought you here if I didn't trust this place with my life," I said. "She is safer here than she is in Solvane."

I let the next words come plain, without gentling them.

"But you need to know that taking entire families below is rare. It is a risk, and because of that, it isn't something we do often. We only do it when the cost of leaving someone above is worse."

She didn't miss a beat. "Isn't it always a greater risk?"

God, she was impossible. But also right.

My mouth twitched, the closest thing she'd get to a smile right now.

"Touché," I said quietly. "For most people above ground? Yes."

Her shoulders tightened, the weight of the decision already dragging at her.

"But selfishly?" My voice dropped, dark and unvarnished. "In *your* case, I don't want you up there at all."

Her face was unreadable.

"I want you here," I said, letting the truth bare its teeth. "Where I can find you. Where I know you're breathing. Where nothing touches you."

The flicker in her eyes said more than her smart-ass mouth ever could.

"If moving your sister below is what keeps you close," I went on, "then I'll take on every risk. Every precaution. Every route. I'll do whatever it takes to keep you from walking back into a world that would happily devour you."

Her mouth parted—just barely. The bond surged, hot and

unmistakably hers.

"So yes," I murmured. "She comes with you."

She lifted her chin then, those silver-blue eyes cutting.

Those fucking eyes.

"Has anyone ever told you you're an intense man, Rhaelin?"

"Once or twice," I said, a slow curve pulling at my mouth.

"And you don't plan on changing that?" she asked.

"Not a chance. I refuse to tone it down. Intensity serves me. Especially when I want something."

She swallowed. Rattling her was a pastime I had no desire to give up.

"And with you? I have no intention of softening."

Her pulse kicked—I felt it, clean as a strike.

"But don't mistake that for recklessness," I went on. "I know exactly where to put my restraint."

Her breath stuttered but she didn't look away.

"I'm an intense man, little flame…" I let the words brush the air between us, controlled and certain.

"But I'm also a patient one," a dark laugh escaped me. "And that means I am perfectly capable of waiting for the exact moment you stop pretending you don't want this."

A smirk settled across her face, then she huffed a laugh.

"You think I'm pretending?" she said, tilting her head. "No. I'm choosing. If I wanted distance, you'd know."

She leaned in, her breath a ghost against my ear.

"Maybe," she whispered, "I'm just enjoying watching you try not to break first."

Veil take me.

For one beat—one—my control slipped.

The tether blew open like she'd punched straight through my ribs. Heat. Want. A darker kind of hunger.

I shut it down fast, slamming the restraint back into place. But the damage was done.

"Careful sweetheart," I said, too measured for the chaos she'd just lit in me. "You throw challenges like that, and I stop pretending patience is for your sake and not mine."

Her mouth curved—slow, victorious. Then she rose to her feet.

She stood over me, chin tilted, silver-blue eyes cutting down like she knew exactly the reaction she'd just wrung out of me.

She shifted her weight, turning toward the archway.

"I'm going back to Solvane tonight."

The words hit harder than any staff strike.

Before she could take another step, I was standing too.

"Sorry," I said, tilting my head like I'd misheard something. "I thought you just said you were going back to Solvane tonight."

Her eyes narrowed. "I did."

"Right," I murmured, letting my smile sharpen. "Except that would mean someone is flying you."

I tapped a finger against my chest. "And I don't recall you asking me."

I shrugged, deliberately unbothered. "Must've been a slip in your memory. Happens when you're tired."

Her lips parted.

"Solena said she knows someone—"

I laughed. Actually laughed. The sound echoed off stone.

"No," I said when it faded. "You can just stop there. I will take you."

Her silver eyes snapped to mine. "That sounds a hell of a lot like an order."

"It's not an order," I said, stepping in until her back grazed the pillar behind her. "I just won't feel another man's hands on you when I can feel it burn through my veins."

Her mouth tilted. "Protective much?"

"Possessive," I corrected with a wink. "Don't mistake the two."

That earned me the smallest huff that might have been a laugh if she'd let it. The tether warmed in an approval she wouldn't admit.

Her gaze snagged on mine and held. I've been alive a long time. Limited things still steal my breath, but the way she looked at me was one of them.

"If you are planning on staying," I said, "we need to mark you for entry—so you can get in and out down here without me."

Her brows drew together. "Mark me how?"

"Not a chip," I said. "Something we call the Embermark. It binds to bone and answers only to our walls. You press your palm to the stone and the Embers read you as one of ours. Aurelian created it for us. I'll bring what's needed tonight."

"Commander," Darius barked from three paces behind us. I hadn't heard him return. He's good at that.

"Don't," Zyrenna told him without looking. "He's unbearable enough."

Darius's mouth twitched. His gaze flicked to her stance like he couldn't help inventorying it. He didn't like many people, but he liked her. Probably because they both carried their tempers like loaded weapons.

"We need you when you have a minute," Darius finished.

"Be right there."

He moved off, already shouting at a pair of trainees whose staffs were slapping instead of striking. The hall's noise rose around us.

"I'll be at the south corridor in eight hours," she said. "If you're late, I'm leaving without you."

"Best of luck to you, sweetheart," I shot back.

She stuck her tongue out and started for the door. She paused and rotated her head to the side, not fully turning.

"Thank you," she said. The word was enough.

"You're welcome." I didn't reach for more. I've learned when to let a good moment stand.

She left. The hall swallowed her footsteps and returned to itself. I stood in the center of it and let the room's weight settle back onto my bones. Then I moved.

"Darius," I called.

He appeared from a column of shadow like he'd been waiting. He usually was, he had a specialty in lingering.

"Double the watchers near Solvane tonight," I said. "Loose perimeter. Keep them out of sight lines. If you see Spire scouts, tell me."

"Understood," he said, then paused. The corner of his mouth twitched. "You're screwed, you know that?"

I gave him a look. "*Well fucking aware*, Darius."

"Just saying. That one's going to set fire to more than the Spire."

I didn't answer. He wasn't wrong.

"Can you be at the Embers Council in ten?" he asked.

I nodded. "Yeah. Be there shortly."

Turning away, I stopped at the armory—the familiar weight of steel waiting for me. Whatever softness she'd left in me, I buried it.

There was work to do.

CHAPTER NINETEEN

RHAELIN

It had been two nights sincc I returned from Solvane without Zyrenna.

The Spire Council's meetings dragged—another round of rotting politics dressed as order. I sat silently through ledgers and speeches spoken like prayers, merciful only because no one else had died this month. I cut away after to put out the fires that actually mattered underground. I tried to catch up on sleep, but it came the way it always does—like chains, not mercy.

Her absence made the bond quiet. I hated the quiet more than the noise.

When my eyes finally shut, the dark didn't soften. It pulled me back by the throat.

Back to the Trials.

* * *

The arena wasn't in the Spire. It stood on the edge of Nocthallow, a tower of stone with multiple levels. They called it a ring, but it was closer to a pit—walls high, sand raked flat.

Two hundred vampires went in. One came out. They

gathered two hundred of Nocthallow's strongest vampires, men and women. Whoever was the last standing earned the final seat in the Spire Council. Courtesy of the Veil.

On each level, there were viewing tiers. The powerful watched from shadowed boxes placing bets on who would survive. The rest of the city watched from the cheap benches, but everyone knew one thing: last one standing earned the seat.

There were only two ways to end a vampire. Steel through the heart, or a clean sever at the neck. Anything else just bought time—and time always belonged to us.

Alliances were spoken about like strategy, but everyone understood what they really were: delays. Sooner or later, there would only be one winner. Trust bled out first.

Food came just often enough to keep you standing. Water arrived in rusted buckets, sometimes tipped over on purpose. Weakness was currency. If you showed it, someone collected.

If you were careful, you slept sitting up, spine to stone, blade wedged beneath your thigh where no one could strip it from you.

If you were wiser, you didn't sleep at all.

Elias was with me, my older brother. We were forged from the same streets, running through smoke-black alleys of Nocthallow, learning to hold blades before we could write our names. He was the only one who could make me laugh when the world didn't deserve it. Where I carried silence, Elias carried light, even when there was none left to find.

"Side by side," he'd said the night they threw us into the ring. His voice shook but he smiled anyway, like his grin could keep the ground from opening under us. "We'll figure it out. We always do."

I wanted to believe him.

We worked together. Where his sword struck high, mine cut low. When I slipped, he steadied me. When he stumbled, I pulled. We had spent our childhood building a language that took people years to learn.

After the sixth day of staying alive, killing every day, fighting for water, for food, the air began to feel thicker. Like it knew how many had already died. One night, three competitors tried to cut our throats in our sleep. Elias woke to the first sound of a footstep. He always woke first. He broke a wrist before he was even on his feet, while I took the other two. Afterward he laughed low, the way he always did when we survived something we shouldn't have.

But hunger ate at us by the ninth day. Some fed on the fallen. That's part of the test—the Council wants to see what you become when you're given what they consider to be the easy way out. So I refused to feed. Not because I felt noble, but because I knew the shape I take when I do. It was the last shred of dignity I had left in that pit—a choice that was still mine. Elias didn't feed either; we starved evenly. We moved slower because of it, but we knew that didn't matter if we lost ourselves first.

Over time, faces blurred and names stopped mattering. I tried to hold each one for a breath anyway—a habit I taught myself in the alleys so the dead didn't turn to numbers. The ring hated that, all it cared for was numbers.

On the eleventh day, the shouts changed. Crowds got quiet. We were down to six. Then four. The third-to-last died laughing. I still don't know why. I can only assume deprivation got the best of him.

And then, when the sand had taken enough blood, when

only two of us remained, our pact became the blade drawn between us.

"Rhaelin."

Elias's voice was broken glass in the silence. His face was cut, dark hair plastered to his skin with sweat, his chest heaving. His sword trembled in his grip, though his eyes did not.

"Only one of us walks out," he whispered. His voice was raw, torn out by screams. "You know that."

"There's a way," I said, panic rising in my chest.

But he was already smiling, hollow and ruined. "You'll make it out."

I dropped my sword and reached for him. "Don't you fucking dare—"

Elias raised his weapon, not toward me, but inward. His hands were steady for the first time since we'd been dragged into that pit. He met my eyes, and something in me shattered.

"I love you," he rasped. "Live, Rhaelin. Do not allow your soul to die here."

"No—"

My scream tore out too late. His sword drove through his heart, his body collapsing before I could reach him.

The pit erupted. Cheering. Screaming. Applause.

I heard none of it.

I remember falling to my knees, clutching him while the warmth drained from his body into the sand. Pressing my palms to his chest as if I could shove the life back into him through sheer refusal.

His eyes were already glassing, unfocused, staring past me at nothing.

His blood soaked my hands, my chest, my throat, until I couldn't tell if it was his life or mine spilling away.

I stayed on my knees long after he was gone.

That was the moment the Council marked me a victor.

One survivor. One seat.

And that was the moment the ghost of Elias Morrain carved himself into me; a wound that never closed.

CHAPTER TWENTY

Midnight draped itself over the Embers when I returned. Outside, rain slicked the stone; down here, the air held a cool damp like the tunnels were breathing. It had been two days since I told Alira almost everything. She said she understood the danger of knowing truths like these. I wasn't sure anyone could, though. Some days I'm not sure I do.

She knows about the bond, about Rhaelin. About the Houses and the contracts and the Council. I told her where I'd been going, told her about the people under the ground who train and bleed and believe they can remake a world that decided what we were without asking.

Her face had gone pale. "You said there was nowhere you'd go that I couldn't follow," she said, her voice shaking not with fear, but with anger. "Mom and Dad are dead, Zyrenna. You think I didn't already live with danger? You thought keeping me in the dark made any of this better?" She took a step closer. "You took it upon yourself like it made you noble. It didn't. It just made you selfish."

I didn't answer because I would have reacted the same way. There was an anger in her that I knew well; I would not blame her for it.

"Do you know what it's like, watching the last bit of family you have left disappear and have no idea if they are coming back?" Her eyes glossed but she didn't let a single tear fall. "You don't *ever* get to make a choice like that for me again. You thought you were protecting me, but all it did was rip me apart more."

There was no begging, no theatrics—only truth, and it struck me.

"I'm sorry, Alira. I made the wrong call," I said. "It felt like the only one at the time. I didn't have answers—I still don't."

"You do not vanish. Not anymore. I'm done being left in the dark." She froze for a moment. With that, she went to her room to pack her things.

Before we left, I went to see Aunt Kaelen. She sat at her kitchen table like she'd been waiting, hands folded, lamp turned low. I told her we would be back, that it would be safer. That this was what she'd asked of me from the first day she said, "*don't leave that girl behind.*"

She didn't ask questions. She never did when she knew the answers wouldn't help. She'd told me she didn't want the details—that not knowing might keep Alira and me safer if ever pressed for the truth. It was one of the many things I respected about her.

She looked at me then, her eyes softening just slightly, and for a moment I saw the exhaustion she carried in her bones— the loss that never fully left her.

"I would hate to lose you both," she said, voice frayed at the edges. "You and Alira are the last of me. Don't make me bury what's left. And don't be a stranger. Whatever shadow you've stepped into, don't let it swallow your memory of home."

Her words lingered in me long after we'd embraced, long

after I'd led Alira away from the only home we'd known.

I had been prepared to send for Rhaelin—that was the plan. I would push to him, let him carry the burden, let him decide the route and the risks. It was the logical choice.

But when I pictured reaching for him, I didn't just think of him—I felt him. Not the usual hum at the back of my ribs, not the quiet static of knowing he existed somewhere. This was pulled, directional, like a compass between us. My body answered before my mind did, as if it had already marked him as *home*.

I forced a breath. "I can… I think I can get us there."

We began walking, Alira following close behind, and within the first mile I knew it wasn't memory or nerves guiding me. It was him. I could track him. The realization buckled something inside me; my knees nearly gave.

Alira noticed. "Zyrenna?" Her brows knit. "How?"

I couldn't explain it without sounding mad—without admitting that every time I tried to shut him out, the bond found a new way to drag him back in. But I couldn't deny it anymore either. The connection had deepened, honed itself, until it felt like the earth itself would bend before it let me lose him.

My voice trembled only slightly. "I can feel him."

I would not lie to her anymore. She said nothing, and the silence told me she understood.

So I followed it—the pull instead of the fear of it.

Every step through the fields, every turn along the dark roads, I felt him nearer. Not with sight or sound—with certainty. A thread under my ribs, taut. My hand brushed the dagger he'd given me at my thigh, as if that steel tethered me too.

By the time the hidden entrance to the Embers came into

view nearly two days later, my hands were shaking.

The bond hadn't just deepened—it had changed, and whatever this new thing was, Rhaelin was not going to take it lightly.

* * *

When we arrived around midnight, they gave her a small chamber right next to mine in one of the quieter halls. Alira set her pack down carefully and looked at everything, as if memorizing where it all went.

"You'll be safe here," I promised. "His people will look after you." *His people.* It sounded insane. "I'll be close."

Alira searched my face. "I'm not worried, Z." I didn't know what to do with the relief that line carried.

My smile felt fragile.

I brushed her hair back, kissed her forehead, and left before she could see how shaky my hands were from pure exhaustion.

Kaelen had packed a bag before we left—dried meat, bread wrapped in cloth, two skins of water. Enough to keep us upright, but not comfortable. She hadn't known we'd be walking—we hadn't either—she'd only packed what would keep us fed if we were delayed. And somehow it was exactly what we needed. The hardship over those two days wasn't the hunger; it was the miles. We walked without pause until the sky turned black, stopping only once to sleep in shifts. Two hours at most.

I could have called Rhaelin and avoided all of it, but I needed the time. The weight of the walk forced my head quiet, forced my body to earn whatever decision waited at the end of it. I wasn't going to put my sister's life in someone else's hands without bleeding for the choice first.

I stepped straight into the shower, scrubbing away the weight of the past two days until the water ran lukewarm and my skin was clean. Exhaustion clung to me like a second skin. When I finally dragged myself out, I threw on a loose linen shirt and shorts.

My hair dripped down my back as I stepped out into the corridor.

The moment I stepped into the hall, it hit me like a wave.

An overwhelming sensation of fear. My chest constricted, fear that wasn't mine. The kind that steals air and keeps it.

Rhaelin.

I didn't think. I ran.

The Embers stretched endlessly, torches blurring past as I tore through the tunnels. The tether pulled harder with every turn, guiding me until his keep loomed like black stone at the end of the passage. I pressed my palm to the carved slab beside the door. Heat sparked under my skin as the Ember-mark answered the stone, and the wall cracked open on a low groan.

I shoved the heavy doors open and sprinted up the steps two at a time—bursting inside.

Rhaelin thrashed on the bed. Sheets tangled at his waist, sweat soaking around his naked torso. His breath was ragged, strangled, and his hands—Veil save me—were clenched in fists tight enough to bleed.

"Rhaelin," I uttered, crossing the room.

He didn't stop. His body jerked like something invisible had struck him, lips parting on a low, broken sound that hollowed me out.

I gripped his shoulder, shaking. "Rhaelin, wake up!"

His eyes flew open, green wildfire. His arm came up on reflex—then focus slammed back into him. He dragged in a breath like he'd been underwater for hours.

"What the fuck are you doing here?" His voice was raw, cracking, nothing like his usual control.

"I felt you. Through the bond. You were drowning in it, I couldn't ignore it."

His stare hardened, half fury, half something else. "But how are you *here*, Zyrenna?"

I began, and absolutely fucking hated the way my voice sounded when I spoke—a reminder of how exhausted my body had been.

Guilt and defiance hit me at the same time. "I was going to wait for you," I said. "I don't know how to explain it…" My throat closed up, but I forced myself to push through. "I was going to have you come get us. We left two nights ago. I was ready to wait. But…" My voice broke again, shame tearing through my chest. "Then I thought of you, and it wasn't just a thought. It was like… like a thread wrapped around my ribs and pulling. I knew where you were. Every turn, every step, all the way from Solvane."

Rhaelin sat up slowly, the shadows clinging to him, his face hard and unreadable. But the bond betrayed him. Fury, relief, and a thread of fear tore through the bond.

"You tracked me," he said flatly.

"I just listened," I corrected. "I didn't fight it, and it just led me to you."

He pushed a hand through his hair, stood, paced, turned, every movement too controlled for someone who'd just clawed himself out of a nightmare. "Two days across open ground, Zyrenna?" The anger was his armor. The fear was the truth underneath. "Do you have any idea what could've happened? Two fucking *days!*"

The bond pulsed between us, furious. My hands curled into fists at my sides. "I don't know why you're pissed at me, Rhaelin. I have to learn what I am capable of eventually, right? I mean, you aren't telling me anything! And what was I supposed to do? Lie in bed while your nightmares drown you? Pretend I didn't feel your pain ripping me apart from the inside?"

His chest heaved. His silence said what his pride would not: *He was glad I came.*

Something in him eased. Not much, but enough. "I'm not angry at you," he said finally, voice rough. "I'm angry that I wasn't there to make it easier. And I haven't told you more because this—" he gestured between us. "—is the first time I've lived through anything like it. I only have what the archives say. Anyone else who ever lived through it…" his mouth twisted, "we'd have to dig up their fucking grave to ask."

I swallowed, the weight of it thick in my throat. "I don't know what I'm doing. I don't even feel in control of my own body anymore, Rhaelin. I feel like I'm going *fucking crazy.*"

His eyes softened, his expression easing just enough to show something like understanding. "I know. Sit down. You are exhausted."

Against my better judgment, I did. Because for some fucking reason I had no restraint left when it came to him. And my knees were done pretending they could still hold me after the miles I'd walked.

He dragged a chair across the floor and sat opposite me. "I've read everything I could find about this bond. It's a blood-forged tie. And it doesn't just connect hunger, pain, and nightmares. It's deeper," then he went quiet.

"Well fuck, Rhaelin—please, don't stop there. I'd hate to see you run out of dramatic pauses."

A breath of a laugh escaped him. "You really can't help yourself can you?"

He leaned forward, elbows on his knees. "It alters both sides. I'm supposed to draw from you—your strength, your blood, your fire… in order to fuel me. Makes me faster, sharper, more dangerous than I've ever been. But it doesn't stop there." He gestured faintly toward me. "In return, you're supposed to *feel* me. Think of it as a safety feature; it allows you to detect when my emotions become too overwhelming so you can help me contain them. Fear spikes, you get the warning. Rage builds, you feel the pressure. Heat—" his mouth tightened, "—you already know what that does. I draw from you, and you feel how my body responds to it."

My fingers locked together until the tremor calmed. "That's… baseline?"

"In what's documented, yes. From what I have seen personally, yes." His gaze held mine. "What those reports don't mention is anyone following a fucking pull across two nights like it's as simple as breathing. That isn't written anywhere."

He rubbed a knuckle once over his jaw; the movement brought attention to the ink covering his neck.

Veil save me, almost his entire body was on display. If discipline were a test, I was failing spectacularly.

I cut him off, "Rhaelin for fucks sake, please put a goddamn shirt on." It didn't matter how exhausted I was; I'd have to be dead not to notice his body.

The smallest smirk that said he knew exactly what he was doing. He stood up and grabbed a shirt, and threw it over his head. As if a piece of cloth was doing a thing to cover the muscle beneath it.

He hit me with an exasperated look and said, "May I continue now, sweetheart?"

When I said nothing, he nodded once, then went on.

"There are things you don't know. The Spire has always sold the lie that blood is payment—a mercy. But blood isn't just payment, Zyrenna. It's power. Different human blood types change vampires in different ways. Without humans, our kind would wither—not from hunger alone, but from weakness. Vampires only stand as superior because humans bleed it into them."

My lungs seized. "The Treaty—"

"—was never about peace," he cut in. "It was about control. Humans are kept alive not out of mercy, but utility. If all we needed was blood, we would drain livestock. But every drop taken from a mortal makes us stronger—every vein becomes a weapon for our kind. The Council keeps it quiet by paying off the human Council and Houses."

"What do you mean a weapon for your kind? What are you saying to me right now, Rhaelin?" I pleaded.

"Every human blood type carries a different kind of power," he said, almost like he was reciting something. "And when we feed, we take more than just blood; we take that strength into ourselves.

"Type A sharpens the *body*. Reflexes, speed, reaction time. Not every vampire is fast; only those who drink A-blood move like lightning, like they see the strike before it comes."

"Type B steadies the *mind*. Focus, precision, clarity under pressure. Those who feed on B are harder to break, and far better at breaking others. That's why the Spire hoards B-types; they shape generals and strategists."

"Type O fuels the *body itself*—endurance, stamina, healing. Vampires who drink O can take a dozen blows and keep moving. Their wounds close faster, their strength lasts longer. The Council breeds soldiers on O-blood, feeds their legions until they're nearly unkillable. Another reason why we've never been ready down here. Not enough Type O."

"Then AB," he said. "Rarest of the common types. A balance of A and B—speed *and* clarity. Fighters who move quickly and strike with precision. Their blood is the most valuable in the Crimson Houses. Humans with AB never live long."

My stomach turned. I blinked, the words heavy, almost too much to swallow at once. "So people don't know this? Not even the ones in the Embers?"

He didn't give me time to drown in it.

"Everyone knows the truth down here, just not up there," he muttered.

"But Zyrenna—your blood isn't just rare—it's forbidden. The old archives call it *Type S*. Any bond ever formed is only recorded through a human who has a Sanguis blood type. It is the blood type that doesn't just strengthen, it binds."

Rhaelin's stare cut straight through me. "But you're not just type S, Zyrenna—you're something more. The archives…they describe S-blood as a weapon. A bond that made vampires nearly unstoppable. But always one-sided. The vampire gained power, speed, clarity, and strength that rivaled armies. The human remained almost the same. Still fragile, still mortal."

His voice dropped lower. "But you're not fragile. You're

changing. I feel it right now—every time you move, more defined than the day before. Your instincts have grown." Your body is faster, too. Even your observations—you catch things other people wouldn't notice. There are no records of humans improving in this way. No record of a human feeling the power in return. None."

My breath was tight and burning. "So… what does that mean for us?"

"It means," he said, jaw tight, "that you and I are rewriting what the bond can be. And if the Council finds out, they won't just kill us. They'll kill just about anyone who knows."

The bond thrummed as if agreeing.

Rhaelin leaned closer, his voice raw. "What we already know is dangerous enough. The bond lets me feel your emotions, lets me know your fear, your rage, your desire, and most of all your strength. That much the archives confirm. But with you? It's growing. You found me through it. That's more than feeling. It's tracking, Zyrenna."

I swallowed hard. "And what if it keeps growing?"

His green eyes burned brighter than ever. "That's the question I don't have an answer to. There is no way to tell if there's no record of it. But I can only assume the unimaginable. We may speak through thought instead of voice. We may strike as one; two bodies, one force."

Silence stretched, the air thick enough to choke. My heart was pounding, every word sinking into my veins.

Rhaelin's mouth curved, but it wasn't a smile. "What this bond can become is beyond even the Veil's whispers. But I'll tell you what I do know, if we survive it, if we master it, we'll be everything the Council has spent centuries trying to bury. You will have been the key to this revolution all along."

CHAPTER TWENTY-ONE

RHAELIN

Her face would've been enough to break me.

"The rule is, the first blood test goes out with the first offering. A sample of your blood is saved and sent to the Spire."

"Then why didn't they test me?" she asked. "I'd be dead by now if they had."

"Because your parents never let them," I said, and the mention made her flinch the way I knew it would. "They took every vein contract they could so you'd never have to step inside a Crimson House. They shielded you—never gave them the chance. That's why the Council has nothing on you. Why no record exists." I held her gaze. "And the only reason they still don't is because I was the first to drink from you—and because I intercepted your blood sample before it reached the Spire. I dumped it before anyone could test it."

Her eyes hit mine.

"And I knew how to hide it," I added. "I knew how to smother what your blood did to me. The attendants are trained to clock the tells—the pulse in our throat, heat under the skin, the change in the eyes. They're paid to notice when a vampire leaves differently than when he entered."

"How did you hide it?" Her voice was a thread.

"Ended it early," I said. My mouth tilted without humor. "And I've practiced control longer than I've had a name that mattered."

I could see her mind working by the second.

"Any vampire can drink from any human," I went on, leaning forward, voice roughening. "If it isn't their aligned type, it won't kill them. They leave fed, satiated, just not changed. And apparently that was all Varik needed that day—an appetite quieted. That's why he made such a big deal of it being your first offering."

Her face went pale as stone, the silence between us dragging long enough that I swore I could hear her heartbeat.

She sat on the edge of my bed—my bed—fingers digging into her knees like she needed to anchor herself to something that wouldn't move. "So all this time, all these years, humans thought it was just survival. That we just needed to keep your kind alive."

I nodded once, slowly. "Because that's the lie they needed you to believe—also why the Blood War dragged on as long as it did."

Her gaze cut to mine, with the eyes that could bring me to my knees. "Why would you wait this long to tell me?"

The question speared me. I dragged a hand across my jaw, the weight of the truth heavy. "Because I wasn't sure you were ready to hear it," I admitted. "You hated me. You hated what I am. And the truth of this bond—of what your blood means—it would have felt like chains. Like another way I was trying to own you. And I would rather you hate me for silence than think I was using you. But then you started to feel it back—your speed, your edge, your instincts. I realized this wasn't only about what I take. It's what you're becoming."

Her lips parted, fury sparking hard and clean. "You should've told me. It wasn't just yours to know."

"I know." The admission left my mouth. "And still I didn't. Because the truth terrifies me too, Zyrenna. What I feel when I drink from you—fuck—it's nothing I've ever known. I'm stronger than I should be. It isn't just feeding; it's being rebuilt from the inside out. And if the rest of the Council knew…" I trailed off, jaw tightening.

She breathed through it, anger and confusion bleeding through the tether like smoke through a cracked door. We sat in the weight of it for what felt like forever, the fire speaking in low pops from the hearth.

Then, steadier, she asked, "The nightmares… show me. I'm done, Rhaelin. I am done being left in the dark."

My throat locked. I should've told her to leave it. Should've turned her away before the walls broke further. But she leaned forward, her voice low, almost breaking. "Show me, Rhaelin. Please. If we're bound like this, stop locking me out."

It was the *please* that broke me. Mostly because I knew I'd never get one from her again.

Not until the circumstances were… considerably less appropriate. Which I knew, without a doubt, they one day would be.

I reached across the bond and unbarred the door—not all the way, not enough to drown her—just enough.

Her inhale snapped quick. But she took it with strength, she held on.

Blood in the sand, walls covered in it. The arena at Nocthallow made out of stone. Elias's laugh at the start, that easy, reckless sound that got us out of trouble when we were boys. Elias's mouth at the end, set in a line I still wake trying to smooth with my hands.

"Side by side," he'd said the night they dropped us in. And for days we were. Until there were only two.

The night I walked out of that pit alone, my veins full of victory and my soul hollow. Her hand tightened on mine. She flinched, but she didn't pull away—she stayed.

When I finally severed the memory, sweat dampened my hairline. I kept my eyes on the floor until her voice, quiet and shaking, forced me up.

"I'm sorry, Rhaelin," she paused. "If I had known—fuck..."

A ragged laugh tore out of me before I could stop it.

"What?" I said. "You wouldn't have been such a stubborn, unyielding pain in my ass?"

Her mouth curved—just a flash of a smile. Beautiful.

Her hand lifted, hesitated. Then she touched my jaw, light enough to be lethal. Not command. Not pity. Something far worse.

Understanding.

The bond burned, curling around us like smoke. I swore I could taste her pain for me on my tongue.

"I hate you," she whispered, voice shaking. "I hate you because you've made it absolutely impossible to hate you at all."

"Zyrenna." My voice scraped low, a warning. "Careful."

If she understood what her words did to me, she'd know she could dismantle me without ever raising a blade.

I'd spent over a century perfecting restraint. Survived trials meant to break men. Wars that left cities burning. Losses I carried like scars beneath armor. I'd stared down generals, slit the throats of monsters, and walked away whole. I'd been trained from childhood to wield violence like a blade, precisely, and without hesitation. Weapons in my hands were never toys, but simple expectations.

And still, this woman existed. She was fucking ruinous. Not just the cut of her cheekbones or the silver-blue in her eyes, but the way she looked at me like I was both her ruin and her salvation. Like she despised herself for wanting to see which one I'd choose to be.

One more look and I wouldn't choose at all.

"Come on, Rhaelin," she said, eyes flashing. "We both know I've never been onc to yield just because you say so."

And that—

that was my undoing.

CHAPTER TWENTY-TWO

ZYRENNA

His warning was still on his lips when his hand came up, rough fingers framing my jaw. Heat surged low in my stomach, and before I could think or breathe, his mouth found mine. It wasn't gentle. It was fire, desperate and starved. His kiss dragged a sound from my throat I didn't recognize, something between a whimper and a gasp. My hands shot up to his chest, pushing him away for only a second.

"Yeah, so… about the whole 'put a shirt on' thing," I said, voice rough. "I need to retract that. It was a lapse in judgment."

His mouth curved. "I was wondering how long it would take you to rectify that particular oversight."

"*Shut up* and take it off, Rhaelin."

He laughed—quiet, like he couldn't help himself—canines flashing as he threw his shirt aside.

For the first time, I truly let myself see him—all of him.

Every line of him looked carved with intention, muscle shaped the way weapons are shaped—nothing wasted, nothing ornamental. His chest was broad, tapering into a stomach ridged with hard definition that shifted with every measured breath, each one too controlled to be accidental. His shoulders were massive, thick cords of strength that made him look even larger than he already was. And god, his height. He didn't just fill the room, he consumed it, towering, built for wars that left histories broken in their wake.

Black ink crept from his throat and spilled down his arms and across his chest, tattoos winding over his biceps and forearms like living things—symbols I didn't yet understand etched against a body I wanted to. Firelight caught along the lines as he moved, the ink shifting, breathing with him. At his sternum, the markings converged and ran straight down the center of his torso into a single, stark blade—an unforgiving sword carved into skin, like something driven through him rather than placed there.

It all only made him worse—danger inked onto something already lethal.

Veins cut beneath bronzed skin, subtle but unmistakable. Beauty and brutality, bound together so tightly they were impossible to separate. The kind of man who didn't need to threaten. The damage was already implied.

"Careful, little flame," he murmured, voice all steel. "You keep staring at me like that, and the bond will start screaming your secret loud enough for both of us to hear."

A flare rushed up my neck, but I didn't look away. I refused to miss a thing.

His hands found me again, guiding me back onto the mattress. His weight braced above me—not crushing, just close enough to cage. My legs locked around him on instinct, my body betraying every wicked word I'd ever thrown his way. The hard line of him settled against me through the thin layers left between us, unmistakable, but still leashed. A low sound rumbled in his chest—approval and warning all tangled together.

His palm slid to my throat, thumb tipping my chin up until I had no choice but to meet his eyes—not to claim me, but to remind us both who I was bound to.

His voice dropped.

"You have no idea how long I've dreamed of these eyes looking up at me from this position."

The words shouldn't have undone me the way they did—one sentence, and my body answered like it had been waiting to hear it.

He didn't ask for anything. He kissed me like the question was already answered. His mouth moved to the angle of my jaw, then lower, to the notch where my pulse beat.

"Breathe," he said against my skin, as if he already knew I couldn't. My lungs wouldn't obey—not when his weight caged me in and every inch of me betrayed how much I wanted him there.

His hand slid beneath my shirt, the heat of his palm stealing mine. He mapped me with the backs of his fingers first, drawing slow lines up my ribs, down my side, learning the shape of me like a path I knew he would learn. When I arched, my breath hitched—a sound that felt like victory and my downfall at once. His knuckles grazed the underside of my breast, a whisper of contact that wasn't nearly enough. The bond snapped taut, feeding his tight inhale straight into my bloodstream.

He pressed a light kiss to my collarbone, then dragged his mouth lower. He paused there, breath fanning over skin he hadn't yet tasted, before catching the delicate spot just above my breast between his teeth—gentle, possessive, and gone way too soon.

"This is mine to learn, little flame," he murmured.

My body had never responded to someone's words the way they did his. Just his look alone could unravel me.

"Don't get cocky," I somehow managed, though it came out thin.

"Too late. I've waited too long to be humble now."

He had every right to be, not when I was already coming apart for him.

His knee eased between my thighs. I made a sound I didn't try to hide. He didn't grind, he gave me something to move against instead. The seam of my shorts dragged exactly where I needed it, and the tether lit up. I felt his reaction roll through us—a tremor in his control. His hand slid to the back of my thigh, fingers curling, urging me closer without ever giving me everything. I felt everything that he wasn't allowing himself to take, a dark, hungry echo that made my hips roll again just to feel it spike through him.

"Look at me," he said.

I did exactly that. Because I could not for the life of me think of one justified reason why I would ever look anywhere else. He didn't gloat, he simply watched my face like it was a map he refused to misread.

"Rhaelin," I breathed, a plea.

He pressed his forehead to mine, held there a second like he needed the contact to stay breathing.

"Not until you say it," he said across my skin.

The truth rose, hot and ready to scorch.

And in an instant, he went still.

The rhythm he'd given me with his lips and hands faltered; his hand at my hip tightened once, hard, then eased. He closed his eyes like it hurt.

"Rhae—" The word caught in my throat, my pride clashing

with the heat building between us, because I've never needed anyone. And when I have, it has brought nothing but pain. His mouth found me again and trailed down, tracing across my jaw, and I broke on a gasp.

"Zyrenna." His voice was steel and a plea all at once, vibrating through me. "You think you can hide it when this bond grants me every secret you try to keep?"

The tic amplified it all, every brush of his lips, every graze of his fingers, like sparks catching. It wasn't just me feeling it, it was him too, pleasure whipping back and forth between us, sending waves crashing against one another.

"You'll ruin me, Zyrenna," he murmured.

At that moment, something inside me finally cracked.

The need wasn't heat anymore—it was certainty. Solid. Inescapable. My lips parted, breath catching as I reached for the words I'd fought so hard to bury, ready to give him the truth we were both circling, the confession pressing against my teeth like it had always belonged there.

But his hand stilled against my cheek.

He pulled back first.

His mouth left mine, his forehead coming to rest against my temple instead, his breath uneven. The bond surged—pain, restraint, desperation crashing through me all at once.

"Not yet," he whispered.

The words weren't denial. They were restraint carved raw.

"Not until there isn't a single trace of hesitation in you." His thumb brushed my skin once—gentler than it had any right to be. "Because if you say it and take it back…" The sound wrecked. "That might be the greatest injustice of all."

And in that space between us—so close it hurt—I understood the cost of what he was refusing to take.

CHAPTER TWENTY-THREE

ZYRENNA

I woke up with the taste of him still in my mouth.

The echo of his voice in my ear, the feel of his body pressed against mine. The bond didn't let me forget; every heartbeat still hummed with the memory. It was like carrying fire in my chest, a constant reminder of everything I hadn't said.

I damned myself for it.

It wasn't hatred that had sealed my mouth. It was fear. The kind I knew too well. Everyone I'd ever allowed myself to need had been taken from me, and every loss had carved something out of me I hadn't known could be hollowed. I'd made a promise a long time ago—never again.

Apparently, my body hadn't been part of that agreement because wanting him lingered anyway.

The sheets clung damp to my skin. I scrubbed a hand over my face, muttered a curse, and shoved out of bed. Alira being in the room next to me was the only thing that grounded me. That was all that mattered, I told myself. Not the man with green fire in his eyes. Not the way my body still hummed with every touch of his.

At the basin, I splashed my face. The water shocked me back into my skin, but it didn't cool anything that mattered.

When I lifted my head, the mirror threw my betrayal back at me: eyes too bright, lips bruised the soft pink of surrender. I braced my palms against the stone until my knuckles went bloodless. The bond pulsed once as if to say, *you can lie to yourself, but you won't lie to me.*

I looked away first.

* * *

By the time Alira and I reached the dining hall, it was loud with morning: steel scraping wood, boots on stone, laughter spiking. We took a spot at the long table near the fireplace. Maris set a chipped mug of tea in front of me and Alira with a smile before sweeping off to terrorize a line of soldiers taking fruit above their rations.

Alira wrapped both hands around the mug, warming her fingers. Her eyes cut to mine.

"*So,*" she said, drawing the word out like thread, "where were you last night?"

I groaned into my mug. "What is that look?"

"The look," she said, stirring her tea, "of a sister who knows she's being lied to. And don't you dare answer my question with another question. So, where were you?"

I shot her a glare across the rim of my mug. "Showering."

"Sure," she said sweetly. "And I'm secretly the Veil."

My lips twitched.

Smart ass, I muttered to myself. "Ali—"

She leaned in, her voice dropping low, "You came back late. And you look… compromised."

Embarrassment shot through me. "Alira."

"Oh don't you dare say my name like that." She smirked.

"I'm not oblivious, Z."

"Okay, well, I'm done getting chastised by my fourteen-year-old sister." I stood, scarfing down the rest of my food. "I have to train anyway. I know you wanted to catch up with Solena, she'll be here soon to show you around."

"Uh-huh. While you're at it, don't forget to tell Mr. Tall, Dark, and Broody I say hello."

"Insufferable." I turned and walked out the door.

* * *

Hours later, the training hall stank of sweat and iron as it always had—an ugly, honest smell I was learning to crave. Rings of sand scored the floor; racks of weapons stood against every wall. Sweat already slicked my skin, and the staff dragged in my palms, heavier than it had any right to be.

"Higher," Darius barked. "You're dropping your wrist. Again."

Rhaelin watched from the far edge, arms crossed, expression neutral as stone. Only his eyes moved—tracking, not missing a damn thing.

I swung. Sloppy—too slow. The staff smacked the dirt. Heat climbed my throat, half exertion, half humiliation.

"Again," Rhaelin said calmly. I hated how unaffected it sounded.

I snatched the staff up, bit down hard on the sound my frustration wanted to make, and lunged into the sequence Darius had drilled into me until my shoulders burned. Spin, step, strike—

The staff slipped in my grip and smacked against the floor with a hollow crack.

183

I bit back a curse. My jaw clicked. Sweat ran down my spine in an itchy path I couldn't reach.

All the while, I could feel his gaze branding me.

Out of nowhere, the bond flared—violent and alive.

It didn't rise; it struck. The world narrowed to a line of light. My hands tightened on the staff until the wood groaned. Sound thinned to a hum—Darius's commands, the shuffle of feet, even the laughter in the room—all drowned beneath the drum of my heartbeat syncing with his across the space. I felt him at my back, though he hadn't moved. Breath for breath. Pulse for pulse. A current pulling both ways at once.

I moved.

This time the sequence flowed—spine to shoulder to wrist— like the staff had grown from my bones. My sparring partner lifted his weapon a heartbeat too late. Mine knocked it clean from his hands. The follow-through cracked across his jaw, sending him flat into the sand.

Silence slammed down.

"Ah—fuck," he groaned from the floor, hand to his face.

The staff trembled in my palms, but the weight no longer felt like weight. With that hum under my skin, I could have broken stone.

"There she is," Rhaelin said, low but carrying. Pride tugged at his mouth before steel shut it away. "There's the fury I need. You need to wield it, Zyrenna."

The words punched deeper than the blow I'd landed. Pride wasn't all that came through the bond. Want burst sharp and unguarded, there and gone in a breath, and my pulse stumbled in answer.

I looked away from him like that might save me and found Darius watching—not me, but Rhaelin. The old scar across his mouth pulled tight, like a man who'd just solved a riddle and wasn't sure he liked the answer.

* * *

The hall had mostly emptied when I jammed my staff into the rack hard enough to rattle the whole row. The crack echoed through the room. My palms were raw. Stray hairs stuck to my damp neck.

"What the hell was *that*?" I demanded.

Rhaelin didn't flinch. "What was what?"

"Don't," I hissed, stepping closer.

"Whatever happened out there—it wasn't just me. They felt it. Darius *saw* it. And you stood there like you wanted them to."

His jaw ticked once. Silence from him was heavier than most men shouting. When he finally spoke, it was quiet and certain and infuriating. "So let them see."

I went still. "What?"

He closed the space between us, not touching, close enough that the air seemed to bend. His figure swallowed the light from the training hall.

"Let them know what they already suspect."

I shoved at him. He moved before I did, fingers closing around my wrists with a quick firmness. For a second my shoulder threw toward him on its own, but the shove never landed—his grip held me there, immovable. It felt like pushing against a wall.

"Really, sweetheart? All this training and that's what you're going with?" he asked.

That made my teeth clench and my hands pull harder. "You

185

don't get to decide that for me," I spat.

"I'm not deciding," he said, voice like steel. "I'm telling you the truth when I say I didn't hand you that strength in the ring. The bond did. I told you it would get more intense." His gaze flicked over me, unapologetic, taking inventory of every tremor. "You need to learn to use what it gives you."

"I don't want them—" I swallowed. "I don't want them staring like I'm a problem to solve or a weapon to aim. I don't want them knowing. It will only get us *and* them killed."

"First of all," he said dryly, "I'm wounded. Truly. And highly offended that you think anyone in this fucking place could kill me." His mouth twitched. "Including you."

I opened my mouth—

"Secondly," he continued smoothly, voice dropping to remind me who he was, "if anyone here decided to test that theory, their lives would end before the thought finished forming."

"They're not blind, Zyrenna," he went on. "You think Darius hasn't noticed the way I snap when you're too far from me? You think Maris doesn't see the way I burn when you walk into a room?" He huffed a laugh of disbelief. "They know something ties us. They'll follow you because of it."

His words landed.

"Is that what you want?" My voice came out softer than I meant, which only made me angrier. "Their loyalty because of *you?*"

"Because of us," he said without hesitation. "You don't borrow power from me, you already have it. The Spire will learn your name because it has to, not because I say so."

Fury tangled with something hotter. "And if I don't want them to know?"

"Then they will still know," he said simply, like saying the sun will rise. "You can't hide this. Neither can I. Nor will I try to. I would happily let every person in these halls know who and what you are to me. I will respect your decision of not telling them, but what I am trying to emphasize is they *will still* know."

The world felt unsteady. The noise from training was gone, and somewhere far away a door slammed shut. My face was hot, my chest tight. He looked at me like someone who'd already taken the leap and was waiting to see if I'd follow or just watch him fall.

A shape detached from the archway.

Darius—of course. The man could move like a sliver of night when he wanted, fold himself into shadow on demand.

He didn't speak right away.

He stood there, arms loose at his sides, gaze moving between us with unnerving precision. Measuring. Cataloging. As if he'd been listening long enough for the last pieces to click into place.

Something in his expression shifted, marking confirmation.

"Figured as much," Darius said at last, his voice dry as paper. Relief edged the words, thin but unmistakable. "About time someone called the mess what it is."

I opened my mouth—what would've come out, I had no idea. Denial. Agreement. A threat to anyone stupid enough to spread this faster than Rhaelin or I allowed.

Darius didn't give me the chance.

"And I'll pretend I didn't see half the barracks already betting on whether you break his nose before sundown." The scar tugged into something wry. "For the record, my coin's on her."

"Your faith is noted," Rhaelin said, not looking away from me.

Darius's boots whispered against stone. He vanished the way he'd arrived, leaving us the silence I had thought we had before.

I exhaled, realizing I hadn't truly taken a breath since he'd said *let them see.*

"You like this," I said quietly. "You like that he looked at me and then at you and drew lines between us."

His eyes darkened—green gone molten. "If that was your question all along, you should've just said so." His voice roughened. "Yes, Zyrenna. As I told you, I would gladly let every single person down here know exactly what happens if they touch you aside for in those rings. Let them see. Let them wonder. Let them understand what it means to even think of laying a hand on you."

He stepped closer until the heat of him pressed against the edge of my self-control. "It's not something that can be hidden, and that might bother you—but it sure as hell doesn't bother me. I *want* them to see. I want them to know you are not alone, and you are not unclaimed. These are my people and I trust them."

His thumb brushed the inside of my wrist. "This wasn't my choice," he said more quietly, the edge still there but softened by truth. "The bond forced itself into us. But if you can feed from my power the way I feed from yours—if it keeps you standing, if it makes you stronger..." His face was hard—cold. "Then it's the first thing I've ever wanted the world to witness."

I swallowed hard, every word cutting me open. "You make it sound so simple," I whispered, though my voice wavered.

"Because for me it is," he said. "But I understand why it isn't for you."

"The choice will always be yours," he went on. "I won't take that from you. Yes, the truth puts both our lives—and others—in danger, but I would walk into it again and again if it meant you stood beside me stronger than before. They know me well enough to understand what it means when I speak your name, Zyrenna."

He bent toward me with deliberate slowness and set his lips to the crown of my head. The kiss was gentle and certain—a promise spoken without words.

When he straightened, the loss of him hurt more than his closeness ever had. He turned without speaking, his boots whispering over the stone, and the door closed behind him.

I stood there for a long moment. The room held the shape of him—the particular warmth that always followed Rhaelin, the faint trace of cedar.

The bond sat strangely in my chest. Not pulling. Not straining. Just—present, as if waiting. The same way it had been since the feeding that morning. The way I could feel, without asking, when he'd had enough and when he hadn't.

Right now, he hadn't.

I opened the door before I'd finished the thought.

He stopped at the end of the corridor, turning as he heard it. His face was unreadable.

"You didn't finish," I said, lifting up my arm.

"I took enough," he finished.

"I know what enough looks like on you," I said, and the fact that I said it—that I'd learned the difference—was its own thing to reckon with. "This isn't it."

He stayed where he was. The distance between us was only the length of a hallway, but he didn't close it. He was letting me decide.

I walked to him, arm out.

Not because I owed him, not because the bond demanded it, and not because he'd asked.

Because I chose to.

Something shifted in his face before the careful mask came back up. He reached for my arm, slower than usual. Giving me every possible second to change my mind.

I didn't.

When he finally fed, it was different from every time before it. Not rougher, not gentler, just different. Like something between us had unclenched. He kept one hand wrapped around my forearm, and I felt it through the quality of the tether: his relief.

When he finished, he didn't speak right away. He held my wrist a second longer than he needed to, then he looked up.

"Zyrenna."

"Don't," I said. "Not tonight."

His mouth closed as he nodded once and let me go.

I walked back to my room and didn't look over my shoulder. But I felt him standing there in the hallway, watching until I was gone.

CHAPTER TWENTY-FOUR

RHAELIN

The chair groaned under me as I leaned back, the half-empty glass of whiskey warming my hand. Papers for the Embers lay scattered across the desk—rotations, reports, numbers I no longer cared to read. I'd been staring at them so long the words blurred together.

The door creaked.

"Don't bother saying come in," a small voice announced. "I already did."

I looked up. Alira Vaeoria stood in the doorway, small but unshaken. A sweater too big shoved up to her elbows. Chin high. Her eyes were softer than Zyrenna's—Alira's were a calm blue.

"For the record, it's worse than advertised," she said matter-of-factly, stepping inside without waiting for permission. "You're even broodier when she's not around."

"It is." The words came out flat, though the corner of my mouth betrayed me, lifting despite myself.

She crossed the room and perched on the chair opposite my desk, studying me. My chambers were larger than most, warmed by a low fire. A black leather couch sat against the far wall, matched by a chair deeper and sturdier than the rest, its size demanding notice. The desk was broad, papers spread in neat stacks. On the wall, a pair of blades gleamed above the mantle, polished but clearly used. It was the only thing I owned that felt the slightest bit like home.

Alira's gaze swept over the room, cataloguing every surface, lingering on the leather couch before coming back to me. Her look said she wasn't impressed.

"She's with Solena," she said at last. "And I figured it was time I finally spoke to the man pulling the strings around here."

I nodded. "I've seen you around, but I didn't want to push. Figured you needed space—the last thing you needed was feeling like you owed anyone."

She tilted her head, lips twitching. "That's funny. Most people think I should be grateful you let us stay here."

"I'm not most people."

"No," she said. "I'm starting to gather that."

"Look." She leaned forward. "I'll say what I need to say, because I know you probably have important-people stuff to do, and I'm not good at talking in circles."

My brows rose. "I was beginning to suspect that."

She smirked, but it faded quickly. "She's all I have, Rhaelin—Zyrenna. She's strong—stronger than anyone ever gave her credit for. I've watched her carry things that would've broken most people in half. But strength has its limits. She won't tell you where hers are. It's possible she doesn't even know them herself. But if you push her past them..." Alira's voice went hard. "If you break her—"

I let the words settle between us like a weight.

"I won't." I paused, searching for the right words. "I have never—and will never—mistake your sister for something fragile though."

Some of the tension in her shoulders eased. Not much, but enough.

"She doesn't sleep some nights," Alira went on, softer now, as if confessing to the fire instead of me. "Walks the floor, quiet as she can so I won't wake. She thinks I don't hear. She carries the things no one else wants to name, and then she tells herself it makes her strong. Sometimes it does." Her voice thinned. "She was there every night after our parents died—wiping my tears before her own—like grief would obey her if she took mine first." Her gaze flicked to me. "Sometimes it just makes her tired in ways a bed can't fix."

Her words sank deep, leaving me still.

"I've tried to contribute in ways I knew how," she said. "I can work in the vineyard. I can boil water. I can pretend not to notice when her hands shake." A muscle jumped in her cheek. "But here—" she flicked a look around the room, toward the blades, the maps, the closed world of the Embers—"here I can't do the same things. She doesn't need her little sister's shadow. She needs... something else."

"What do you think that is?"

Alira chewed the inside of her lip. "Someone else to carry the strength. And someone who won't mistake her for their own reflection."

I let the words find their place. "The bond doesn't make her mine."

"Does it make you hers?" she asked without blinking.

I almost smiled. "In ways you couldn't measure."

Her gaze dropped to the whiskey in my hand, then back up. "I'm not blind," she said. "She thinks I am—but I've seen the way the air changes around you both. The way the room listens. I've seen you bleed to put yourself between her and anything that doesn't serve her. I've also seen you stand back and make her move her own feet, and I know that costs you. I'm not asking you to be soft with her." She leaned in, elbows on her knees, a child who had taught herself to speak like a general. "I'm asking you to be precise."

"Precise," I repeated.

"About when to push," she said. "About when to pull her out. About what you ask her to carry—because if you hand her everything at once, she'll try, and she'll drown. She's like that. She tries until there's nothing left… so don't hand her everything."

For a moment I could only look at her. The words weren't polished, they didn't need to be. They were clear, direct, truer than anything I'd heard spoken within these walls in weeks. She hadn't hesitated, hadn't bowed her head. She'd walked into my chambers with nothing but a too-big sweater and her sister's name on her tongue and had spoken like she belonged here.

"You're too old for your age," I said at last.

Her eyes didn't flinch. "Death will do that to a person."

A low chuckle escaped me, rough and short. "Yeah," I muttered, more to the fire than to her. "I suppose it does."

Alira's mouth twitched, and then she went still, studying me like she was deciding whether to lay down her last card. "You watch her," she said finally, voice gone careful.

"I do," I said.

"Not like the others though," she continued, shaking her head. "They look at her and see a story they want to tell. You don't." Her eyes narrowed, testing. "You look at her like she's the sun."

The truth moved through me. I refused to lie.

"Because she is," I said—simple as breathing.

Alira blinked but didn't look away. "You mean that?" she asked.

"I do." The glass of whiskey felt heavy in my hand. "I grew up where daylight never touched the ground. Needing anything was how you got killed. Then your sister walked in and ruined all that. She made me want to need something."

The words came easier than they should have. "I can promise you one thing—we both want the same thing: to keep your sister alive."

My hand tightened around the glass until I thought it might shatter. "She doesn't even know half of it. Because if I say it wrong, or if I say it too soon, I'll ruin it. But you need to know this, Alira—what she means to me. I would burn myself out before I'd let her be broken again. I don't care what it costs me. My blood, my body, my name—all of it. I'll throw it into the fire before I let her fall."

I finally looked at her. "And I don't mean that as if she's someone fragile I have to guard. As I said, your sister isn't fragile. She's the strongest person I've ever met. But as you said, she's tired. Tired in ways she won't admit. And that's why I'm here. Not to smother her—but to make sure she doesn't have to carry it alone."

I exhaled, rough and low. "So yes, Alira. I mean it. She is the sun to me—the only light I've seen in years. And I won't let it go out. Not while I still have breath in my body."

She stared at me for a long heartbeat. Then, quietly, she said, "I like you, Rhae."

The words were small, but they landed hard.

Rhae. No one had called me that in years—not since Thalia.

It shouldn't have meant anything, but it did.

I let out a quiet laugh. "I'm glad," I said. "Because you are the world to her. Don't ever doubt that. If anything ever happened to you…" My voice went rough. "She would be lost. Gone. By all means, everything we're building here would shatter."

Her eyes flickered.

I leaned forward, elbows braced on my knees. "As much as I respect you walking in here tonight—more than you'll ever know—I need you to hear me. You don't have to, Alira. Not now. Not yet. You've been carrying weight that isn't yours since you were a child. Death has already taken enough from you. You deserve to be fourteen. You deserve to enjoy what you can, while you can. That's not weakness."

Her chin trembled once, but she kept her gaze on mine.

"I've watched you," I went on, quieter. "You're older than your years. I know how hard it must have been—pretending not to hear her at night, standing between her and everything that wanted to take more."

A single tear slipped down her cheek before she could swipe it away.

"I'll try to hold it," I said, voice low. "Not just for Zyrenna, but for you too. Let me carry some of it. Because I promise you—that's all Zyrenna wants: for you to be able to stop carrying the world."

For the first time since she'd walked in, Alira moved. She rose from the chair and crossed the space between us. She paused beside me, hesitated only a second, then folded her arms around me.

My hands hovered, then settled gently at her back. She was so small. Zyrenna's fire, but in a smaller frame.

CHAPTER TWENTY-FOUR

"I've got you," I murmured. "Both of you."

She stepped back, sniffed once, trying to pretend she hadn't just done it. "If you tell her any of this, I will kill you."

A corner of my mouth lifted. "I wouldn't dare."

She held my gaze a second longer, like she was fixing something inside herself. Then she turned. Her steps were light as she crossed to the doorway.

"Before you go," I said, voice steady, "you'll start training. Whenever you're ready."

She froze with a hand on the frame, eyes narrowing. "You're putting me to work?"

I let one corner of my mouth tug higher and gave her a slow wink. "Call it insurance. If you're going to threaten me, might as well make sure you can back it up."

For the first time all night, she cracked a real smile. As she reached the doorway, she glanced back and, without any grandness, said, "I'm glad it's you."

Then she left.

CHAPTER TWENTY-FIVE

ZYRENNA

Weeks blurred into one another.

Days bled into nights. Training. Bruises. Sweat. And I was learning to love every second of it. Every ache in my muscles felt like proof, another lesson carved into me. For the first time in years, I didn't feel powerless. I learned to welcome the strength building in me, the keenness in my instincts, the way my body moved faster and surer, with each passing day.

But it wasn't only my body we were training.

Rhaelin had made it clear early on that if we didn't learn to master the bond, it would master us. So our nights were spent in quieter wars—sitting across from each other on the floor, knees brushing, hands steady, breathing in time. Learning to feel the surge of power without drowning in it. Learning how to build walls in our heads so the bond wouldn't spill into every thought, every heartbeat, every reckless impulse.

It didn't escape me that it all came easier for him.

Two or three tries, and he had it—control snapping into place like it had always been waiting for him.

It took me longer. More missteps. More bruises to my pride.

Which, frankly, pissed me off.

The man couldn't stand not being good at something immediately—apparently failure offended his ego.

My words, not his.

And somehow that made it worse, watching him rein himself in with infuriating calm while I fought every instinct screaming at me to either bolt or break something.

I told myself I hated it.

That I hated how easily he adapted, how naturally the bond bent to him.

But somewhere between frustration and exhaustion, I started to accept the truth I didn't want to name: this was who he was—controlled, relentless, built to survive anything thrown at him.

And whether I liked it or not, I was learning to survive beside him.

He taught me how to ground him, and I taught him how to anchor me when my fear tried to choke the air from my lungs. Sometimes it worked. Sometimes it didn't, and the energy flared between us until objects cracked, candles snuffed out, or one of us—mostly me—ended up flat on the floor, panting.

It was humbling.

But every night, no matter how many times we failed, I felt something shift. The bond wasn't just a chain tying us together. It was a language. One we were learning to speak in tandem.

Alira started training too, though Rhaelin insisted hers would be lighter, slower. She took to it in her own way, smiling through corrections, asking questions even when she was breathless, with that stubborn spark that mirrored mine so fiercely it sometimes frightened me. Where I met resistance with teeth bared, she met it with an almost infuriating optimism. Watching her learn how to plant her stance, how to hold a blade, laughing when she stumbled and trying again without shame, gave me a peace I hadn't realized I was starved for.

And god, I was so grateful.

Because knowing she was here, not hidden away in Solvane, meant my heart didn't have to tear every time I left her behind.

* * *

Rhaelin asked me a week ago if I was ready to make it official and inform the Embers' inner Council about the bond. He made it clear it would be my choice, that he wouldn't force it, though most already knew anyway. They'd been asking him questions he didn't know how to answer. Because in the Embers, nothing stayed secret for long.

He didn't keep things from his people—not truths that mattered. What was spoken at the Spire Council table always bled into the barracks down here, the kitchens, the training rings. Not out of recklessness, but because he believed they deserved to know what they were fighting for. What they were risking everything for. I used to think that kind of honesty was dangerous—reckless, even—especially when you were leading something as fragile and volatile as a rebellion. Trusting that many people felt like inviting disaster. Like handing them the blade and hoping they wouldn't turn it.

Now I understood it wasn't ignorance. It was faith.

Faith that they would keep choosing to stand, to fight, to do the right thing—not once, but every day.

And that was how loyalty survived. Not through secrecy, but through shared risk.

So when I finally said it aloud—when I admitted the bond in front of his trusted inner council—there were no gasps. No flinches, only nods. Confirmation of what had already been suspected in corridors and carved into knowing glances.

Still, something shifted.

The way people looked at me when I passed them in the halls. The way silence rippled when I entered a room: not cruel, not mocking. Just weighted.

And I started to realize it wasn't only because I was tethered to Rhaelin Morrain. It wasn't pity or envy, as if I were some extension of him. No, their eyes followed me because of the bruises I earned in the ring, because of the strikes I landed that no one thought I could, because I hadn't broken under the truths I'd been handed. Because I showed up the next day and the day after that, even when it would have been easier not to.

They looked at me like someone who had chosen to stay when she could have run.

I wasn't just Zyrenna Vaeoria—the vineyard girl who used to swing a staff too slowly, and now landed blows that made trained men stumble. And I wasn't just Rhaelin's bonded human either. I was no one's shadow. I was something more— and for the first time, I welcomed that thought, I started to believe it.

* * *

The fire crackled low, throwing red light across the thick crimson carpet in Rhaelin's room. I sat cross-legged, knees brushing his, the heat from the fire nothing compared to the warmth where our legs touched.

He'd kicked his boots off the second we came in, and I'd done the same. He was down to a soft black shirt and loose training pants. I'd shed my leathers before coming here and thrown on a worn linen top with shorts. We looked like two people who'd done this a hundred times—comfortable in ways that couldn't be forced.

"Look at me, not the flames," he said, voice light but laced with that familiar tease.

I lifted my gaze. "Worried I'll decide the fire's prettier?"

He laughed a true laugh. "Let it try. The fire's never had you on your back."

I snorted. "You're unreal," I said. "Come on, focus. No more stalling."

He closed his eyes first, and I followed. I drew my attention to the constant pull in my ribs that I had grown accustomed to now.

"Okay," he said. "Start breathing."

I did. We built the rhythm together—always in four, out six. Then it hit me first.

A flicker of his day slammed through the tether—the sound of steel clashing, the snap of someone's nose breaking under his hand, the way his temper had flared before he forced it back down. It wasn't a memory so much as the emotional imprint of it, and it lit through my chest. He'd been in training earlier—I was seeing it the way he'd felt it.

My heart rate started rising. I felt my own jaw tighten like I'd been the one swinging.

His eyes were still closed, but he felt it. Of course he did.

"Your temper's rising," he murmured. "Plug it."

"I'm trying," I said.

But the anger bucked under my grip, too big, too quick. It

crawled up my spine. And it wasn't just his anger—it was mine. The bond twisted it, braided it, made it feel personal. Feeling him fight through the tether didn't feel like observation—it felt like trespass. The possession of it made control feel impossible.

He didn't soften. He opened the door wider.

"Control it, Zyrenna. Cage it."

The command scraped something raw. His mental door was now almost fully open, the emotions completely consuming me.

"Son of a bitch!" I shouted.

It tore out of me before I could stop it—not elegant, not restrained, just pure reaction. My pulse was in my teeth, my vision hot.

His eyes opened at that. Not angry. Worse—amused.

Pink crept up my cheeks. "Sorry," I muttered.

"Sorry, what? I didn't hear y—"

"Fuck off, Rhaelin. That's the only one you're getting."

He laughed—really laughed—head tipping back.

The sound cracked something in me. I tried to hold onto indignation, but it slipped; a small, unwilling laugh escaped me too, soft and breathless.

"That's what happens when you let emotions run the room. Again."

He didn't even give me a breath of warning this time.

Another surge slammed through me—the *shape* of a memory built entirely from feeling. Rage so powerful it formed pictures on its own. The Blood Trials rose in my mind fully formed: the flash of steel, the brutal certainty of the moment his blade drove clean through a vampire's chest. Ruthless and immediate.

The fury that had powered the strike carved the image into me anyway, lightning cracking straight down my spine as if I were the one holding the sword, as if my hands remembered the weight of it.

Underneath it all burned the reason.

Elias—bloodied, staggered, a blade having kissed him moments before. Rhaelin's control snapping not because he'd been challenged, but because his brother had been touched. Hurt. The bond carried that too: the instant calculation, the loss of mercy, the decision that there would be no second chance for this vampire.

My pulse spiked hard enough to hurt. The instinct to react—to finish what he had started—surged up my throat like an order I hadn't chosen, like my body already knew how that kind of violence was supposed to end.

"Plug it," he said.

The pulse hit again—and for the first time, I didn't let it sweep me under. I caught it mid-break, hands shaking as I hauled it inward like it had weight, like it could tear loose if I lost focus for even a second. It fought me, pressure screaming behind my eyes, every instinct demanding release. My breath stuttered. My vision blurred. I dragged it down anyway, forcing it into the same vault I'd built for the others, holding it there while it slammed once—twice—against the walls.

Then it locked.

The tether shifted, contained now, the violent edge dulling into something tense but quiet.

His eyes opened slowly.

"And that, little flame," he said, voice lower now, "is what it looks like when you win."

Pride consumed me in that moment.

CHAPTER TWENTY-FIVE

"Your turn," I said.

One brow lifted—faint surprise—but he obeyed. I closed my eyes and dug through my mind, lifting the door that went from me to him. I knew exactly what I was looking for. The point was to test each other—to share the things that should fray control, so that outside this room we could contain them.

I lifted it.

A silent room. A body too still on the barn floor. My father's face slack in a way it never was in life. My own hands shaking as I touched him. The sound I made—small but broken—echoed through the tether.

He didn't move. Didn't reach, didn't interfere.

He controlled it absolutely perfectly, didn't let a breath bleed back into me.

"Name it," I said.

"Your father," he whispered.

I plugged the memory, forced it back down, locked it beside the others.

But even as the vault sealed cleanly—*too* cleanly—frustration scraped up my spine. I didn't want it contained. I wanted it *answered.* I wanted to rattle him, to see if anything could shake the iron he kept so carefully in place. If I had to learn how to cage the things that could undo me, then he would learn too. He wasn't exempt. Not from this. Not from me.

So I went digging again, not for pain this time, but for the thing I knew would strike deeper. I found it, wrapped my mind around it, and lifted it into the bond.

That night in his keep. The room swallowed in black, my eyes wide open in the dark. The ache for him coiled, so intense my hands shook as they slipped beneath the sheets. The way

I touched myself, slow at first, then desperate, whispering his name like a prayer. The broken sound that tore from my throat when I came.

I shoved it straight through the bond, raw and unfiltered.

I felt him fracture—just for a beat.

His chest tightened, ragged in the silence between us. I kept my eyes open, forcing the imprint deeper. His jaw locked so tight the muscle jumped, veins standing out along his neck. The bond flared with a surge of want so violent I was grateful we were sitting.

Then, in one ruthless flex of will, he slammed it shut. Caged it. Made it disappear like smoke.

When he finally looked at me again, his mouth parted, voice scraped raw.

"Do not ever send me anything like that unless you intend to finish it."

I tilted my head, letting boredom settle over my face like a mask.

"I don't know what you mean."

The lie hung in the air.

The shift in him was instantaneous, a storm rolling in without warning.

One moment he was sitting in front of me, the next, something ancient and predatory uncoiled behind those eyes. Danger poured off him in waves, power barely leashed.

I devoured every second of it.

He uncrossed his legs with deliberate slowness, the motion rippling through the room, as if he were the heart and soul of the air we were both breathing. Then he rose, tall enough that the space between us shrank without him taking a single step.

I retreated before I could think, spine meeting the thick carpet with a soft thud. He followed, lowering himself over me without a single touch—arms braced on either side of my head, knees caging my hips. The heat of his body hovered just above mine, close enough that my skin prickled with awareness, yet far enough that the absence of contact felt like torment.

I could do nothing but take him in—the cut of his jaw, the cruelty promised in his mouth, the eyes that had lived through centuries and still burned with hunger.

"Tell me," he murmured, voice low, each syllable dragging over my nerves like silk over steel. "Were you thinking of me, little flame?"

The words sank into my blood, setting everything inside me alight. My pulse spiked, fierce and mortifying. I couldn't answer—wouldn't—because the truth would shatter the last pretense of control I clung to.

He tilted his head, a few strands of his dark hair falling forward, and leaned down until his breath ghosted over the shell of my ear. No contact, just the warm rush of air and the promise of teeth. A helpless shiver raced down my spine.

He hummed once, like he'd gotten exactly what he wanted. "That's what I thought."

He lingered there, letting the silence stretch until my body arched toward him without permission, chasing heat it wasn't allowed to have. Need coiled tighter, unbearable. Only then did he close the last fraction of distance, lips barely grazing my ear before his teeth caught it.

The soft, involuntary sound that escaped me seemed to be proof.

His hand settled on my thigh—long fingers, callused from

centuries of wielding blades—tracing upward with agonizing patience. Higher, higher, until the path he carved left no doubt where he intended to end. He stopped just short of where I ached most, palm hovering, the radiant warmth of him teasing without mercy. My breath fractured.

"Look at you," he whispered. "All that defiance—gone the second I decide to touch you."

The bond beneath my ribs blazed, wild and pleading. I arched again, chasing his hand, and he let me feel the full weight of my desperation for one humiliating heartbeat.

Then he withdrew—hand, heat, everything—rising in one smooth motion that left me empty on the floor.

He stood over me, impossibly tall. His gaze lingered, possessive and unreadable, before he turned away.

"One warning, little flame," he said quietly, the words absolute. "Do not ever toy with me when it comes to you."

The truth crashed through me then, raw and undeniable.

I was his—body, fire, soul—and I was done pretending otherwise.

CHAPTER TWENTY-SIX

ZYRENNA

It had been two days, and Rhaelin hadn't been around much
since. When I did see him, it was during training, where
he said little more than "again," or in passing through the
halls—his attention already fixed on the next task. Meetings.
Reports. Strategy sessions.

The Embers buzzed with whispers in his absence—Council
scouts slipping too close to the woods, patrols tightening near
the Spire as if the Spire itself had sensed something.

And every time he left, the bond dimmed—just enough to
ache. Not gone—never gone—but quieter, as if someone had
pressed a hand over my chest. When he returned, whether
after hours or days, it always ignited again—fire flooding
through me before I ever even saw him.

Part of me missed his presence so fiercely it rattled me.

Two days also meant two days of no feeding.

I noticed the absence of it all. My wrist felt strange in a way I
didn't have a language for. Just aware of its purpose. Restless—
the way skin feels in the moment before it's touched, already
anticipating something it hadn't been given permission to
want.

The bond was quieter without the feeding too. I hadn't

understood, before, how much the feeding threaded into everything—his steadiness, the weight of his focus, the warmth that moved through me when he drank. That warmth. I was trying very hard not to think about that warmth. The way it started at the point of contact and spread outward, loosening things I kept locked. The way my breath always came differently after.

Without it, the tether still functioned. It just felt thinner. And I felt… hunger in my own way. For that specific thing he did, for that feeling.

I told myself that this need was the bond. The architecture of what we were. Simply chemistry.

Ultimately, I was getting better at lying to myself.

* * *

Finally finding my rhythm within the Embers, I realized I'd been avoiding something I couldn't ignore forever.

Aunt Kaelen.

She'd raised Alira in the ways I couldn't. Fed her when I was barely holding myself together. Kept the cottage warm, kept the lights on, kept my sister safe while I was drowning in my own shit. She'd never asked for thanks. Never asked for anything at all. And I wouldn't let her feel abandoned now—not when I'd disappeared into the shadowed spine of a rebellion that demanded everything and promised nothing.

So I chose a day to return to Solvane. Not because I had to—but because I wanted to. To step back into the life I'd left behind and prove, if only to her, that I hadn't traded one family for another. That I still knew where I came from.

Alira stayed behind.

She surprised me when she said it—too quickly, too eagerly—but she didn't try to soften the truth. She had meetings with Maris and Solena. Real ones. Learning the slow, unglamorous backbone of survival: supply routes, stock counts, trade negotiations, how to keep the Embers breathing when resources ran thin and tempers ran thinner.

"I'll come next time," she said, bright-eyed, already half gone.

And the sparkle in her gaze told me what she didn't say out loud—she was thriving here. Belonging. Standing in her own skin without apology.

So, I let her have that without protest.

* * *

Rhaelin was gone—swallowed by the Spire again, called into yet another spiral of politics and corruption that never seemed to loosen its grip.

So—I went to my next best bet. Darius.

His face was stone when I asked, and for a long while, I thought he'd refuse altogether.

Instead, he asked if Rhaelin had cleared it.

The reminder was unnecessary. Most people bound to the Embers didn't step aboveground without permission—not when secrecy was survival and loose ends got people killed. I told him the truth anyway: Rhaelin had given it before the Spire called him in. It had been meant as a one-time trip. Something he'd planned to take me on himself, if he'd been here.

What I didn't mention was that he'd said *sometime this week*.

I'd just… accelerated the timeline.

Truth by omission still counted as truth, I told myself—quietly, like the lie might hear me if I said it out loud.

That was enough to fly me to Solvane, against Darius's better judgment and very much on my own responsibility.

The flight there was quieter than I expected. He didn't waste words, but I caught him studying me once or twice, like he was measuring the changes in me since the first time he'd seen me with a staff in my hands.

When we landed in the olive grove outside Solvane, his boots hit the soil with a dull thud. The familiar scent of earth and leaves rose up around us, grounding and unsettling all at once. Wings folded back, he stood still, watchful, every line of him alert, his scars catching the light.

"I'll wait here until you're ready," he said flatly.

I shook my head. "No. Go back."

His eyes narrowed. "Rhae—"

"—is not my keeper." My voice was firm, though my heart pounded. "I need one night in my old home. He would give me a choice if he were here." I held Darius's gaze, refusing to flinch. "I will be fine. I have my dagger if I need it. Now go."

For a long moment, he didn't move. The silence stretched, heavy with everything unsaid. Then finally, he inclined his head in that clipped way of his, acknowledgment rather than agreement.

"I swear, Vaeoria—if anything happens, I am not taking the fall for this. This is on you."

"I wouldn't ask you to."

"Reach through the bond if you need him." His mouth twitched, humor thin but present. "Though I'd appreciate it if you didn't—I'd enjoy keeping my immortal life."

With one last look, measured and unwilling, Darius spread

his wings and vanished into the night, leaving me alone in the quiet vineyard air—with the ghosts of home and the weight of choice settling in around me.

* * *

Aunt Kaelen's house smelled the same as it always had—rosemary, bread cooling on the counter, the faint sweetness of grapes clinging to Kaelen's clothes. Sitting across from her at the table, I felt the ache of familiarity dig into my ribs.

"You've grown stronger," Kaelen said after a long silence, tearing her bread in half. Her eyes were steady, searching—too much like my father's for comfort. "Not just stronger physically. In here." She tapped her chest. "You carry it like a sentence."

I stared into the soup, watching the surface ripple as my hand tightened around the spoon. "Because it feels like one," I said quietly. "Every step forward I take there feels like I'm choosing something else over this. Over you. Over what's left of... us." My jaw tightened. "I don't want to wake up one day and regret it."

Kaelen shook her head. "Listen to me. You don't owe me your roots. This vineyard, this house—yes, they are ours, and they will always be ours. But you have bigger things ahead of you than sweeping floors and keeping my house warm. You don't have to keep coming back here to prove your love to me. I know it already."

I swallowed hard, chest tight.

"I know you'd rather not know where Alira and I are," I said quietly. "But please, Kaelen—I won't be able to live with myself over there if I know you're kept in the dark. I don't even know if I'll be able to come back after today. I just need you to know."

She hesitated for only a moment, then her face softened. "Go on."

So I told her. About the Embers, the rebellion carved into stone and secrecy. About humans and vampires training side by side, bleeding side by side. About the blood types, the lies of the Treaty. My voice faltered, but I kept going until it all spilled out, the truth I had carried in silence for so long now burning free.

She deserved the truth, whether she wanted it or not. I wouldn't lie to one of the few people I had left.

What I didn't say—was that as I was about to plead with her to come, I didn't even know if Rhaelin would allow it. I hadn't asked him. Hadn't tested that boundary yet. But the thought of his refusal never truly formed. I wouldn't accept an answer other than yes from him. Not on this. Not when it came to her safety.

When I finished, Kaelen only stared at me, quiet for a long moment. Then, she leaned back, eyes calculating. "You want me to come with you."

"I want you safe," I admitted, my voice fraying. "And for once, I want you to live without chains. If you came to the Embers, you'd be protected. You'd be part of something that could change all this."

Her lips curved in a sad, gentle smile. "This is my home, Zyrenna. I've buried my sister here, and worked on this land my whole life. I wouldn't know how to breathe without these walls around me." She reached across the table, covering my hand with her own. "You, though—you were never meant to stay. You've been running since you were a child, and now I see why. You don't belong in the shadows."

Tears burned at the backs of my eyes. "I don't want you to feel abandoned."

"You've never abandoned me," Kaelen said firmly. "Not once. You've given me you and Alira, you've given me reason when I might have let grief win. And now you gave me something else."

"What?"

"Hope." She squeezed my hand, warm and sure. "Don't look back, Zyrenna. I'll be here when you return—I always will. But don't keep tearing yourself in half because you think you have to stay close to me."

Her thumb brushed my knuckles.

"I'm not the one who needs you most anymore. You don't have to become a stranger," she went on gently. "Just don't chain yourself here out of fear. Forget where home is, and you'll lose yourself." She met my eyes, unwavering. "But go where you're needed—and you'll find who you were always meant to be."

Her words gutted me, but also stitched me back together in a way nothing else had.

* * *

The night air was cool when I stepped outside Aunt Kaelen's door. The vineyard stretched before me, rows of twisting vines under the moonlight. It was quieter here than in the Embers—no clatter of weapons, no hum of strategy murmurs. Just the hush of the fields and the faint rush of the river beyond them.

I'd planned to walk to my old house and stay the night, one

last breath of what used to be mine. Maybe I thought I could still belong to it, even for a few hours.

But the moment I stepped onto the dirt path, the hairs on my arms rose. That crawling awareness. Predator's eyes.

"Out past curfew, Vaeoria?"

I froze, every instinct screaming before I turned. I knew the voice. I recognized the hunger in it anywhere.

His figure detached from the dark between two dead olive trees, taller than I remembered, his red cloak catching faint moonlight. Fangs gleamed when he smiled, but his eyes were the real danger—cruel, glinting with the smug hunger of someone who'd already won. My dagger made its presence known where I kept it on my thigh almost always now.

"Varik," I said, cool and cutting. "Always a pleasure."

His smirk deepened. "Pleasure? No, Zyrenna. That's what you gave *him*—what you denied me." His head tilted, eyes dragging over me with open appraisal. "Rhaelin must really like you, keeping you tucked away at the Spire. Out of sight and out of reach."

A pause.

"Or maybe he's just learned how valuable a private supply can be."

There it was.

"I've been looking for you everywhere," he went on lightly, as if discussing a misplaced trinket. "No luck. Eventually, I was able to put it together. Once he got a taste of you, he decided to keep you for himself. Morrain always did like to pretend he was better than the rest of us—more controlled, more principled." His smile turned evil. "Turns out he's no different. Just more selfish."

I didn't flinch. "A disappointment you'll have to live with,

I'm afraid. You know him—he's not much of a sharer. Our first interaction proved that well enough."

He laughed softly. "Sharp tongue. I see why he keeps you so close." His gaze hardened, pride sliding back into place like armor. "But don't forget who I am, Vaeoria. Varik Draevan—son of Kalor Draevan, one of the Seven."

I tilted my head, unimpressed. "You'll have to forgive me—I've never given much of a shit about titles."

And at this he lunged.

The air shifted before his body did, the force of his speed stirring the dirt at my boots. Instinct drove me sideways, my dagger flashing free from the sheath at my side. The steel caught a sliver of moonlight just before I slashed at where his ribs should have been.

I was fast, but he was faster; his hand closed around my wrist with an iron grip.

I reacted, driving my knee up. It connected with his thigh—not quite as high as I would've liked, but enough to make him grunt. His hold loosened just enough for me to twist free, spinning to slash again. This time the blade kissed his jaw, a shallow line of blood springing across pale skin.

His eyes lit with cruel delight. "Now that," he said quietly, "is not something a girl like you learns on her own."

My chest heaved. I refused to answer.

He struck back, wings snapping wide, a rush of black cutting through the moonlight. I barely got my dagger up in time to catch his blade. Steel clashed against steel, the vibration rattling my arm to the elbow. I stumbled, boots skidding on loose dirt, but didn't fall.

He shifted left, then slammed me from the right. Pain flared through me as my back smacked against the vineyard wall.

The air left me in a gasp.

But rage shoved me upright. Always rage.

I slashed for his throat, wild and desperate. For a heartbeat, I thought I had him—thought the blade might land true.

Then his hand locked around my throat.

My feet left the ground, toes scrabbling uselessly against stone. My dagger clattered across the cobblestones beneath me.

Varik laughed.

It wasn't loud—just a soft, breathy sound against my ear, like he was savoring a private joke. His grip tightened.

"This," he hissed, amusement curdling into something vicious, "is how it should've ended that night at the House."

Another breath of laughter.

"You in my hands. Your blood in my mouth." His smile pressed close, cruel and intimate. "Like mother, like daughter."

Rage ripped through me like I'd never experienced. Piece by piece the memories snapped into place until the picture locked: his voice—the way it carried a cruelty, the same one I heard outside the Crimson House the day my mother was murdered. It wasn't a threat; it was a confession.

Understanding crashed in, cold and absolute. Varik had killed my mother. Bled her dry for his own gratification and walked away, leaving two little girls to grow up around an absence that never stopped hurting.

My nails tore at his wrist, skin splitting beneath my claws, but his grip only tightened. The world narrowed to the pressure at my throat, to the dizzy hum flooding my head.

The bond screamed.

Rhaelin's rage detonated against the back of my skull, green fire sparking in my vision though he was nowhere in sight. I knew he felt it—I knew it was tearing him apart.

I kicked, my heel catching Varik's knee. His hold faltered just enough for me to drop, choking, gasping as air clawed back into my lungs. My dagger was in my hand again before I thought, driven into his shoulder with every ounce of strength I had.

He staggered, blood darkening his coat.

He looked confused at first, eyes flicking down to the thin line of red on his skin. For a heartbeat, he didn't seem to understand how a mortal girl had drawn blood from him. Then the confusion shifted into something else.

He laughed—dark and hungry.

"Good," he said, voice dripping with amusement. "Fight harder. It makes it more fun."

Anger collided with something colder inside me. My arms shook, strength bleeding out in uneven bursts, my breath tearing loose and ragged. The truth landed like a blow to the chest—I couldn't keep this up. Not like this.

The bond flared in answer, sudden and feral, roaring to life like wildfire.

And in the next heartbeat, the air split open.

Rhaelin dropped behind him, landing on one knee with a force that fractured the ground beneath it. Stone split outward in a spiderweb of cracks. His wings tore open, vast and black, veins igniting with a molten gold fire that hadn't existed before. They eclipsed Varik's completely— larger, darker, more commanding—the kind of wings that were meant to strike fear.

The look on his face—unhinged, murderous, wrecked—was nothing I had ever seen him wear.

Varik barely had time to register the shift before Rhaelin's hand closed around the back of his skull and *ended the thought*. Stone rang as Varik's head was driven down, the sound echoing like a bell struck for the dead.

"You touched her?"

But it wasn't a question.

His voice wasn't a voice. It was animalistic, vibrating the air itself, every syllable crawling across my skin.

His eyes blazed as he wretched him up by the throat and hurled him. His body moved through the air, smashing into the vineyard wall, dead vines ripping from their roots as the entire section collapsed.

Varik clawed to his knees amid the rubble, blood pouring from his jaw, gasping. "Rh—

"Do *not* speak my fucking name," Rhaelin growled. The words came guttural. "You lost that privilege the moment you laid a hand on her."

Varik spat blood, lip curling in defiance. "You've lost yourself to a girl. Elias—"

The second I heard the name, I looked away.

I knew what it would awaken in him. I'd felt it before through the bond—the place where grief stopped aching and hardened into something merciless. Varik had just stripped away the last restraint Rhaelin might have been considering, the last flicker of control that separated punishment from annihilation.

Rhaelin's roar split the night.

In less than a blink, he was on Varik again—driving him into the dirt with a force that caved the ground beneath them. I looked back just in time to see his face: not rage alone, but something terrifying seething beneath it. Eyes burning, jaw locked, every line of him drawn tight around a single, violent purpose.

His fury poured into me raw and untempered, not pain but power, a tidal wave that pressed against every nerve until I could hardly breathe. It wasn't only his violence I felt—it was his fear. His desperation. The bone-deep terror of what might have happened if he had been too late.

And for the first time, I saw him as he must have been in the Trials.

Not the Commander or Councilor. Not the tethered man holding himself together for me. But the creature who had carved his name into Nocthallow's bones, the predator who had taken down stronger men and women and left them broken in the dirt.

He stopped striking for only a moment.

Then he seized Varik by the hair and dragged him across the earth toward me, Varik's boots carving useless lines through the dirt. Rhaelin hauled him upright in one brutal motion, forcing his bloodied face toward mine.

"Look at her," Rhaelin snarled, leaning close to his ear. His gaze flicked to me, eyes searing. "Do you see her? She's fucking beautiful, isn't she? The kind wars are started over. The kind that unmake empires." A controlled breath. "Men kneel to her without realizing they're already on their knees."

His hold tightened.

"You almost took that from me." His voice lowered, stripped of everything but promise.

"Pray," he said, leaning closer, "pray to whatever fucking god you still believe in, Varik."

"Because if you had," he went on, voice calm, "I would have kept you alive just long enough to watch me dismantle everything you've ever loved—slowly—until the only name left in your mind was hers."

Every inch of me burned at his words. No one had ever spoken of me like that. Not as prey. Not as fragile, but as if I were unstoppable.

Varik gagged on blood, spit spilling down his chin.

"Apologize," Rhaelin demanded.

His voice cracked. "S-sorry..."

"She didn't hear you." The words came calm. Measured—lethal.

"I'm sorry!" Varik rasped, coughing blood.

Only then did Rhaelin release his hair. His hand stayed locked on the back of his throat, chest heaving, the feral light still burning in his eyes.

I felt something inside me twitch at that moment. The fury that had been burning me shifted into something cold—something that sought vengeance. The reality of it settled: Varik had killed my mother, and he'd almost taken me in the same way.

And with that recognition, I rose in one slow motion.

"Rhaelin," I said, voice flat. "Grab his wings."

He obeyed in an instant, fingers clamping around them with an iron grip, before Varik could put them away. He hissed, shock and pain tearing through him, thrashing uselessly as he realized there was nowhere left to go.

I stepped forward.

The dagger in my hand felt light—too light—like it had already decided what it was meant to do. I didn't look at the blade. I looked at Varik. At the echo of pleasure that had crossed his face when he spoke of my mother, like her death had been a story he still savored.

When I reached him, I bent close enough that both Rhaelin and Varik could hear me.

"There will be no end for you, Varik," I said quietly. "No mercy. No clean escape."

My voice didn't shake or rise.

"When you think it's over—when you start begging whatever gods you believe in to let you die—that's when it will begin." I met his eyes, unblinking. "You will remember this night. You will remember what you took from me. And you will never be granted the quiet you gave my mother."

The whisper left my lips like a verdict.

Varik's expression fractured—bravado collapsing into raw, naked fear. Beside me, Rhaelin went still. He watched my face, my posture, the steadiness in my hands. I felt the moment his understanding locked into place through the bond—the realization of what I was about to do, and that nothing in him wanted to stop it. Awe gleamed in his eyes, completely unguarded.

Then I cut.

The blade drove through both wings with one deliberate motion. Rhaelin's hand sealed over Varik's mouth at the same instant, swallowing the sound before it could break free. What escaped was only a strangled, wet gasp—more vibration than noise—lost quickly among the vines.

I had learned long ago what this meant for his kind. To a vampire, wings were more than flesh—they were pride, freedom, the equivalent of what passed for a soul. To cut them was to unmake him.

Varik collapsed, body folding in on itself, something essential torn away. The air went unnaturally still, as if the world itself had drawn a breath and forgotten how to release it.

I stood over him, black blood slicking my hands, the bond humming with Rhaelin's silent, stunned reverence. There was no triumph in it. No relief.

Only finality.

The verdict had been carried out.

His scream echoed faintly between the rows of vines when Rhaelin finally moved. He released his hold on Varik's ruined wings, voice cutting through the sound.

"Leave," he said. "Crawl back to your father. Tell Kalor Draevan what happens when his son overreaches. Tell him I spared you only because killing you now would start a war none of us are ready for."

Varik staggered, clutching what was left of himself—face a mask of hatred and humiliation. He cast one final, venomous look my way before limping into the dark.

Rhaelin didn't watch him go. His chest rose and fell like a storm still breaking against its own restraint. His hands trembled with the effort of control.

Then he turned to me.

The fury cracked—breaking into something else entirely.

And I felt it. Through the tether, his rage bled into agony— his agony into relief so heavy it nearly broke me. His need clawed against mine, wild and possessive, and beneath it all ran the unspoken vow: *never again.*

I could barely breathe, but it wasn't from Varik's grip anymore.

It was from him—from the way his need tore through the bond and wrapped around me like armor. From the way he looked at me, like he might burn the world for ever allowing it come close.

And in that moment, I knew the truth of him.

He would.

CHAPTER TWENTY-SEVEN

ZYRENNA

The flight back to the Embers was a void of silence.

Rhaelin's face was unreadable. His wings cut the night in hard, perfect beats—each one measured. I didn't try to speak; there was nothing left to say. The air between us vibrated with everything he wasn't saying.

When we landed, I whispered a thank you—feeble, hollow. His eyes didn't even flicker. He inclined his head, a ghost of acknowledgment, and turned away, leaving me at my door.

His silence drowned me, pulling me under until I couldn't breathe.

I reached through the tether—tentative at first, then desperate, clawing. Not emptiness. Barriers. Rhaelin, rigid as a fortress, barricading every thought, every flicker of emotion behind impenetrable walls.

I bathed, steam curling around my shoulders, trying to wash away the memory of Varik's hand at my throat—the sound my body made when air was taken from it. The water ran too hot; I let it, welcoming the sting.

It wasn't the bruises blooming across my ribs or the revelation of my mother's killer that clawed at my soul. I'd armored myself against that unknown for years, forged a life from the hollow ache of it. No—the ghost that haunted me was the night fracturing open, Rhaelin descending like vengeance incarnate. His hand crushing Varik's skull against stone with a sickening crack. His voice, raw and feral, wrapping around my name like a curse and a prayer.

I should've been horrified. I was, a little.

But beneath it, buried deep down, something else burned.

Seeing him that unmade in my name didn't extinguish the fire in me. It fed it.

I dragged on loose pants and a black tank, hair dripping cold trails down my back. Sleep was a cruel joke; every blink summoned him—the savage command in his voice, a death sentence for anyone who dared stand between us. The hidden beast he leashed every dawn, now bared for me alone.

I lay there listening to the Embers breathe. Far-off clatter in the halls. A door closing somewhere—this place never fully slept. The bond hummed low, barely present.

We'd wrestled that tether into submission, failed spectacularly a thousand times, rebuilt it into something sacred and unnamed. Tonight, it had twisted into a weapon. Our shared walls lay in ruins, shards glinting in the silence. And that quiet? It was a torment worse than screams.

I twisted in the sheets until the ache gnawed through my bones, louder than any fear. So I rose.

The stone remembered every step we'd taken in these corridors. Torches hissed when I passed them. Someone's laughter rose from a lower passage and died quickly. The closer I came to his room, the warmer the air grew—as if the fire there refused to be contained by a single door.

I ascended the stairs and pushed inside without knocking, the latch clicking.

He sat before the fire, shirtless, hair ravaged by his own fingers, chaos in every strand. Shadows and firelight carved his body into hard lines. The couch held him like it had been waiting. He hadn't slept—I could feel it, his control stretched thin, ready to break.

He lifted his head, and the world tilted. All air fled my lungs.

"I know you're furious with me," I said, words tumbling before doubt could snare them. "It was stupid to ask Darius. But I needed to see her, Rhaelin. I couldn't keep pretending Solvane didn't exist."

His gaze locked on mine, unblinking. Then it dropped to the flames, jaw clenching with enough force to grind teeth to dust.

"Rhaelin," I urged.

He remained statue-still—no pacing, no outburst. Just that lethal immobility, as if movement would unleash hell. Knuckles whitened on the chair's arm, veins bulging.

"One thing," he ground out finally, voice a low rumble that shook the air. "I asked one *goddamn* thing. And you went to *Darius.*"

His eyes snapped back to me, the raw hurt bleeding through his crumbling facade. "Darius, Zyrenna?" The name exploded from him, volume surging like a dam bursting. "For fuck's sake!"

It struck like a physical blow, stealing my breath. Rhaelin didn't raise his voice to me. Never. This fracture in his composure made my heart stutter.

"I asked one *thing*," he snarled, voice straining against the leash he tried to yank back. "Don't fly with anyone else. Don't risk yourself without me." The accusation landed heavy, sinking into my chest.

"Every time you charge into the jaws of death like that," he said, leaning forward, elbows digging into knees, "you're not just betting your life. You're wagering mine."

His jaw ticked, a muscle jumping wildly.

"And not because of any fucking bond." His words fractured, sharp edges glinting. "Because I will come for you. Every. Single. Time. That's the only rule I have left."

He raked a hand down his face, fingers trembling with suppressed violence. "And I'm running something bigger than us. Hundreds of people depending on me. An entire rebellion balanced on whether I keep control and make the right calls." He let out a bitter laugh. "And tonight, I lost it. Not in training. Not in the ring. In the open. Loud enough that Varik *will* carry it back to the Spire."

His voice dropped to a lethal growl. "You severed his son's wings, Zyrenna—and I pulverized half his face before you even raised your blade. Kalor will scream treason, provocation. He'll use it to gut me from the Council, to dismantle everything I've bled for. We won't be able to pull people down here as easily if I am not up there. Do you get that?"

He paused, exhaled through his teeth. "And the worst part?" His eyes bored into mine, dark and storm-tossed. "I didn't even want you to stop. If you hadn't, I would have ripped his heart out myself."

"I nearly threatened to wage war because of you," he finished.

In that moment, I saw it clear: beyond the terror of my loss, he feared the monster he became for me—the one that would raze empires without remorse.

I closed the distance, halting inches from him. "Look at

me."

He resisted, gaze fixed on the fire. Then, slowly, he obeyed.

"I'm sorry," I breathed. "For the recklessness, for the risk. We will deal with the Council and whatever comes of tonight. I held him off, Rhaelin—I did. If I'd known what it would cost you—if I'd known you'd have to bare yourself to him like that, I never would've gone. You have to know I would never risk what you've built."

"*Bare* myself to him?" He surged to his feet, voice booming through the room like a war drum. "Is that what you think this is? You *still* don't fucking get it!"

I recoiled—not from the roar, but the agony laced beneath, raw as an open wound.

He loomed closer, control evaporating like mist. "You think I give a *flying fuck* what that bastard saw? What fragment of me I exposed?" He shook his head, a savage, mirthless laugh ripping free. "You're blind to it, Zyrenna. Blind."

One step more, and he was inches away, heat radiating from him like a forge. "You could have died," he thundered, voice cracking the air. "Do you understand that? Gone." His chest heaved, fury a living storm. "And what then? Then you think the world goes on living happily ever after? That Alira grows up and finds a world that's whole? That she looks at me during those two weeks I'd have left to pretend I'm still breathing and sees a man who can teach her to fight, to survive, instead of a hollow fucking shell dragging himself through the ruins because the only thing that kept him breathing just vanished?"

His voice dropped suddenly—raw, edged with something jagged and final.

"Because surprise, Zyrenna." The words came out quieter, almost a whisper, but they cut deeper than any shout. "I would rather end my own life than survive those two weeks without you. Better yet—I'd fucking *sprint* to meet you at the gates of whatever afterlife this pathetic fucking world likes to pretend exists.

But you think I am furious for *baring myself* to Varik. Because I showed the monster?" His laugh was bitter, hollow. "I'm furious because there isn't a single fucking reality where your name isn't the first thing I think of when I open my eyes. And you—you do something as selfish as you just did. Thinking the lives could just keep going on around you."

I had known what I was to him—what I did to him, what the bond had carved between us. I'd known I mattered. That I anchored him. But this—this was something else entirely.

If he thought I hadn't thought about it the way he was now, he was wrong. I had. I understood it in my bones. Because in this moment, there was no greater torment I could imagine than a life without those green eyes drowning me in their intensity—like gravity, relentless and inescapable— every fucking day of this life.

He didn't try to hide what he felt. For the first time, he let it all go. And somehow, that fury was an offering.

I pressed a hand to his chest, feeling the wild hammer of his heart. "Sit."

He froze, eyes blazing defiance.

"Rhaelin." My voice cut low, unyielding. "*Sit down.*"

A shudder ran through him; the breath exploded out. He collapsed back onto the couch, as if my command had severed his strings.

I stepped between his knees, looming over him.

"You don't get to fall apart over me," I said softly, though my own voice trembled. "Not when I'm standing right here, unbroken."

His jaw flexed hard enough to crack stone. But he didn't look away—didn't rebuild that iron wall between us.

"You terrify me with words like that," I confessed. "Like you'd throw all this away because of me," waving my hand around the room.

His eyes traced my face, agony etched in every line. "I absolutely do get to fall apart over you," he growled. "That's what you don't seem to understand. I don't lose this because I feel something for you. I lose if I pretend I don't."

My breath caught, suspended.

His hand lifted, hovering over the ribs that still throbbed where Varik had slammed me. "You fought Varik Draevan," he said, eyes searching mine. "And you're alive." He swallowed. "I'm furious. But, goddamn, little flame… I have never been more proud."

The bond warmed at *proud,* a spark in the darkness.

"All my life," I said, "everyone I loved has left. My mother. My father. Even Solena, or so I thought. I've talked about it with anger for years because anger was the only emotion I knew how to hold. But it isn't anger—it's fear."

He froze, looking like he wanted to inhale every word I spoke.

"When you need someone," I said, "when you crave someone this deeply, losing them is worse, you know their absence will hollow you out. I told myself if I refused to feel this for you, if I just kept you at arm's length, I could avoid the pain. That I wouldn't bleed when you were taken from me." I shook my head.

I cupped his jaw, stubble scraping my palm like sandpaper. "No more lies."

I slid down onto his lap, my legs settling on either side of him, slow enough that I felt every breath hitch between us. He didn't move. Didn't reach for me. His hands stayed fisted at his sides—as if he didn't trust himself yet, as if the moment he touched me there would be no return. His breath reached my collarbone. The look in his eyes a prayer.

"Zyrenna," he rasped, voice gravel and smoke. "Whatever leaves your lips next—make it eternal. I will not endure you as a fleeting thing."

I leaned in, lips brushing his ear, breath a whisper of surrender. "Listen to me," I said. "I was wrong. Not about the Council. Not about wanting to burn the Houses to the ground. I was wrong about thinking I could want all that and not want you."

His entire body froze at the confession. I would no longer live without him.

"I want you," I murmured. "I *need* you, Rhaelin. Not your power, not your protection. You. All of you."

The words robbed him of breath, his chest seizing.

The bond erupted—heat surging through the tether, a wildfire unbound. He captured my gaze, eyes ablaze.

"If you ever take those words back," he said, voice shattered with command, "if you think for even a second there is a chance in which those words can be reclaimed, you will learn what true hell is, Zyrenna. There is no world where you walk away from this."

"I know."

Because I did. I knew his intensity. Knew every word he spoke carried a promise—especially the ones that were wrapped in threats. And still—none of it did anything but magnify the throb that gathered inside me.

He framed my face with his hands—rough palms cupping my cheeks, thumbs brushing the high curve of my cheekbones—and his mouth found mine in seconds.

It wasn't a kiss. It was consumption.

He devoured me like I was the first air he'd tasted after centuries drowned. Tongue invading, teeth catching my lower lip hard enough to sting, a low growl vibrating from his chest into mine. I kissed him back like he was oxygen and I'd been suffocating—clawing at his shoulders, nails digging into his skin, pulling him closer until there was no space left.

My body moved on instinct, hips settling closer—thighs parting wider to straddle the thick, insistent ridge of him through his pants, his toned muscles flexing. The hard length of him pressed against my clit, sending a strike of need straight through me. The couch groaned as he lifted me—one arm a steel band around my waist, the other cradling my bruised ribs with reverent care, as though even in his ruin he refused to let me break.

"Slow," he commanded against my mouth, the word edged in steel and trembling restraint. "I've waited too long to rush this. I want to feel every inch of you surrender."

His hands skimmed the hem of my tank, fingers hooking the edge. The fabric dragged slowly over my skin, cool air hitting the flushed peaks of my breasts before firelight touched every speck. He looked—truly looked at me—the way a soldier studies the battlefield before stepping onto it—gaze raking over me from the lines of my arms, over the swell of my chest to the dip of my navel, hunger sharpening those eyes. His pupils dilated, darkening the green to near black, and a low rumble vibrated in his chest.

The next kiss was slower, deeper—the kind you could

drown in and never want to surface from. His tongue stroked mine, deliberate, claiming, and the bond ignited like dry tinder. I felt the quiver of his fraying control beneath my own skin; he felt the dull throb in my ribs. I let him take the pain. He was already carrying everything else.

"You're shaking," he murmured, thumb tracing a slow, possessive line down my spine.

"I'm alive," I whispered.

"Then eyes on me." The order was absolute—impossible to disobey. The warmth of his skin pressed against me, a faint gleam of sweat making his hair stick to his temple.

I looked. The world narrowed to him. Eyes that had watched me patiently from shadows, waiting for this very moment to ruin me.

He kissed lower. Lips ghosted the frantic pulse at my throat, teeth scraped the edge of my collarbone until I gasped. Stubble rasped against sensitive skin, igniting trails of fire that arrowed straight to my core. He stripped the rest of my clothes away with lethal patience—pants sliding down, cotton whispering to the floor—until I was bare before him, vulnerable only to the monster who'd sworn to die for me.

His eyes flicked up, catching mine with a ferocity that nearly undid me—a raw hunger edged with something tender.

"You have no fucking idea how beautiful you are," he rasped. The words were low, almost accusatory, as if my beauty was a weapon I'd wielded against him all this time.

My hands flew to his face, pulling him back into me, fingers tracing the strong line of his jaw, then threading through his black hair, down over the ridges of his back—muscles honed from years of wielding a blade.

I needed to feel him everywhere, every muscle forged by

blood and battle, every scar that made him. The scars told a story my hands tried to memorize. And the tattoos… god, the tattoos snaked over his skin like living shadows: thick black vines coiling up his arms, blooming into runes across his chest that seemed to shift in the firelight. I traced one rune with my fingertip, feeling the subtle hum of power beneath his skin, and he shuddered under my touch, his breath catching as if my exploration was its own form of sweet torment.

His hand drifted down with murderous certainty and found me drenched. A dark smirk curled his mouth.

"Already ready to burn for me, little flame?" he murmured against my skin, "aching for my touch all this time, and just like that you're ready to come apart on two fingers?"

His smirk sharpened, as if he'd orchestrated every drop of my desire. "But you haven't even begged out loud yet."

And that was almost enough to finish me. His finger brushed me in a way that made my hips jump—a firm circle over that tight bundle of nerves, sending heat spiking up my spine. He watched my reactions intently, learning every gasp, every twitch, adjusting his pressure until I was writhing, the slick sounds of his fingers filling the air between us.

I spread my thighs wider, shameless, the sound of my own breath breaking around his name. He stroked me slow at first, patient, fingers curling just right to hit that spot inside, palm pressing flat against me so every thrust sent sparks crashing through nerves, my pleasure twisting with his satisfaction until it all blurred into one rhythm.

The bond throbbed in perfect rhythm with his hand. He answered every unspoken need. My back bowed off the couch.

"I could live a thousand lives," he growled, eyes locked on

mine, "and I'd still die from wanting you like this. You're mine, Zyrenna. Every gasp, every shiver, every drop of you that's dripping for me right now—mine."

The confession hung between us, heavy with the weight of all the moments we'd denied ourselves, making this one feel like salvation.

Then his mouth replaced his hand. Broad shoulders forced my thighs apart; tattoos flexed like dark wings as he settled between them. Tongue flicked with devastating precision, dragging me to the edge in long, slow strokes. I clutched his hair, thighs trembling against unyielding muscle. He hummed approval, the vibration shattering through my core, hands pinning my hips so I couldn't escape the onslaught.

"Eyes on me when you come," he commanded, voice vibrating against swollen flesh. "I want to watch you break for me. I want every second of it, Ren."

At that name, on his lips, I came apart. I let out a moan I couldn't contain, my vision blurred, my body shaking, the bond flooding until it felt like the entire world burned down around us. He didn't stop, tongue gentling to soft drags, drawing out every aftershock until my thighs quivered against his jaw. Waves of pleasure rolled through me, each one amplified by the bond, his own arousal echoing back like a mirror, making me feel utterly claimed.

His fingers left my skin only so he could strip, firelight pulling over every line of him. Broad shoulders, hard chest with that beautiful tattooed sword, falling down to a stomach carved in muscled planes. Built like he'd been made for someone to fall to their knees over.

Then my gaze dropped, and my breath snagged.

His hand wrapped around himself, fingers curling with a

slow, certain stroke. Thick and heavy in his palm—enough to make my stomach flare. Veins traced the length, pulsing under his grip, and the sight of him touching himself sent a fresh wave of desire crashing through, my body clenching in anticipation. He held my stare the entire time, unashamed, letting me see exactly what I did to him.

He stood there like a promise—restrained, dangerous, and absolutely certain of the effect he had.

And all that strength was aimed at me.

"Rhaelin," I gasped, half plea, half prayer. "I need you. All of you. Now."

"I will give you every fucking piece of me, Ren." The vow cracked through me, his free hand reaching to cup my face, thumb brushing my lower lip like a promise.

His thumb lingered, pressing just enough to part my lips; I tasted salt and smoke and him. Instinctively, I drew it into my mouth, sucking gently, a guttural sound escaping him as he watched.

And then he was moving, propping himself up on one arm— the muscle of his bicep bulging next to my face, veins standing out like ropes under his skin, the coiled serpent tattooed on his forearm flexing with the effort—the other guiding himself into me.

My eyes lifted to his, and in the same instant he entered me. The world detonated. Every nerve lit at once—walls clenching around him as he sank deeper. My breath caught so quickly it felt like I'd been split open and remade. He started slow, each thrust deliberate torment—hips rolling smooth and controlled, the honed ridges of his abs tightening with every push. The stretch was inconceivable, bordering on too much, yet exactly what I craved, filling me in ways that went beyond the physical, the bond weaving our sensations into something of shared ecstasy.

He paused, buried fully, forehead pressed to mine. "Your ribs," he rasped. "Tell me if—"

"No. Make me feel it," I whispered, and rolled my hips to prove it, grinding down until the stretch of him bordered on pain and perfection in the same breath.

A growl tore from his throat, low and animal. It reverberated through his chest into mine, primal and possessive, unlocking something wild in me.

The bond surged, doubling every sensation: the blistering heat of his body fused to mine, the way pleasure spiked and ricocheted between us until I couldn't tell where his want ended and mine began. His fear of losing me tangled with raw awe at finally having me—crashing through the tether. His chest pressed to my breasts, nipples dragging against sweat-slick skin with every shallow thrust. His hand slid to the small of my back, fingers splaying wide, lifting me just enough to angle deeper—every roll of his hips dragging the thick head of him against that devastating spot inside until stars detonated behind my eyelids.

Each movement opened another door between us until there was no separating us.

"Your hair, Zyrenna..." His voice faltered, rough with awe. I followed his gaze. At the edge of my vision, strands lifted and shimmered—molten silver in the firelight, glowing like moonlight had poured itself into me and set every filament ablaze. Whatever it was, it didn't matter. I had no room left for thought.

Veil, I had never felt so whole. My legs wrapped around his waist, heels digging into the curve of his lower back, pulling him deeper as my nails raked down ridges of muscle and scar.

"I can't—Rhaelin—fuck…" My voice splintered as the rhythm turned brutal—harder, faster, his thrusts snapping with barely-leashed violence. Sweat gleamed on his tattoos, making the black vines and runes look alive. "You're ruining me."

His free hand shot up, fingers clamping my jaw, forcing my eyes back to his. "You were never meant to survive me whole, baby."

I couldn't take it anymore—the tenderness warring with the brutality, the way he filled me so completely I could feel him everywhere. I needed more. I needed *him* to break too.

I shoved at his shoulder. "Let me—please."

He stilled instantly—eyes blazing emerald inferno. For one heartbeat, I thought he'd refuse. Then, with predatory grace, he rolled us. The shift drove him so deep we both groaned—long, guttural, shared agony. My hands braced on his chest, fingers splaying over the inked runes that pulsed hot under my palms. I moved slowly at first—savoring the stretch, the way his hips jerked involuntarily beneath me, the way his breath sawed out like I was killing him.

His hands clamped my thighs—hard enough to bruise. He didn't guide. He just held. My movements grew bolder—grinding down, circling my hips in slow, cruel figure-eights that made his abs lock and his throat work on a choked sound.

"Ren," he rasped, head falling back, throat bared in offering. "You're—you're fucking killing me."

"Good," I whispered, leaning down to bite the corded muscle of his neck. "Now you know how it feels."

I rolled harder, merciless, chasing the edge for both of us. His breath punched out; stomach muscles locked under my palms.

I smiled down at him—an unguarded, wicked smile I knew would shatter him. His eyes flared black. The last thread of restraint snapped.

A sound tore out of his throat, and in one fluid motion he sat up, arms banding my waist like iron. My knees left the couch; and the world tilted. He lowered me onto the carpet like he was about to worship. The soft fibers against my back contrasted with the hard planes of his body, grounding me as he loomed above. Control reclaimed in a heartbeat—effortless, inevitable.

His lips hovered at my cheek, breath shaking. "Smile like that again," he growled, voice shredded, "and forget I ever let you take the lead."

He drove back in. One hand pinned my wrists above my head, the other pressing my hip down. The dominance in his hold sent a thrill through me, my body arching to meet him, surrendering completely to him.

Each thrust dragged me closer to oblivion. His low, broken breaths unraveled what little control I had left—grunts rumbling from his chest, vibrating where we were joined.

"Don't you dare hold back," he groaned, pressing his forehead to mine. His words seared hot across my mouth. "Break for me. Let me feel every second of you falling apart."

My body had never obeyed anyone the way it obeyed him. Every syllable burned through me, ripping reactions I couldn't hide. The way he looked at me—like I was salvation and destruction in the same breath. The way he filled me—thick, relentless, owning every inch. The way his need tangled with mine through the bond until we were one pulsing, desperate thing.

And then I shattered. The world cracked open, stars exploding behind my eyes, every muscle trembling in bliss that bordered on pain—my core pulsed around him, thighs clamped tighter, my gaze shattering. I cried out against his lips, swallowed by his moan, both of us coming undone together.

He tore his mouth from mine, gaze locking onto me with wild, almost desperate intensity. "On me," he rasped as he tilted my chin up.

I couldn't deny him. My body arched one final time, soul split wide, eyes fused to his as the aftershocks rolled through us both.

The world returned in pieces: crackle of fire, taste of sweat and salt and him, the heavy burn of him still buried deep.

He rolled onto his back, dragging a hand over his face like he wasn't sure if the world we'd created would still be here when he opened his eyes again. I sat up slightly, watching the lines of strain soften across his jaw. For once, he looked almost breakable, the defined angles of his face softened in the afterglow.

I reached for him, and with my fingers I began tracing the serpent on his forearm.

"Months of blue-balling each other through the bond, and the second we give in you turn my hair into a fucking beacon," I glanced at a glowy strand still faintly shimmering.

What the fuck.

"Next time, maybe warn a girl when whatever *this* is decides to announce we're finally fucking."

A deep, rich laugh tore out of him—completely unguarded. His whole body shook as he rolled toward me, a smile breaking fully across his face.

CHAPTER TWENTY-SEVEN

Beautiful. Infuriatingly so.

"Yeah," he said, still smiling, "unfortunately, that's something we're going to need to address."

I just stared at him for a long moment. Let the silence stretch.

Then, quietly, honestly, I said, "You undo me more with every breath, Rhaelin Morrain."

Something flickered in his eyes, bright and fragile all at once, before he bent to press his lips to my forehead like he'd been given permission to breathe. We drifted, and just before sleep found us, he murmured, "Little flame."

"Hm?"

"You burned beautifully." His arm curled around me, pulling my form against the solid wall of his chest, warm under my cheek.

I moved closer to him, lost in every word he spoke. I slept in the arms of a monster who would burn the world for me and dreamed of the day I'd hand him the match.

CHAPTER TWENTY-EIGHT

When I woke, I wasn't the same.

Everything felt heightened, like the world had been cut open. I could pick apart every sound—the faint clink of a kettle far off in the kitchens, the scrape of boots two halls away, the firm beat of Rhaelin's breathing beside me. The sheets tangled around my legs felt like nothing at all, too light to hold me. Energy buzzed under my skin, restless, like a second heartbeat I couldn't calm.

Beside me, Rhaelin shifted, voice a low rumble that curled through the bond. "You're restless." His eyes opened, alert in a way that said he'd never truly been asleep. "You've been moving like you're training in your sleep."

I pushed myself upright, the blanket sliding down my naked skin. "I feel… different."

His gaze narrowed with something unreadable before concern softened his features. He sat up with me, studying me too closely, like he'd noticed something I hadn't.

"Different how?" he asked.

I ignored the weight of that look, brushing it aside as though it didn't matter.

"Everything's too loud. Too bright." I flexed my fingers;

sparks seemed to run through the tendons. "My body feels—" I broke off, shaking my head. "Like every nerve has been lit."

He cupped my jaw with one hand and set two fingers of the other against my carotid. "It's faster," he murmured. "Your heart. Your blood." His jaw tightened; the bond snagged on a thread of unease. "The tether must still be evolving," he said, the uncertainty in him clean and new—he didn't doubt much. "Zyrenna, go look at yourself."

I slipped free and crossed to the mirror. Silver-blue eyes burned brighter than yesterday, as if starlight were caught behind my irises. Strands of hair glimmered where they fell across my shoulder. For a breath, a faint ripple moved through my pupils, then faded.

"I'm not imagining this, am I?"

"No." He was already on his feet behind me, reflection a tall, dark figure over my shoulder. His eyes traced mine in the glass.

"You're changing, Ren."

His voice slid into my ear. "And now it's even harder to look away."

He tucked a strand of hair behind my ear and pressed a brief kiss to my temple.

Something in me shifted at the words. The thrill of it mixed with fear. How far would this go? How far could I let it go before I ceased to recognize myself?

* * *

Maris delivered my final set of altered leathers that morning— the last adjustments finished. She lingered longer than she should have, her eyes flicking over me, catching on something

245

she didn't name. Her mouth pressed thin, but she said nothing. Rhaelin had already left to walk the rounds with Darius, leaving me alone to drag the leather over newly restless skin.

The change was immediate. The dark set hugged without choking, sculpted close along my waist and thighs, looser at the shoulders for movement. Black seams traced patterns down the sleeves and along the ribs. High boots laced just below my knees. A dagger belt rode low on my hips along with two twin sheaths hugging my thighs.

Twin blades—now the first language my hands reached for. My instinct and my preference.

They hadn't been my first weapons. That had come later, earned through bruises and muscle memory and hours in the ring where balance mattered more than brute strength. I'd taken to them fast—too fast for some people's comfort—and apparently fast enough for Rhaelin's notice.

This morning, when I'd dressed, there had been another waiting on the dresser.

Same weight and balance as my original one.

A perfect match.

The hilt was purple—deep, unmistakable. Rhaelin's doing. A quiet decision made without ceremony, without explanation.

But now I had two.

I slid the new dagger into the empty sheath, the twin weight settling against my leg like it had always belonged there.

When I straightened, the mirror didn't give me the vineyard girl I'd been. It gave me something cut for fire and blood. The leather emphasized every line of me, the curve of my hips, the lift of my chest beneath the fitted V-neck.

The corridors buzzed when I stepped into them, sounds

carrying. But the sounds separated rather than crowded—this person had a limp, that one was humming off-key, the door's latch needed oil. My body moved like it knew the routes before my mind did, angles opening and closing around me as if I'd walked them a thousand times.

When Rhaelin appeared from the hall, striding toward me in his own set of black leathers, the bond roared awake. His gaze swept over me once, and the corners of his mouth lifted up with no shame.

He leaned close enough that only I could hear. "Little flame," he said, "you look absolutely fucking lethal."

Heat pooled at the base of my spine at his words, a reminder of last night.

"Come," he added more evenly. "They're waiting."

I didn't move. Not when he looked at me like that—all quiet hunger. He was truly the most beautiful man I had ever seen. "Keep staring at me like that and they'll be waiting a while."

He tilted his head. "Ren," he said, my name weighted like a vow. "You're playing a dangerous game, sweetheart."

As much as I wanted to push, I knew better. Rhaelin didn't make statements he didn't mean—and when he warned me, it was never empty. I tilted my head in return, matching him without challenging him, and chose—deliberately—to leave it there. His gaze lingered one second longer before his mouth curved into a faint smirk and he turned toward the hall.

We walked side by side into the training hall. Heads turned, conversations ended. The clang of steel hit the ground and every single eye turned our way, not just on him, not just on me, but us.

It wasn't that I looked entirely different. Whatever had awoken in me this morning had dulled before I left, dialed down to almost something human again. Almost. My hair had slowly—but not fully—retreated to the same black that caught in the firelight while I was getting ready. My frame no different than it was yesterday. But something in me shone brighter now, like the night always seemed to cling to me, bleeding into the edges of my skin. It wasn't just seen; it was felt, like the first shift of weather before a storm breaks.

People stiffened as I passed, gazes catching a second too long. Even the air went still, as though the Embers themselves paused to listen.

Darius's scarred brows furrowed, sizing me up like he couldn't decide if he was impressed or worried. Solena tilted her head, a grin creeping across her face—like one of her hunches had just clicked into place. Alira's lips parted, her blue eyes going wide, staring at me like I was her sister… and someone new all at once.

Others watched too—Maris with open satisfaction, a few soldiers with wariness, a handful of humans with relief that read like hope. It struck me then: it wasn't only Rhaelin's shadow they were reacting to. It was power—still-forming—and the fact that it wore my face.

For all the terror bristling under my skin, something in me settled. As if whatever was happening had finally found a home that fit.

Minutes passed and people finally settled back into what they were doing after Rhaelin so helpfully reminded them there was—in fact—shit to do besides gawking. Poetry in motion, that one.

Darius barked, "In the ring." His tone had an edge I'd heard only a few times; he wasn't just testing me. He was proving something—to them, and maybe to himself.

I stepped forward—the sand took my weight. The twin daggers rode easily against my thighs, now as familiar as breath. My opponent was a broad-shouldered mortal soldier with a staff, older than me by a handful of years.

He struck first downward, hard enough to crack a wrist. My body moved before thought, in fluid motions. My blade caught the wood, and I pivoted, sliding close enough that my second dagger pressed the air just shy of his ribs.

Gasps rippled around the circle.

From the edge, a soldier's voice rang out, smug and cutting: "Careful, Bren, she's making you look like a recruit."

The man in front of me flushed darker. "Fuck off," he snapped without looking away from me. Whoever he was talking to, it wasn't someone I recognized, but the tone said it wasn't the first time they'd taunted each other.

"Again," Darius ordered, his scarred face unreadable.

This time the soldier lunged with a low sweep meant to take my legs. The world slowed. I saw the shift of his weight a breath before he moved; my feet were already going. I sidestepped, spun low, dragged both daggers across the grain of the wood. The staff splintered along the cut. Half of it hit the sand; the other half sagged in his grip. My blade was at the hollow of his throat before he processed the loss.

He swallowed; I stepped back. Quiet throughout the whole room.

Two vampires replaced him—both with blades. I didn't wait for them to close the gap. I charged first, boots pounding the stone, my arms pumping as I closed the distance in three heartbeats.

Steel met steel. I ducked the first swing, drove my elbow into one man's gut, and felt his breath leave him. My dagger bit along the second man's sleeve, close enough to draw a hiss without blood. The crowd stirred, disbelief threaded through the noise.

One soldier came at me again, blade high. I deflected, pivoted, and swept the second dagger low across his knee. He crumpled. The other raised his, but I was already behind him, the tip of my dagger pressing to the back of his neck before he even realized I'd moved.

I had gotten better since training began; I knew that. But this was something else. Not brute strength—though strength ran through me—nor only speed. It was rhythm, the sense of seeing the opening before it existed, as if the air itself revealed where the strike would pass. Like my body had been rewired for it.

"Enough," Darius said when a third soldier stepped forward, raising one hand. His voice was dry as gravel. "It's confirmed. She's a fucking badass." A few laughs cracked the stillness.

He slanted a look at Rhaelin. "I see why you're tied to this one. You both fight like mad bastards."

Solena's laugh rang brightest, her head thrown back, blonde braid swaying. Maris shook her head, smiling like a kid. Rhaelin didn't flinch. His mouth curved—pride flickering through the tether like thunder, warm and electric against my chest.

"You have no idea," he responded, and there was no question in it.

I slid both blades back into their sheaths, fingers steady. Even I was rocked by what had just happened—but I didn't let it show.

I'd always been more athletic—built for movement, for motion, for using my body instead of sitting still—but today it felt like something else. I walked off the sand with a sureness I'd not yet earned yesterday and somehow had today.

"Well, damn," Solena said, pushing off the pillar. Her braid swung as she crossed the floor, eyes bright with mischief and a glint of approval she didn't bother hiding. "Remind me to stay on your good side."

I tilted my head. "You mean aside from the fact that you disappeared into an underground rebellion for years and never told me?"

Solena grimaced. "I deserved that."

Alira slipped in on my right, fingers catching my sleeve. "You didn't even look like my sister," she whispered, awe and fear braided together. "You looked… like you knew what was going to happen before it did."

The words cut deeper than she knew because they were true. I squeezed her fingers. "I'm still me," I said, and hoped it was true enough.

"Clear the ring," Darius called. "Pairs, then fours. And if you're staring, you're not working." The hall stirred back to life under his barked corrections. "Higher. Tighter. Stop dropping your wrist," he snapped at someone else, then—without looking at me—"Don't get proud, Vaeoria," It was grudging praise. I nodded even though he wasn't watching.

Rhaelin drifted closer as the circle broke apart. He kept a commander's distance, but the bond ran a thumb over my pulse. "Walk with me," he said under his breath.

We took the long side of the hall, past racks of weapons and the dozens of punching bags lining the wall.

"How are your senses?" he asked. "Any pain? Disorientation?"

"No pain. I can hear too much, but I can separate it. Sight

is… bright, not blinding." I paused. "I feel like I could run to the river and back and not be winded."

He nodded once, jaw easing a fraction. "You were fucking mesmerizing in there, Zyrenna." His eyes didn't leave mine. "I lost track of everything else."

"I hardly recognized myself, to be honest. I was good before, but not like that," I said.

"You've always been good. Better than most down here. Don't doubt that."

He stopped beside a rack and plucked a short throwing blade from a shelf. Balanced it on his finger, then flipped it hilt-first toward me. I caught it without thinking.

"Targets," he said, chin tipping toward a painted board across the room. "Three. Left to right. Then reverse. Breathe on the release."

I took stance. The room's noise dropped to a hum. Left, center, right—metal thunked, neat in the ring each time. Reverse—right, center, left—one after another, as clean as if a line had been drawn for me to follow.

Rhaelin's pride slid through the bond again, brief. "Again," he said, tone even, like he hadn't just watched what I did. But I did it again. The last throw landed off-center; relief tugged at me. Imperfect meant I was still me.

"Good," he said. "Now close your eyes." I did. "Listen. Name five sounds."

I breathed. "Darius scolding somebody for missing a target." His snort from across the hall proved me right. "Solena talking to one of the fighters. Alira—chewing a peppermint she thinks I can't hear. Maris—counting numbers under her breath. And you." I smiled, eyes still closed. Voice now a whisper. "Breathing like it kills you to let them look at me."

His silence warmed; the bond flicked with reluctant amusement. "I asked for sounds, little flame—not mind-reading." A beat passed. "Eyes open."

When I looked, he was already watching the doors at the far end of the hall, thoughts turning toward patrols and supply and the thousand invisible threads he pulled tight to hold this place together. He looked like command again. It should have made me feel smaller; it didn't. It just made me want to carry what I could with him.

"Rhaelin," Alira said, appearing at my side again, light on her feet despite the boots. "Can I—" Her eyes dropped. "Can I run laps with the morning squad, like the recruits? Not the whole route," she added quickly. "Just… part. Solena says it's time."

Rhaelin didn't look at me, just at Alira. "Two laps," he said. "With Maris or Solena on your shoulder. And you stop if your chest burns. We don't have healers for hearts that give out down here."

Alira's grin cracked open. "Yes, Commander," then she did a mock salute.

"Next week," he continued, as if it had always been on the schedule, "we start you on daggers. We will work slowly. You'll hate it—hate is allowed. Quitting is not."

Alira's eyes went wide. "Really?"

"Really," he said, then lifted a brow. "If you tell your sister I'm soft, I will make you memorize the names of every commander under the Spire since the founding."

A laugh bubbled up from my chest before I could stop it.

"I wouldn't dare." She beamed at me, then dashed off toward Solena, who caught her in a noogie that sounded like a small brawl.

"Thank you," I said, voice raw. He didn't answer with words. He pressed his hand against my lower back: *Of course.* It said more than speech could.

Darius's bark cut across the room. "Commander! If you're done parading your terrifying little shadow, we've got reports to run through."

"I'll never be done," he said to only me with a wink. "I will come find you later after lunch," he said as he turned and jogged off—something that should not have been as sexy as it was.

When I looked up, Alira was jogging the perimeter with two recruits, cheeks flushed, hair bouncing. She caught my gaze on a pass, lifted two fingers to her temple in a salute that made my throat feel small. Solena shouted at her to swing her arms; Alira stuck her tongue out and did it anyway. A normal moment. A needed one.

I stood at the edge of the ring, hands braced on the railing, and let the noise of the hall move through me. The restlessness hadn't gone; I didn't think it would. But it wasn't a frantic thing anymore. It was fuel. A current I could learn to ride.

A flicker of caution threaded the bond—Rhaelin, thinking of Spire eyes and ears, of how quickly rumor travels when you need it least. I sent back steadiness the way he'd taught me: breath down to the ribs, count four then out six.

For the first time since stepping into this world, I didn't feel like an outsider, or prey. I felt like I belonged.

CHAPTER TWENTY-NINE

RHAELIN

The Embers Council had never felt small to me, but tonight it did.

It was stone that had been patient for a century. Tonight, the table looked longer. The torches burned lower. Every step toward the head of the table pressed on my body.

I called the council at dawn. Days had passed since the vineyard—since the moment I fell into that courtyard and found his fingers at Zyrenna's throat.

I'm not proud of how completely I surrendered to that anger.

But if I ever saw that hand there again—those fingers closing where they had no right to be—I wouldn't stop at breaking him. I would dismantle him, piece by careful piece, until the memory of her skin became something his body rejected.

I stepped in first, Zyrenna at my side. I wouldn't hide her behind me, or pretend we were anything less than what we were.

The tether between us made itself known as always—stronger than ever. She changed a little more each sunrise. She walked sure and unafraid at my side. I let my council see all of it. The only thing I kept to myself was my fear; the kind that lived in the thought of losing her.

If I can say one thing though, spending every night with her since our first had been torment and salvation all at once. She burns me alive with a look, yet steadies me in ways I never thought possible. She allows me to tear open my restraint that I've spent endless hours mastering, as long as it's with her in my hands.

The doors to the Embers Council chamber opened, spilling torchlight in, and the six faces I knew well followed. The Embers inner circle. My *chosen* circle.

Darius sat closest, arms crossed over his chest, an expression that was almost always carved from stone. He didn't bother hiding the smirk when his eyes slid from me to Zyrenna. Fucker.

Solena lounged half sideways in her chair as she sat, grin as cutting as ever, already calculating angles the rest of us hadn't considered. She earned her place at this table years ago, when I smuggled her out of the Crimson House that would've bled her dry. I hadn't asked for thanks, but she gave it anyway, not in words, but in loyalty deep enough to gut anyone who spoke ill of me. She swore if I ever called, she'd answer, and she has every time. Most importantly, she earned a spot here with her mind—it can twist strategy faster than most men can draw a blade. Now, I'm just grateful Zyrenna has someone in these halls she can trust that isn't me.

Maris had parchment spread before her, ink-stained fingers flying quickly over the page, tallying supplies even as her eyes measured the room. She's my record-keeper, my numbers woman, always weighing cost against survival—turning scraps of grain and steel into lifelines, her quiet mortal focus the glue that holds our edges from fraying.

Theron didn't sit. He lingered in the shadows, wings always out, lean frame folded against the wall, gaze restless as if he'd already run through every possible outcome and hated them all. I did too.

He's my spy, my ears—always keeping watch outside so we can keep breathing down here. His network snakes deeper into the Crimson Houses than anyone here cared to know.

He also had a tendency to push me further than anyone else in this room ever dared. Arrogant on the surface, sharp-tongued and relentless—but it was only a cover for the fact that he gave a shit.

We went at each other often because he was an instigator by nature, and because he refused to let me go quiet when pressure mounted. I tolerated it because when Theron pressed, it was never without purpose.

Lennan—human—took the far end with quiet authority—older, hands folded on the table, her calm gaze enough to hush a room faster than any shout. When she spoke, people listened—not out of fear, but because ignoring her would be flat-out stupid. She's our most talented healer, a scholar with more knowledge tucked in her head than half the Spire's dusty archives. Book smarts, sure, but the hands-on kind that's stitched us back together more times than I can count.

And then there was Brannic. Young, restless, his knee bouncing under the table, boot tapping a rhythm only he heard. He tried to hide the awe in his eyes when they darted to Zyrenna, but he failed—wide and unguarded, like she'd hung the damn moon. He's our youngest member in the room, reckless but brave, bold enough to voice the opinions for his entire generation down here. He idolizes us more than he should, but sometimes I let it slide. The young need something—someone—to pin their hopes on. It's clear Zyrenna's shot straight to the top of that list now, her silver-blue fire pulling him in.

I didn't sit. I stood at the head of the table, Zyrenna one step to my right. I let my voice carry.

"The Spire has called a council. I received a summons at my keep in the Ring of Thrones. They've requested my presence." I paused and let my gaze pass to her, lingering on the line of her jaw, and the tone of her frame, then back to the table. "And hers."

Silence fell heavy.

"It's a trap," Darius said simply. "The Spire doesn't summon, they order. The moment she steps into their sight, they'll measure where to cut."

"They will not lay a hand on her." The words were out before I could temper them—ripping from my throat. The bond surged, hot and possessive: mine—a fierce, coiling heat that wrapped around my gut and hers, echoing back her quiet resolve like a shared pulse.

Every head turned to me—Solena's grin fading to a tight line, Maris's ink-stained fingers pausing mid-note, Theron's lean shadow shifting against the wall. Zyrenna's eyes locked on mine—silver coins and calm.

"We won't go in blind," I added, forcing the steel back into place. "That's why you're all here. We map it, we arm it, we turn their game into ours."

Solena leaned forward, elbows hitting the table. "If they wanted her dead, they would've tried to reach her by now. This—" She waved her hand at the air between us all, "This is theater. They want to see how far they can push you before you break."

"We don't know if they've tried to reach her. She's been buried down here with us. You'd gamble her life by calling it theater?" Darius pressed.

"I, out of anyone, would never gamble with her life," Solena snapped. "What I'm saying is the Spire doesn't waste blades in the dark when they can bleed you in the open. They're baiting him on purpose."

"She's right. I've had patrols on Zyrenna's street for months," I cut in. "People have lingered on the streets as they always have, but no one's actually tried to approach her house in that time besides Varik."

Her gaze flicked to me then—searching—and I watched the realization settle behind her eyes. She saw it—understood it.

It had never been the Spire Council guarding her street.

It had always been my people. My orders. My resources spent on her long before she ever stepped foot belowground.

Something in her expression shifted—not fear, not shock. Something softer. A quiet, dangerous understanding that brushed against the bond and burned.

Outwardly, I was stone. Inwardly though, the fire clawed. Because Solena wasn't wrong; the Spire wanted to test me, prod at the frayed edges of my control until I snapped. And Darius wasn't wrong either. Every trap they set ended in blood.

Maris's voice slid in. "It doesn't matter what it looks like. The cost will be the same. Nothing is free with the Spire. Not food, not soldiers, not lives. Whatever they ask of you there, we'll pay for it down here. In rations or blood."

Theron's voice slipped out of the shadow, his lean frame unfolding from the wall. "You're all speaking as if they won't use the Severant." His eyes flicked to me, then Zyrenna. "If they suspect, they'll set it in the room to see if you flinch."

Theron's words landed like a blade. The Severant—the name alone made my jaw lock. Fury pressed under my ribs, intense enough to shake my control. If they used it on her—if they so much as let its shadow touch her—I would not stop at breaking the council. I would burn every stone in the fucking Spire.

I forced my voice even. "Ther—"

Zyrenna's voice came clean, cutting through the air. Her eyes flicked from me to the others. "What is the Severant?"

The chamber shifted—tension coiling tight in the air. Even Solena's smile thinned. Lennan answered—her voice calm but laced with an unsettling quiet.

"The Severant is a device created long before the Spire. It was made for one purpose: to expose and, if possible, destroy the Sanguis tie for those who saw it as evil. They set it between the bonded pair and feed it blood from both of them. Once awakened, it forces the tether out into the open."

Zyrenna's brows furrowed. "Forces it how?"

"Through pain," Lennan's voice stayed calm, but the weight in it pressed. "If the bond is weak—which it rarely ever is— the Severant will snap it clean. Quick and final. That's the mercy in it. But if the bond is strong…" She paused, her gaze flicking between the two of us. "Then it fights back. The device tears and claws, trying to force it apart. The pain is said to be… unbearable. Few survive it whole. And my guess, just based on what I've seen, the bond you two share is anything but weak."

Her eyes flicked to me, then back to Zyrenna. "Either way, you lose the protection of secrecy. And once the Spire knows, they can decide whether to break you apart, or use what you are for themselves."

Theron added, "There are stories. Once, a pair endured. He came out blind. She mute. They forgot how to move in the same direction. They stopped breathing within a day of each other. The Spire easily could've killed them—"

My blood boiled.

"Theron, shut the fuck up."

"No." Zyrenna cut in, her voice firm. Her eyes poured into me—absolutely no fear there.

"You don't get to do that," she said. "Hopefulness isn't a tactic anymore, Rhaelin. Not for us."

The table went still.

I held my silence a beat too long. Long enough for the past to claw its way up my spine. For the smell of iron and smoke to settle at the back of my throat. For the memory of bodies that had tried—and failed—to endure what the Spire demanded.

I nodded once.

Because she was right. Because hope had never saved anyone.

"I was there," I said.

I didn't need to say more. The room tasted like ash after the words left my mouth. "But it will not happen," I said. "Not to her. Not while I still draw breath."

Darius spoke first, hands curling into fists on the table. "We don't take her. We don't walk into a snare. The Severant is a blade at both of your throats, why hand them the chance to use it?"

Solena's grin changed into something else entirely. "And if we don't go? The Spire will paint it as guilt… as weakness. They'll whisper she's a danger they can't control."

Brannic leaned forward, restless energy spilling out of him. "Then let her go," he said, words tripping over each other. "Let her walk in and look them in the eye. They think she'll hide behind you, Commander. If she walks into that chamber unflinching, it'll rattle them harder than any threat."

With every passing second, I felt my composure slipping again. Before I could stop myself, the words tore out, raw and louder than I intended. "I will not just hand her over to them."

Darius looked grimly satisfied, Solena looked like she'd been waiting for me to crack, and the rest watched in stillness.

"Enough," she said—her voice cutting clean through the room. "Look at me."

Every head turned. She didn't look at any of them. She looked at me—eyes finding their mark.

For a heartbeat, it was only us. She intended for this.

I forced my gaze up, the anger still burning in my chest. And suddenly, the bond shifted. Her calm pressed into me—like her hand sliding through my chest to hold my heart still until it remembered how to beat. All I could do was breathe her in; she pulled me back from the edge.

This woman would end me.

She didn't look away. "You are not handing me to anyone," she said. "You've trusted me every step of the way—let that stand here too. I decide."

She turned her attention to the rest of the council now, away from me. Her gaze tore through everyone at the table. "You all speak like I'm not sitting right here. Like I'm a cost on parchment or a pawn on your board. It's my blood they want, my bond. And I will not have you deciding for me whether I walk into that chamber." She exhaled. "You will not speak for me—not ever."

Darius shifted, uncomfortable—he didn't agree, but he respected it, his scarred face tightening in that silent nod. Solena's grin widened with real approval, like she'd just bet on the right horse. Even Lennan's gaze softened, as if she'd been waiting for Zyrenna to take the floor.

I turned to her then, the words breaking out like surrender. "What do you want, Zyrenna?"

"I'm going to the Spire," she said, eyes holding mine without a flicker. "You can weigh the risks however you like, but I'll stand with you."

For a moment, everything in me rebelled.

I had wanted choice for her—freedom, not chains disguised as loyalty. And here she was, choosing to walk into the lion's den.

It destroyed me.

But it swelled something fierce and aching in my chest all the same.

"Okay," I murmured. She would always have her choice. Even when it terrified me—even when it cost me.

Then I let my voice harden back to command. "Then we face the Spire." I paused, letting the weight settle between us. "But hear me: if they so much as lift the Severant from its cloth, if anyone in that room breathes wrong toward her—" Silence cut the room. "—we start this war."

I stood, every line of me coiling. "I am done waiting. I am done letting threats circle at the edges of what I care about." My hands clenched until the knuckles whitened. "I am done using all our resources down here and dancing around the inevitable. I have kept my temper in check long enough."

No humor in my voice—it split through. "I draw the line at her."

The silence that followed wasn't fear. It was resolve.

Zyrenna got up to walk away, nearly in the hallway now. I got up to follow her, caught her wrist before she could slip free, my fingers light but holding. We were outside the hall, just the two of us, the air cooler and quieter.

"I'm sorry, Ren," I said without hesitation. "I should have asked."

She didn't pull her hand free. "You always act first," she said, voice low and soft, like a blade sheathed in silk. "It makes sense—after everything. I won't pretend it doesn't scare me, you deciding for us both." She paused, her thumb brushing slow over my knuckles. "But I'm here. I'll remind you every time that I get a say too. This mess is on me—I pulled us into it. You won't pay for my fuck-up alone."

She met my gaze without flinching. "Anger's always been my first instinct," she said. "You know that. I don't fault you for it—I won't. But there's a difference between feeling it and letting it answer for you."

She tilted her head, the small, practical motion that could smooth a dozen tempers. "Don't let anger answer for you," she added. "It's honest, but it isn't always wise. Breathe. Think. Be the man who keeps people whole, not the one who won the Blood Trials because he had to. Be the leader they've stood behind for decades."

There was a gentleness in her voice I hadn't expected. It wrapped around the jagged edges of my chest.

"Be better than them," she said.

I wanted to tell her I already tried to be that man for her, that the vineyard had frayed something in me I hadn't mended. Instead, I let my thumb drag once across the back of her hand.

She squeezed my fingers and, in the same breath, let go.

"I'm going to Alira," she said. "I need to be with her. Spill another promise I can't guarantee I can keep. I need her to hear it from me—no one else."

"I'm sorry, Zyrenna. For all of this." My chest cinched tight. Alira—it hit me then. I'd promised her. How do I bow to the will of the woman I see as my God and still keep her sister's promise? The two truths cut against each other until I felt sick.

Zyrenna's fingers came up and rested against my cheek, the tips brushing the stubble along my jaw, grounding me even as her touch trembled just a fraction. "Before I say this," she breathed, voice catching soft, "I'm sorry for the pressure I'm piling on you. None of this is yours to carry alone."

Her gaze pinned me like a hand laid over something that might otherwise fall apart. But I saw the flicker in there, the crack she hid from everyone else. She was at her limit—the limit Alira warned me she'd reach.

She let out a short breath, her chest rising quicker now, uneven like she was fighting not to break. "If staying in that room all night means I get to come back to Alira—then you better stay and map every ending until the sun comes up." Her voice cracked on the edge—equal parts command and plea, sharp as a blade but laced with that quiet ache, the fear she'd never voice plain: *I need to make it back. Don't let me leave her alone.*

She was struggling, but she pushed through. "You can lead without losing yourself to them. Don't let the Council twist you into the monster they need you to be—not when you're the one who keeps us whole."

I got it then, clear as the bond's pull—her words weren't just advice; they were her gripping onto hope, handing me her fear so it wouldn't swallow her whole. This woman, who'd clawed her way through everything alone, was trusting me with her breaking point. And that alone would've chained me to the table until dawn cracked the sky.

She stepped back then, precise as a commander issuing an order. I could see her eyes glossing over by the second. "I will be here again and again to remind you who you are."

The words cracked something in me—the pressure and anticipation I'd been grinding between my teeth since the vineyard. My chest eased, remembering my purpose. I bent, closing the last breath between us, and pressed my mouth to hers. She exhaled against me, a soft shudder rippling through her body.

"Go," I whispered into her hair, fingers lingering on the curve of her neck before letting go.

Her eyes lingered on me for one second more, shining like she saw every vow I'd never spoken aloud. Then she slipped from my hand and turned, shoulders squared, leaving the chamber with a grace that carried both our burdens.

I took a minute to gather myself before walking back where the rest of my council stood. They were already muttering preparations, urgent voices around the table.

We did not leave the table. We sat, shoulders nearly touching, and unrolled the maps that mattered: the streets and shadows where the Embers could breathe unnoticed. We marked watchers outside the Spire—two teams, staggered shifts, the main watch posted at the bend where the light falls and the towers can't see. A runner would circle every hour; a messenger would carry the signal if anyone so much as crossed the outer ring.

We planned routes that kept us out of sight: which roofs

gave a quick exit and which alleys looped you back to the river. We traced the ways the Spire scouts would think and then placed our shadows just beyond their sightlines. Maris mapped supply lines—tallying rations and routes.

And we made plans for worse. If the Severant was brought out and the worst came—if it touched Zyrenna or me—we would not let them turn suffering into spectacle. She was right… hope wasn't a strategy, not here. I said it aloud so no one could misunderstand: "If it kills us, we wage this war even if I'm not there to see it." It was a promise drawn into strategy.

The torches guttered low. Outside, the Embers moved through their ordinary rhythms. Maps lay on the table like a future we might or might not get to walk.

I was never afraid of the Spire for what it could do to me. What I feared now was smaller and truer: the device they worshiped not because it could break me, but because it could touch her. And for that one thing, I would see cities burn before I let her be measured by their cruelty.

CHAPTER THIRTY

ZYRENNA

I lay in my bed that night, staring at the ceiling while sleep refused to find me. The air was heavy, the kind that made every breath feel borrowed. Rhaelin hadn't returned, and I knew he wouldn't. I'd seen it in his eyes before I left him in the hallway—his vow to stay there until dawn, until every route and every risk had been cut open and measured.

I had gone to Alira as I promised. I told her the truth, or as much of it as I could bear to give: the summons to the Spire, the Severant's shadow looming over us, the way it could snap the bond like a dry twig if they chose. She wasn't happy— far from it. Her face had twisted from shock to fury in a heartbeat—blue eyes blazing as she bolted upright, fists balled in her blankets like she could punch through the fear clawing at her. "You're walking into that?" she'd spat, voice cracking, tears already streaking hot down her cheeks. She gripped my arms hard, nails biting into my skin, trembling with that raw terror of losing the only family she had left—me, her anchor in this shadowed world. Why wouldn't she rage? I was risking it all, and for what? A bond that might drag us both under. I held her through the storm of sobs and pleas, murmuring half-promises I couldn't fully keep, but the guilt lingered heavy in my chest long after her breaths evened out.

And in all honesty, I wasn't pleased either. My own words sat bitter on my tongue. I hated the taste of them, hated that I couldn't shield Alira with more than empty promises and hollow assurances. I hated that she saw right through me, those blue eyes full of knowledge that her sister was marching into the lion's den, and no vow—no desperate grip on her hand—could make it feel safe.

A soft knock echoed at the door, pulling me from the dark loop in my head.

"Come in," I yelled.

I turned to find the last person I expected standing there: Lennan. She eased the door shut behind her, moving with that quiet calm that made people listen. The light emphasized the grey of her hair and the lines around her eyes.

"They're still at it," she said with a dry tone, a faint curve tugging at her mouth like she was sharing a secret. "I lost my patience for it all three hours ago. Rhaelin's got them tripping over themselves trying to keep up."

"I came because I needed to speak with you," she added, and something in her tone sent unease down my spine.

"What about?" I asked, sitting up straighter.

She crossed to the chair near my bed, lowering herself with deliberate care. Her hands folded neatly in her lap, the image of composure, but her eyes held the heaviness of someone who'd carried knowledge too long without saying it aloud.

"About the Severant," she said.

My pulse kicked. "Tell me."

"There were records," she continued slowly, "the Spire burned after the war. Whole archives gone. But some pages, some stories, didn't die. A handful of scholars—quiet ones, people no one remembers now—passed them down. I was a student of one. I spent years gathering the fragments, memorizing what I could before the Spire caught wind of them."

Her voice thinned, but her gaze stayed cutting. "What those scraps told me is this: before the Council twisted its claws into everything, bonds weren't rare. There were dozens—maybe hundreds. They weren't hunted down; in some places they were sacred. People believed a bonded pair bred the finest warriors, the strongest healers, leaders with sense enough to see past themselves. But that's not to say everyone thought that way. There were always whispers in the corners, folks who saw the bond as a curse—unnatural. They called it evil, a crack in the world's order. And that fear? It birthed the Severant."

The room shrank around me, each word pressing the air tighter.

"And then?" I asked.

"Then," Lennan said, "before Rhaelin's time in the Council, before the Blood Trials, the Spire began killing bonded pairs as soon as they took their places on the thrones, like a machine— efficient, merciless. But one record—one whispered through those scholars—spoke of a pair who endured the Severant. They survived not because of strength or chance, but because of something called the *Third Breath*."

Lennan leaned forward slightly, voice lowering, as if even the stone walls might betray her. "The tether between you and Rhaelin stretches between two bodies. Two souls. The Severant tears at that thread. The Third Breath is not a spell or a potion—it is an act. One of you can collapse the tether inward, draw both halves into a single vessel. For three breaths."

My mouth went dry. "You mean… I would hold his half of the bond inside me?"

"Yes," she said simply. "For the span of three breaths, you would carry both your lives. The Severant claws at nothing, because there is no thread stretched between you to sever. When the breaths end, you release it, and the tether returns."

It sounded impossible. "And if I cannot let go? Or if I hold it too long?"

Her expression softened, though her words did not. "Then your body will break. The nerves burn out. The mind fractures. Your heart may fail outright. That is why it is called the *Third Breath*. No one has ever survived a fourth."

The silence between us thickened. I wrapped my arms around myself though the fire was still warm. "So you're telling me the only way I might survive the Severant is also the way I might die by it."

Her gaze was unwavering. "Yes."

I let out a jagged laugh. "And you think this is supposed to make me feel better?"

"No," Lennan said. "I think it is supposed to give you a chance. That's all any of us can offer."

I paced to the mirror across the room, catching the faint shimmer in my eyes. The tether hummed faint and alive beneath my skin. "Why are you telling me and not him?"

"Because Rhaelin would never allow it," she answered without hesitation. "The moment he knew, he would chain you to the wall before he let you attempt it. He would rather see himself broken than risk you carrying him like that. You know I'm right."

I hated that she was right. I saw it in him already, the way his restraint burned thin every time my name left someone else's mouth. He would never let me hold that kind of risk.

Lennan rose then, coming to stand beside me. Her reflection in the mirror was calm, composed, but the hand she placed lightly on my arm was warm with human gravity. "I see what you would do for him," she said softly. "But I also see what he would do for you. He would tear down the world stone by stone rather than let you take this on yourself. That is why you cannot tell him."

I met her gaze in the mirror. "And if I try it and it kills me?"

"Then it kills you," she said, blunt but not cruel. "But listen to me, Zyrenna. The Third Breath is not meant to kill. It is meant to shield. Those who died by it were the ones who tried to hold too long. The point is to give Rhaelin time to fight back. His pain will disappear in those three breaths, you just need to make sure he knows at that moment to fight. Sanguis is sacred, no amount of death or murders caused at the hands of the Spire will ever change that. It is a safety feature meant to protect you. But with that, the bond will protect itself. If you hold too long, it will be too much for the host."

Her certainty steadied me more than I wanted to admit.

I turned to face her fully. "So if the Severant is raised, I collapse the tether into myself. Three breaths. And then release."

"Put simply—yes. But it takes focus, you need to envision the tether moving inward." She hesitated, then added, "You must understand—collapsing it means you will feel everything. His half and yours together. His rage. His pain. His need. You may not be able to tell where you end and he begins. That is why it is so dangerous."

I drew a shaky breath. "I can handle his rage. I've felt it

before."

Her eyes searched mine. "Not like this. I beg you not to underestimate the power of it. Imagine drowning, but the water is fire. Imagine carrying two hearts that do not beat in rhythm. Imagine every memory, every scar he has pressed into him, suddenly yours as well."

The air felt thinner now. I gripped the edge of the table behind me. "And you think I can survive that?"

"I think you are the only one who can," Lennan said. "The bond has already begun to change you in ways that are undocumented. In the documented case of the Third Breath, the pair that endured it—the human was the one who collapsed it inward. The weaker of the two."

For a moment, I let her words sink in. Preparation. Maybe that was what all of this had been. The bruises, the sleepless nights, the training until my bones ached. Not for the ring— not for the Council. For this.

Still, my voice came out hoarse. "I'm terrified, Lennan. Even if we survive it… he wouldn't forgive me for keeping this from him."

"I would be worried if you weren't." She reached out and squeezed my hand once, the gesture firm, anchoring. "Fear means you still value your life; and his."

She studied me then, her lined face unreadable for a moment. When she finally spoke, her tone gentled—more confidante. "As for forgiveness… child, he already loves you. He may not have said it aloud—not yet. But I've never seen him—never seen anyone—react the way he does when it comes to another person. He burns hotter, as if you've rewired what his temper even is. He is a man remade in your presence. That is love, whether he gives it a name or not."

Her mouth curved faintly, weary and knowing. "And if you don't believe me, watch him the next time someone so much as looks at you wrong. The truth will be plain enough."

I stared at our joined hands. "So if it comes to it, and I fail—if the tether snaps—what then?"

Lennan's eyes grew distant, as if recalling something too old and painful. "Then the bond dies with you. And he will not last long after. But that happens regardless."

We talked after that—the words coming slow at first, then faster. Time slipped; an hour might have passed, maybe more. We spoke of the Third Breath—what I would see, how to contain it, what to do when it came. Of Rhaelin. Of everything that lived between us.

Finally I asked, "Why are you telling me this at all? Why trust me with this?"

"Because you already chose him," she said quietly. "And because I see the way you carry yourself—you'd rather die fighting than stop and look weak. You won't yield in the face of pain. This, at least, gives you a weapon instead of just a sacrifice."

Her words broke something loose in my chest. For the first time since the summons, I felt something that was not only fear. It was resolve.

Lennan stepped back toward the door. "Remember—three breaths, no more. If you feel yourself falter, if the bond fights you, let it go. It is better to be torn apart together than to burn alone."

I nodded once. "I understand."

Her hand lingered on the doorframe. "And Zyrenna—do not tell him. If you do, all of this becomes useless. You won't even make it to the Spire."

"I won't," I said. My voice trembled, but the vow was true.

When she left, the chamber felt colder. I stared at the fire until my vision blurred, the word *three* echoing in my head like a drumbeat. Three breaths between survival and death. Three breaths to carry the weight of us both.

CHAPTER THIRTY-ONE

RHAELIN

The Embers carried a heaviness in the air that could not be ignored since the summons. The sound of steel rang sharper in the training halls. Boots struck the stone with more purpose. Every soldier honed their blades as if we were already at war, as if they could sense something moving above the surface.

All I could see was her.

Zyrenna moved across the ring like air, her daggers flashing. She was faster and cleaner than ever before—every strike cut a line exactly where it should have landed. Every time she moved, the bond moved with her, feeding me until my veins burned.

Pride burned to the point where I ached.

She turned on me then, those fucking eyes doing what they do best—unraveling me with a glance. "Don't just stand there watching me, Commander," she teased, the title as loaded as ever. "If you're gonna stare, get in here."

My brow arched. "Commander?"

Her grin widened. She didn't bother with an answer, just a wink.

Lethal.

I stepped into the ring. "You think you're ready for me, little flame?"

"Always," she shot back without hesitation.

I stepped into the ring, sword sliding free in one clean motion. Her daggers sat in her hands like they were now extensions of her. Forgetting everyone was watching, it became just her and I. The murmur of the room continued but I heard none of it.

The first clash was sharp, steel singing as it met steel. She struck hard and fast—faster than most soldiers I'd trained, her toned arms whipping the daggers in a blur that cut the air.

"Not bad," I muttered.

Her face twisted into a challenge, silver eyes flashing hot, lips curling in that way that always hooked me deeper. "Not holding back, are you?"

I smirked, the bond humming like a warning in my veins. "Not yet."

She lunged, her eyes distracting me, while her blades flashed for my ribs. I twisted, deflecting one dagger with my sword in a shower of sparks, the other now in my free hand as I wrapped my fingers around the hilt. Her back hit my chest again, her body fitting too perfectly against mine.

"Too slow," I whispered into her ear, lips brushing against it.

Her grin spread wider, cheek brushing mine, as she shifted just enough to grind against me—hip rolling deliberately into the ridge of my thigh, sending a jolt straight to my core. "Cocky," she whispered back, voice low. "For someone who sure doesn't feel half as in control as he thinks."

The tether surged, spreading sparks straight down my spine.

She knew exactly what she was doing to me, that wicked glint in her eyes saying she'd play this game until one of us broke.

I shoved her daggers back, only for her to twist free—toned legs flexing as she pivoted. Her blade kissed the line of my throat, cold edge hitting the skin just above my collarbone. I should've been furious, instincts screaming to counter. Instead, I laughed.

"Dangerous game, baby."

Her eyes gleamed. This time, her voice dropped low, only for me. "You never wanted safe, Rhaelin."

I twisted her until her back hit my chest again, arm banding around her waist, my blade sliding against hers in a grind of metal. I whispered into her ear, lips grazing the curve, "You're right. Safe doesn't look half as good holding a blade."

Steel rang, sand kicking up with her feet. She moved fast, too fast for only a few months of training. For a moment, I let her believe she was pressing me—let her see the fight she wanted reflected back in my grin, in the way I danced just out of reach.

Then I ended it.

In a blur, I knocked one dagger free—hilt clattering to the sand—kicked the other aside with my boot, and spun her until her back hit the ground, shoulders flexing as she landed, breath coming out in a quick gasp. I was above her, knees bracketing her hips, my blade resting steady across her collarbone—tip tracing the hollow of her throat where her pulse hammered wild, sweat glistening on the flushed skin there.

"This was over before it started, little flame," I murmured against her ear. "But my god, did I love watching you try."

Her laugh came quick, bubbling from her chest. "Arrogant

bastard."

"True," I said, pressing closer. "Better you get the arrogant side of me than the feral one. At least this way you're still breathing."

The bond flowed, want and restraint tangling together.

And then she cut it all with one line: "For now."

The words cracked me open. Rage shot through me so fast my vision blurred. My sword slammed against the dirt, her wrists caught in my hands before she could ready another strike.

"Enough," I snapped, my eyes locking on hers with an intensity that made air thicken.

The room stilled, but I didn't care.

"With me," I rasped only so she could hear, voice rough with the fire I couldn't contain.

Without giving her a chance to answer, I helped her up from the floor—one hand sliding to her waist, pulling her flush against me—and dragged her from the circle, past the now-staring eyes. The tunnels narrowed as we walked back toward my room, walls closing in, torchlight flickering shadows over her glowing hair. She didn't ask where I was taking her. She didn't have to—I knew she felt the storm in me, her free hand brushed my arm in silent anchor.

Inside my chambers, the fire burned low. I closed the door harder than I meant to, the bolt clicking in the quiet.

"We can't," I rasped, turning to her, backing her against the door. "We can't just act like this is any other night. Tomorrow, Ren, if they bring the Severant—" I broke off, losing composure by the second. "I have no control here. I don't know what the fuck to do. You want me to just place you in the line of fire—watch them drag that thing out, feed it our blood, tear at you until you scream? You haven't seen what it does!"

She looked up at me, and pressed her palms up to my chest. The touch grounded me, her heat seeping into my skin still buzzing from the training.

"Rhaelin."

I knew by her pleading tone that she needed my eyes, so I gave them.

Looking up at me, she said, "You think I don't know the position I am putting you in? The position I am putting myself in? If you don't, then you are wrong. I know the danger. But what is the alternative?" She reached up. "We hide here?" she said, voice quiet but unbreaking. "Let the Spire get so suspicious they send soldiers sniffing around until they figure out you don't crash at the Ring of Thrones every night? Enough suspicion to realize there's a war brewing under their feet? You know that's not an option. This is bigger than you and me—hundreds of people have followed you for almost a century, bet their lives on your promises, their kids' futures on the world you're clawing to build. I love everything you stand for, Rhaelin—the way you fight like the world owes you blood—but devotion to me alone doesn't keep them breathing. You have to be smarter here."

Her eyes burned into me, pulling at the edges of my control. "I'm stronger now," she pressed on. "You made me stronger— you know it, you saw it in the ring today, every twist and strike. I can hold my own in that room if it comes down to blades. What I need from you isn't rage—it's restraint. Do not be the one to light the fuse first—don't give them the excuse to call it treason before we're ready."

Her thumb brushed across my cheek, the motion grounding.

"But—" she said, voice tightening just enough to make the word real, "you have to promise me: if they start it, and you get even a second to fight in that room, you take it. Do not hesitate, just promise you won't be the first to initiate anything."

Her words hit me. She wasn't just talking strategy; she was handing me the reins to my own leash, trusting me with the line between protector and destroyer.

"Promise me," she said. It sounded more like a plea.

I let out a breath that steadied me more than any armor. I drew her thumb into my palm and curled my fingers around it like a soldier taking an oath, the calluses on my hand rough against her smoother skin. "I promise. I will not be the one to strike first. If they move to harm you, though, I will answer—without hesitation. But I will not hand them the advantage."

"When the time comes," she continued, "we will bring them to the ground—but not tomorrow. They come from bloodlines too deep, too many strings tied to their power, pulling puppets in every shadow—you've said it yourself. If we fight them there, in their lair, we lose everything you've built. You already know this."

She hesitated, her mouth trembling before she forced the words out. "If the bond breaks tomorrow, know this—I will still choose you. Again and again, with or without it. It is not the bond that holds me here. It's you. And if it kills me—if it kills us…" her voice dropped even lower, "then at least you'll know I chose you until the end."

For a long beat, I couldn't speak. Couldn't move. Her words hollowed me out and filled me all at once—stripping away the rage, leaving raw want and ache that bordered on worship.

And she wasn't wrong. We both knew it wasn't the bond. I

felt the pull in that House before her blood ever touched my lips.

"You'll ruin me, Ren," I whispered, voice raw from holding back, my free hand coming up to cup her face.

Her eyes softened, and before I could take another breath, she kissed me with a gentleness I'd never known from her. No anger or fury. Just a quiet that broke me more than any sword.

Then she slipped her hand into mine, tugging me toward the couch. Her fingers caught the edge of my shirt on the way, a silent command in the hook of her nails, and I obeyed without a word, stripping it away in one fluid motion.

"Give me tonight," she whispered, edged with the same plea I'd heard before. "Please. I need you here with me."

I nodded once, no hesitation, and pulled her into me, my tongue claiming her mouth without mercy. Her leathers came undone beneath my hands, stripped away like they were nothing.

She stepped back just long enough for the firelight to paint her skin, and when her lips parted, the words gutted me.

"You have no fucking idea how beautiful you are," she said, smiling, stealing the vow I'd spoken the first night I ever took her—the first night I saw her come undone in my name.

I stepped toward her, pressing my forehead to hers. "You're the only thing I wouldn't survive losing, Zyrenna."

And with that, I lifted her into my arms, carrying her into an oblivion only we knew how to create.

CHAPTER THIRTY-TWO

ZYRENNA

I woke to warmth and silence. Even the bond was quieter under my skin, like it wanted to give me this moment. Rhaelin lay beside me, one arm heavy across my waist, his chest rising slow and even. In sleep, the lines carved into his face softened. He looked younger, almost mortal. Like a man who hadn't just spent a century carrying the weight of his people.

For a heartbeat, I let myself just watch him.

His hand flexed against my hip. "You're staring," he murmured, not opening his eyes.

"Shh," I whispered. "Don't ruin it for me."

He smirked, then let his eyes slide open. In one smooth motion he rolled me so I was straddling him, his hands on my hips anchoring me in place. We both knew what waited beyond this chamber, but what were a few more stolen breaths?

His voice dropped, rough, almost guilty. "I need your blood, Zyrenna."

I went still. He almost never asked; he'd push himself for days before admitting the need. I'd offer before he'd ask, but for him to say it out loud meant he was already at his edge.

I brushed his hair back where it had fallen over his brow.

"Then take it," I said. "You don't need to ask."

His gaze locked on mine. "Not your wrist," he said, his hand sliding over the curve of my neck. "Here. It will give me more. Enough for today… more than usual." His thumb found the vein and held there. A corner of his mouth lifted. "And because I'm selfish," he added, "I need the Council to see it."

"Won't that just add to the Council's suspicion about what we are?" I asked.

"Vampires feed from humans every day," he said. "Us going there isn't about proving or disproving anything. The moment we walk into that chamber, they'll know what we are."

He paused, thumb pressing to the vein at my throat. "It won't prove anything they're not already whispering," he went on. "But it will show them what they already fear—that the bond answers to neither laws nor their bargains. Going there isn't about unmasking us. It's about seeing how far they can push."

His gaze lingered. "We walk in to measure them as much as they measure us. To find out where their lines are, and how far they'll push before they reach for the Severant."

"Then take it," I said. He hesitated just long enough to make it a choice, his breath hitching as he searched my face for any trace of doubt. I tipped my head back to bare the curve of my throat to him. "Let them see."

He shifted, sitting up straighter, my legs draped across his thighs. A sound tore from his chest, a raw, guttural noise— half groan, half prayer—as if he were pleading with some higher power for strength to hold back. His lips brushed the side of my throat, soft as a whisper at first, sending a shiver racing down my spine. The warmth of his breath against my skin was a stark contrast to the cool edge of his fangs, grazing ever so slightly, teasing the line between danger and desire. "Tell me to stop," he rasped, his voice rough, as if the words themselves were a battle against his instincts.

"No," I said, my voice unwavering, a spark of defiance in my tone. "I won't need to." My words were a vow, a challenge, and a surrender all at once. I knew what he was, what this meant, and still, I chose him.

The bite came sharp and sudden, a piercing jolt as his fangs sank deep into the flesh of my throat. Pain flared, like a burn across my skin—but it lasted only a heartbeat before it transformed, melting into a molten wave of heat that surged through my veins. My breath caught, a gasp escaping as the sensation shifted from agony to something else entirely, something intoxicating. His arm tightened around my back, anchoring me against him as if I were his salvation in a world that had tried to break him. The other hand tilted my neck just slightly, fingers threading gently through my hair.

I gasped, fingers tangling in his hair, keeping him there, not out of fear but need. Each pull of blood fed him, strengthened him. Pleasure shivered through me, electric and overwhelming, until my legs trembled against his hips, my body responding in ways I couldn't control. His groan rumbled low in his chest, vibrating against my skin. It felt unreal. The bond between us, that strange, shimmering thread of magic or fate or something older, hummed to life, amplifying it. The room around us seemed to fade, the world narrowing to the press of his lips, the rhythmic pull of his feeding, the feel of his body against mine.

My heartbeat thundered in my ears, syncing with his, a

shared rhythm that felt like it could unravel me entirely. His grip tightened briefly, possessive, as if he sensed how close I was to losing myself in the moment. And yet, there was no fear—only a wild, reckless trust that this, whatever it was, was worth every risk.

When he finally pulled back, his lips hovered a breath away, as if reluctant to part from me. His tongue traced the twin wounds on my throat, sealing them. A bead of my blood clung to his lower lip, vivid red against his skin. His hand rose, slowly, deliberate. His thumb brushed his lip, catching the crimson smear, and my pulse jumped as he brought it not to his mouth but to mine.

His gaze burned me as he murmured, "You are fucking astounding."

My breath caught, fingers still tangled in his hair, holding him close. His thumb lingered on my lip, the taste of my own blood electric.

His mouth curved, almost a smirk. "Do you feel it?" he asked, voice rough. "How much I would destroy to keep you?"

I did. God help me, I did.

"I do," I said without hesitation, my voice steady despite the storm in my chest. "And Rhaelin—if you ever take from anywhere else again, I might actually kill you."

His chest shook with a dark laugh. "Let's get through today. Then you can have whatever you want."

We sat in silence for a shared moment, the world narrowing to the warmth of his arms around me, the steady rise and fall of his breath. For a minute, there was no war, no Spire, no Severant. Just him and the charged air between us, thick with unspoken promises and the faint metallic tang of my blood still lingering on his lips.

"Rhaelin?"

His palm cupped my cheek like he needed the contact to keep me there. His thumb moved slow over my cheekbone, the eye contact so intense it made it hard to breathe.

"You said I was the only thing you couldn't lose," I said. "Tell me why."

He went still; panic stung through the tether—then the walls rose. He looked away. "Zyrenna... I don't—" The words snagged. I gave him the silence—gave him time.

Moments passed and when he spoke, his voice was quieter, shaped by something older than anger. "You never asked me why I did all of this," he said, a small, helpless sweep of his hand over the chamber. "Why any of this exists."

"I assumed it started with the Blood Trials," I said, careful.

A nod of his head followed. "My father taught me and my brother from a young age how to survive. We had no money, could barely stay fed, but one thing he made sure of was that his sons knew how to protect themselves. My sister was too young, but I've no doubt he would've taught her the same."

He stopped—his jaw flexed like the words burned coming out. "I don't share this," he said, voice roughening. "No one knows these pieces of me. Not even Darius."

I shook my head gently, my voice quiet but steady. "You don't have to explain, not if it hurts," trying to anchor him. "But I want to hold it with you. Whatever it is."

He looked at me a long time, green dimmed to something raw and fragile. He leaned in, stole the softest kiss, and pulled back before either of us could chase it.

"We struggled financially our entire lives. Nocthallow is a tale of two cities—gold and riches, hunger and steel. The noble houses sit high in their polished quarters, while the rest of us survive in the parts no one wants to touch. So when two letters were left at our door, one with Elias' name, one with mine, it was terrifying but I knew it could also be freedom. It was the letter for the Blood Trials. If Elias or I sat on a throne, our parents would breathe again. So we trained as we always had."

He stared past me and kept going. "They gathered two hundred names from across Nocthallow; sons, daughters, the poor, the desperate. They dress it up as a lottery—fortune." His breath hitched. "The Blood Trials—it's survival. There's no rules, barely any allies except for me and Elias. Just a blood-soaked arena built to amuse the Spire and find the final seat."

My chest tightened, the bond thrumming with echoes of his pain.

"They starve you first. Strip you of everything until you'd cut your own flesh just to taste food again. Then they send you into the pits. One trial at a time. Sometimes the very ground split under you and swallowed the weak."

His eyes burned back into mine. "By the last trial, there were three of us left. Elias. Me. And a boy from Nocthallow that was bred for this. They threw us into the ring together. The crowd screamed for blood, chanting names like we were weapons, not children. The boy lunged for Elias first. And something in me broke. I killed him, before he could touch my brother. But then the Spire ordered the fight to continue. Only one could walk out. You already know how this ends."

I nodded in agreement.

"When it was over, when my hands were shaking and the sand was wet, I tried to convince myself it was worth it. That at least I could go home with coin. That my parents could finally rest—if that could even exist in their world past this point." His mouth thinned. "Somehow I made it back home, Elias' body with me. When I walked through the door, the kettle was still whistling."

He looked down at his hands. "When I walked through the door that night, the first thing I saw was my sister's—Thalia's—body across the floor. She was so small... too small. Her eyes open staring at the door as if she'd been waiting for me to come home. My mother lay just beyond her, her dress soaked through with blood, her hand outstretched like she'd tried to reach her daughter in her final breath. And my father—" His jaw tightened, voice cracking. "I will save you the details, Ren. But all of them... just gone. The house was silent, except for the sound of the fire still burning, and blood dripping."

My stomach lurched; bile rose. I pressed my hand to my mouth and forced it back down. The ache in my chest a physical thing.

"Rhae—"

"I moved them," he went on, voice rough. "One by one. I straightened Thalia's hair, wiped the blood from my mother's hands, tried to make my father look less broken than he was. It was madness, I knew it, but I couldn't stop. The grief hollowed me out until I slipped into something else... a kind of psychosis. I saw things that weren't there. Heard screams that had already gone silent."

His jaw flexed hard. "By the time I left that house, I wasn't thinking, I was consumed. I went to the Spire ready to kill them all. It had to be them, who else? It was a message meant for me: that I might have been the strongest of two hundred, but power is bloodlines, not victories. That I was never meant to sit on the throne. The Blood Trials were a result solely of the Veil, the other five wanted no part of it. Felt the final seat was owed to someone in line."

His eyes glossed over, haunted. "So I walked, through the city, blood on my boots, on my clothes, on my hands. Every step was a vow to cut them down. I was halfway to the gates when I heard a voice—" He hesitated, swallowing. "My father's. Clear as if he stood beside me: *Wait. Watch. Let it all mean something.*"

His words hung between us. I couldn't breathe. The image of him, younger, covered in his family's blood, marching toward the Spire with nothing left but vengeance, it hollowed me out. My stomach twisted, a sickness clawing up my throat, but worse than that was the ache that spread through my chest. He had carried this alone for decades. And now he was laying it bare in my hands.

"Rhaelin..." My voice broke on his name. My fingers trembled as they brushed over his jaw, the stubble scraping my skin. His eyes met mine, and for once, he didn't try to hide the fracture in them.

He swallowed, hard. "I believed it was him, my father. Telling me to wait. But the truth is, I don't know. Maybe it was madness. Maybe something else. I was too far gone to tell the difference." His hand curled into a fist on the sheets. "But I listened. I didn't storm the gates that night. I waited. And I built the Embers from the ashes and the fury they left me with."

The bond pulsed raw, dragging his anguish straight through me. I wanted to scream for him, to burn the world apart for the injustice of it all. Instead, I forced myself closer, pressing my forehead to his.

"You should never have had to carry that alone," I whispered. My heart ached with every word. "Not then. Not now. They fucking took everything from you."

His thumb dragged across my cheekbone again, slower this time, like he was memorizing me. "And yet, silence has kept me alive. If I had spoken a word of what I saw, if I had dared accuse them without proof, the Council would've struck me down before I even took my seat on the throne. I believe that was the whole point. They already feared me after the Trials. That night would've given them the excuse if I had done what they wanted." His jaw locked, voice rough. "So I kept it. Buried it. Let them believe I bent to their leash. And I swore to myself, I would outlast them. I would watch them rot under their own power."

Tears burned my eyes; I blinked them back. "All this time," I said, "you've been waiting. Carrying their deaths alone. Shaping a rebellion out of nothing. Bleeding for people who don't know half of it. And still, you think you're broken."

"I am broken," he rasped. His hand slid to the back of my neck. "But you—you make me forget the pieces. You have made it feel worth living again."

My chest splintered, both from his words and from the bond that surged between us, drowning me in everything he felt.

"You are not broken to me, Rhaelin," I whispered, trying to hide the burn in my throat. "You are scarred, yes. And grieving. And tired. But you are still here. Still fighting—still capable of loving and protecting when the world hollowed you out again and again. There is nothing broken in that. Nothing broken in you."

"You wanted to know why you're the only thing I can't

lose?" he asked. "Because that night, I lost everything. If I lose you too—" He swallowed, pain traveling through the tether. "Zyrenna—please. I cannot lose you. I cannot watch you die."

"You won't," I said, because there was no other answer I could live with. "You won't."

His forehead tipped to mine; a rough exhale left his chest like my words had given him something to hold. I kissed him, sealing it all.

For that breath, nothing else mattered.

A knock hit the door. Darius's voice cut through the wood. "Commander. It's time."

Rhaelin's jaw tightened, but he didn't move from me. His hands lingered on me like he wasn't ready to let go. I wasn't either. I caught his wrist, grounding him, forcing him to look at me. A silent understanding passed between us, warmth flowing through the bond in both directions.

Then—the instant his warmth vanished and the commander snapped back into place. The heat bled out of him, replaced by that cold, precise stillness that made everyone else straighten without knowing why.

"Make sure they see your neck," he said. It was the last thing he gave me before we broke apart.

Then he let go.

CHAPTER THIRTY-THREE

ZYRENNA

We dressed in silence.

Rhaelin pulled on his usual fighting leathers—dark pants and the sleeveless black shirt that left his shoulders bare, every line of muscle carved by a century of discipline. I slid into the set Maris had finished for me. I twisted my hair into a bun at my crown, strands loose to frame my face, leaving the fresh marks at my throat bare.

Side by side, we looked built for this. Not a Commander and his bonded. Not a man and a woman. Something more—something no one in these halls could mistake.

The Embers' corridors hushed as we strode through them. Boots stilled mid-step. Fighters straightened against the walls, steel at their hips clinking faintly. No one spoke. They didn't need to. Their silence said it all: they knew where we were going and what it meant.

When we stepped into the Embers' council chamber, six heads turned. Six sets of eyes landed on me first, then on the punctures at my throat.

Darius smirked, arms folded tight across his chest. "Bold," he said. Then, after a pause, "I like it, Vaeoria. You two have balls."

The corner of my mouth tilted upward. "Careful, Darius. You keep talking like that and people might start believing you're capable of emotion."

A snort of laughter burst from Solena. "Veil, I live for this," she said, teeth flashing.

She exhaled, the sound shifting as she straightened. "Alright." Then her smile turned into something colder. Talking to us both, she said. "Walk in and don't flinch. They might fear you, Rhaelin, but they'll expect you to bow. And they'll expect her"—she tipped her chin at me—"to crumble. Give them the opposite. Make them question which one of you they should fear more."

Brannic's voice rumbled. "All they care about is politics. They'll talk until their lungs give out. Don't play their game, Zyrenna. Force them to answer on your terms."

Lennan's dry tone slid in next. "And don't waste time thinking you can outmaneuver centuries of arrogance. You can't. But you can make them choke on underestimating you. That's where your power lies."

Maris's words came last, each syllable a command. "Every word in that chamber is a binding contract, signed or not. Weigh your words carefully, and make them pay for every one they steal."

My gaze swept over them—Brannic's stern resolve, Lennan's confidence, Maris's icy precision—before settling on Rhaelin. His presence beside me grounded me more than their words ever could.

"Thank you," I said, my voice clear, meeting each of their stares. "For everything."

Rhaelin's eyes swept the table, his voice iron. "This plays out on her terms," he declared. "It will be her decision."

Darius, silent until now, leaned forward, his voice low but resolute. "We'll be ready, Commander, no matter what." His words carried the weight of loyalty, a soldier's vow to follow.

Their arguments and doubts fell silent, leaving only the weight of their trust. It settled on me, heavy but empowering, bolstered by Rhaelin's unwavering belief.

As we turned from the table, Maris's voice cut through. "Zyrenna," she called. "Unleash the fire we know burns in you."

I glanced back, a fierce smile tugging my lips. "Always."

* * *

Alira found me before I could find her.

I'd barely stepped into the hall when her arms enveloped me, stealing the breath from my lungs. She held me like she could bind me to this moment, keep me from the danger waiting beyond the underground.

She whispered, "they see something in you. As someone who'd tear the Council down brick by brick myself, I know only you can do this." Her voice cracked. "But as your sister, you *better* walk back through those doors."

I blinked, stunned. Her words found their mark.

"I will," I murmured into her hair, though I couldn't promise. My throat burned as I whispered, "I love you more than you know."

Her arms tightened, desperate. "I love you, Z."

A shadow fell over us, heavy as the weight of the moment. I lifted my head to find Rhaelin standing a few paces away. His green eyes, usually sharp with predatory focus, softened as they flicked from me to Alira, a rare vulnerability softening his features.

Alira straightened, though she didn't let go. She met his gaze, unflinching, her voice cutting through the quiet. "You bring her back to me, Rhae."

His expression didn't waver, but his voice was quiet. "Always."

She studied him, eyes narrowed, searching for any crack in his promise. Whatever passed in the silent exchange—something unspoken—was enough. Her shoulders eased, and her hand lingered in mine until the last possible moment.

As we started towards the doors, I glanced at him. "She calls you Rhae now?"

He exhaled through his nose, almost a laugh. "She does."

"And you just… let her?"

"You think I win all my battles?"

I didn't press. But deep down, I knew he liked it—being seen that way, called something smaller, softer. There was a kind of gratitude in it, one that I knew only I could feel.

* * *

We weren't alone.

Darius waited at the end of the corridor, leaning against the wall, arms folded tight. As we passed, Rhaelin exchanged final words with him.

Lennan was waiting farther down, standing alone with her hands folded. She didn't smile, didn't joke. She just looked at me with that steady calm. I walked toward her—alone.

"Remember what I told you," she said softly. "Strength is not just the swing of a blade. It's the choice not to break when they try to tear you apart." Her eyes flicked, just once, to my throat. "You bend if you must. You endure."

I nodded.

Her hand brushed mine briefly as I passed, her only sign of farewell.

When we finally reached the outer doors, the Embers stood gathered in the shadows. Dozens of eyes followed us: soldiers, scouts, healers. Some bowed their heads. Some simply watched. For once, not a word was spoken.

CHAPTER THIRTY-FOUR

ZYRENNA

The wind cut cold against my skin as Rhaelin's arms locked me close, his wings beating. The world fell away beneath us. Higher, farther, until there was only the sky, and the drumbeat of his wings—and the Spire, rising black against the dawn.

It didn't just scrape the heavens. It split them.

The closer we flew, the more I felt it in my bones. The Spire felt alive, like it was waiting. My palm found Rhaelin's forearm and he let me hold there, a small anchor against a horizon that didn't end.

He tightened his hand at my waist as we descended. His jaw was iron, his eyes narrowed on the landing platform below where two perfect rows of guards waited with identical stillness. Not a sound, not a twitch, a hundred eyes tracking us as we touched down on black stone.

He looked almost mechanical, the face of a man who had learned to feel nothing when the world demanded everything. He didn't fold his wings. He created a barrier that I knew he meant for me to see, and only then did he help me set my boots to the ground. He didn't let go of my hand when the guards stepped back in perfect unison, parting to form a path toward the doors—obsidian carved in deep spirals.

Every clang of armor, every scrape of spear against stone, echoed louder than it should have. My throat was bared. His hand was locked with mine. We walked into the center of the Spire together.

And in that moment, I understood—this truly was never about hiding the bond that ran invisibly through us. Anyone who had knowledge of the Sanguis bond would sense it the second they looked at us. It was undeniable—not in light or blood, but in proximity. In the way we existed beside one another, as if the world had narrowed to a single axis.

Inside was colder than the air outside.

The Spire stretched vast and circular, the ceiling lost in shadows. Water fell in sheets from high above along the curved walls, pouring in narrow cascades into twin pools below. The sound was soft but constant, a sacred hush beneath the echo of our footsteps. Red and gold light glimmered across the stone—making the air feel touched by magic rather than fire.

A spiral staircase wound through the center of the tower, ribbed in black metal and gold veinwork, disappearing upward like a spine built by a god. Rhaelin guided me without hesitation, a protectiveness radiating off him that should've been visible. The higher we climbed, the heavier it all felt.

Eventually—after an ascent that stole time and breath—we reached the top, where the space broke open into the Council chamber, the obsidian doors rising before us taller than any cathedral.

Rhaelin's grip tightened once before he pushed them open, and we walked into the heart of the Spire. When we entered, five pairs of eyes turned toward us as we crossed the room— all stripping me bare. At the head of the table, an empty seat rose above the rest—its back a tower of dark wood and bone, carved in spirals that shifted when I tried to follow them. The Veil's throne.

Observing the room, I knew instantly who Lord Kalor was— one of three seated to the Veil's right, the mirror of three to the left. Pale as marble, hair white as ash. His gaze found the bite at my throat and stayed there. His lips curved faintly, tongue pressing to a fang. He was Varik's father, there was no mistaking it. The same hunger lived in his eyes, loud enough for everyone in the chamber to see.

Kalor stood up, his red eyes never leaving my neck as he took a measured step closer. Air bent. Without hesitation, Rhaelin moved, placing himself between us like the most natural motion in the world. His voice cut low, quiet as a drawn bow.

"Careful, Kalor," he said. "You wouldn't want to forget what happened the last time one of yours stepped out of place."

Kalor's mouth curved, savoring the memory like wine. "Ah, yes. My apologies. You'll forgive curiosity." His gaze slipped to Rhaelin, deliberate, taunting. "After all, it isn't every day a man threatens war over one woman." A smile spread slow and cruel. "A bold promise—with no army at your back."

Rhaelin only smiled in return—controlled—as if Kalor had offered him nothing more than idle chatter. His wings stayed half-spread, a shadow that reached the wall behind him and cut the chamber in two.

"If we're all pretending at courtesy, let's do it properly. Introduce yourselves. She deserves to know the names of those who believe themselves fit to pass judgment."

A silken voice—"Shall I?"—from the right of Kalor.

The woman was beauty crafted to draw blood: golden braid

to her hips, lips the color of fresh-spilled wine. "I'm Lady Seraphine of the Northern houses, representing Nocthallow," she purred. She gestured lazily toward Kalor. "And, well, you've already had the pleasure of meeting this one—Lord Kalor—also representing Nocthallow."

Kalor's mouth didn't shift, his face looked unamused.

"Representing the vampire territories are me, Kalor, and of course, your devastatingly handsome—"

I didn't think; I just reacted, jealousy flaring.

"Lord Morrain," I said, before she could finish. I held her gaze. "You were about to say Lord Morrain."

A breathless pause. Then—at my side—Rhaelin's head dipped, just once, and the smallest, wickedest chuckle escaped him. When his gaze lifted again, green fire burned, threaded with pride. His mouth curved in the faintest smirk. Not reprimand. Disbelief—satisfaction.

Seraphine's smile thinned. She inclined her head with theatrical grace. "Of course... Lord Morrain." Her voice smoother now. Her hand pointed across the table directly from her. "And now: Lord Merek, of the human lands." She tipped her chin at a heavy man in crimson and gold, rings catching on almost every finger. "Keeper of the Spire's coin. Every blade, torch, and drop of wine is tallied under his hand. Pray you're not too expensive to keep."

"I'm sure the Spire has wasted coin on far lesser causes," I said.

Seraphine's laughter spilled out, low and delighted, her crimson lips parting in a grin that gleamed. "She has teeth. Perhaps this won't be as dull as I feared."

She went on, pointing a nail toward a woman with short black hair and a face that portrayed no emotion. "Along with

Merek—Lady Cassira, of Solvane, keeper of law."

Seraphine's hand drifted farther, toward the figure who hadn't blinked since we'd entered. Her skin more grey than human. Her eyes were fathomless. "Finally, Orien of Eryndralis," Seraphine said softer. "Of the Veythari. She sees what the rest of us do not, and speaks for her people."

Orien didn't move. She only watched me, unblinking, as if waiting for me to speak first. Then—after a long beat—the faintest nod.

Seraphine's hand swept up at last to the tallest seat. "And, of course," she said, lips curving, "the Veil."

"If you've heard whispers that the Veil is myth, let me silence them," she added. "Our God is real. We have stood in His presence, and it is enough to scar memory. His power should never be doubted. If He were here…" Her eyes found mine. "…you would already be on your knees."

I responded, "Noted. If he's as unforgettable as you say, then I suppose I'll save my fear for the day he actually comes. Until then I'd prefer we get on with it."

Silence settled through the room. In one swift motion, agreement settled through the air. No one wanted to be here. We would no longer waste time on the bullshit.

Rhaelin stepped forward, the weight of him filling the chamber. "I want to emphasize the importance of treading carefully with what you suggest in the next ten minutes that we stand in this room. Because ten minutes is all it will be."

The words slid like a blade.

"Your son overstepped," he continued, eyes tight on Kalor, voice unapologetic. "And I see no reason to keep her in this room longer than necessary."

Kalor surged to his feet, his chair scraping harshly against the stone floor. "She cut my son's wings!" he roared, his voice raw with fury, face contorted as he pointed a trembling finger at me. "He'll never fly again! She will pay for what she did—you both will!"

Rhaelin's jaw clenched, his voice dropping to a dangerous whisper. "Threaten her again, Kalor, and you'll mourn more than just your son's wings."

Before Kalor could retort, Cassira's voice sliced through the chamber, cold and deliberate. "You cannot hide it, Rhaelin." Her eyes, cold and precise, fixed on him before shifting to me, weighing me like a rare artifact. "There's only one reason you lost control with Varik. One reason your restraint unraveled." She paused, letting the silence tighten like a noose. "No vampire bleeds for a mortal this way. No love drives your kind to madness unless they carries the blood of Sanguis."

Rhaelin's voice cut through the charged silence. "And there it is." He neither denied nor confirmed Cassira's accusation, leaving the truth about the blood of Sanguis dangling.

Kalor broke first. His hand slammed the obsidian table, the thundercrack reverberating off the chamber's towering stone walls. "You nearly killed my son!" he roared, his voice ragged with fury. "And now you stand there, silent, as if we're blind? As if you can play us for fools?" He leaned forward, venom dripping from every syllable. "The Veil spared you once, Rhaelin. Treason won't be so forgiving."

Before Rhaelin could respond, Cassira's voice sliced through, strong enough to shatter glass. "Kalor. Sit! I refuse for your lack of impulse control to be the reason all six of us don't walk out of this goddamn room."

The bond between Rhaelin and me flared, a searing pulse of his barely leashed fury heating my chest. Yet he stood motionless, his head tilting slowly, green eyes locking onto Kalor with a calm so lethal it outshone any shout. It was a predator's gaze, a silent command heavier than any roar.

Kalor bared his fangs, a low growl rumbling in his throat, but under Rhaelin's stare and Cassira's order, he sank back into his seat, the obsidian table creaking under his grip.

I finally understood what I was seeing. Their fear wasn't only hunger for proof—it was fear of him—what he could become. Of what Rhaelin had been in the Blood Trials, what he'd done to Varik, and what he'd do again, without hesitation, if they crossed him. He didn't need a blade; he was one, power barely leashed, and every soul in this chamber felt it.

"I see the truth," Orien said, her voice a quiet ripple that stilled the room. Veythari rarely spoke, but when they did, the world listened. Her gaze pressed into me, heavy as a hand on my sternum.

"There's a reason they neither confirm nor deny," she said, her tone gentle but certain.

My mouth went dry. Merek shifted, restless. Kalor's smile was a predator savoring prey. Cassira's chin dipped, a satisfied glint in her eyes.

"Then it must be tested," Cassira declared. "Bring the Severant."

Rhaelin moved like a storm, his voice slicing the air. "Choose your words with care, Cassira. They will be your last to me." His gaze swept the chamber, slow and lethal. "Raise that device, and you'll learn how thin my restraint truly is."

The council froze. Orien alone held my gaze, unblinking. For a fleeting moment, something flickered in her eyes—not malice, but something deeper, almost sorrow.

Anger sharpened my voice before I could tame it. "Why

craft a Severant when you have Veythari?" I demanded, my eyes sweeping from Orien to the others. "Why build a device to torture truth when you can speak it?"

Cassira's reply was cold. "Veythari words are faith. The Severant is proof. Faith bends—proof does not."

"Besides," Seraphine purred, her lip curling, "faith is fragile. But pain never lies."

Her words slithered through the room like oil catching flame. Even the guards' breaths grew shallow—four of them lining the wall.

The bond flared with fire that burned through my veins. He faced the council, his presence filling every shadow until the silence pressed against my skin. "You all watched the Blood Trials," he said, his voice low, etched with memory. "From your high seats, you wagered coin and futures, untouchable, safe behind your bloodlines—certain no harm could reach you."

His jaw tightened. "I never had that luxury. I was forged into a weapon for survival, taught when to strike and when to hold back; because people like *you* exist. But hear me now: I will not hold back. The words you've spoken today will not be forgotten. When the fire you've ignited comes for you, it will show no mercy. And I will aim every weapon I am at you. No Severant, no Spire, no fucking *throne* will save you."

He stepped forward, and the chamber seemed to shrink around him. His voice dropped, calm but deadly. "Doubt me, and it will be my dying honor to remind you why I earned this seat at all."

No one breathed. Seraphine's fingers stilled on the table's edge.

"There will be no Severant," Rhaelin said, final. "We are

done here."

He turned us toward the doors, their carved runes pulsing faintly with ancient magic. We'd nearly reached the handle when Kalor's voice reached us, savoring each word. "Bold, to bare her throat before us."

Rhaelin didn't turn, but his smile was a blade's edge. "Reach for temptation, Kalor, and you'll pray for your family's end." His voice stayed soft, yet the guards averted their eyes.

The chamber shifted.

It wasn't light or sound that struck—it was absence. Every noise vanished, every flame froze in its lantern. The air thinned, as if something vast had inhaled and refused to exhale.

My knees buckled, but Rhaelin's arm locked around my waist, his fury a steel anchor holding me upright. Power surged through my veins, ancient and merciless.

I looked up.

The seventh seat was no longer empty.

The Veil had taken its place.

CHAPTER THIRTY-FIVE

ZYRENNA

The entire chamber stopped breathing.

Shadows poured into the seventh seat, swallowing torchlight and sound. The runes carved along the throne's spine flared white, then bled to black, pulsing like a heartbeat you could feel in your teeth.

Not monster. Not man. Something older—older than Houses, thrones, or time itself—something that drank nightmares and left only silence in its wake. The air thickened, each breath a knife in my ribs. The Veil's face shimmered, features slipping and reforming, as if darkness were its skin. Its eyes—blinding white—burned through me, piercing every nerve, every secret.

No one moved.

When it spoke, its voice was weight, sinking into bone. "The Severant will be used."

The chamber bowed to the words, and so did I. My knees buckled without permission. Invisible fingers closed down my spine and folded me forward. I choked on the air around me.

Rhaelin lunged for me, half-drawing his blade, muscles coiled to strike. The Veil's gaze slid over me, and the world pressed harder, pinning him mid-step. His sword trembled in his grip, his jaw clenched tight enough to crack stone, green eyes blazing with a fury that promised.

The Veil's second command fell, colder than death. "Or I will force it myself."

The force snapped. I pitched forward, caught by Rhaelin's arms, his grip crushing me to his chest. Rage shook him, his breath ragged, every muscle straining against the Veil's will. His eyes locked on it, defiance warring with powerlessness, a predator caged by something older, stronger.

His face was a mask of anguish, eyes determined like he could will the Veil out of existence. For a heartbeat, I thought he might try—damn the consequences, damn the war. But then I felt it: the shift, the choice. His promise from last night, whispered in the dark with my trembling hands in his: Don't fight them here. Don't start the war for me.

Slowly—like the motion dragged a century behind it— Rhaelin lowered his sword. Metal kissed stone with a ringing finality. His shoulders sank, not in defeat, but in deadly restraint, each breath drawn like it hurt to hold the world instead of break it.

Then he moved.

Not toward the Veil, not toward the council.

Toward me.

Rhaelin dropped to one knee, bowing his head—not in obedience, but in allegiance. A vow made in silence, for me alone. My heart stuttered. My gratitude rose, fierce and aching.

I am with you.

Do what you came to do.

I faced the council. Seraphine's gaze gleamed, a cat savoring a mouse. Cassira stood rigid, a statue with a pulsing throat. Merek's fingers twitched over his rings, calculating costs. Kalor's smile dripped with delight, relishing the chaos. Only Orien remained still, her gaze steady, as if she'd foreseen this moment and waited for it to unfold.

Then in an instant, the Veil vanished, its absence a sudden release. Torches flared back to life, their flames gasping as if drowned. For a heartbeat, I thought it was over.

Then the floor split, and the Severant rose.

It came up out of the stone as if the tower had grown it. Black obsidian, the smell of hot metal and old blood. Two curved blades stood like crescent moons facing each other with empty space between—space meant for breath, for light, for our tether. Runes writhed along them, white flaring to red, red to white, endless. At the base, a shallow bowl waited where I could only assume our blood would be collected.

A low vibration began—not a hum, but a pulse, clawing at the space between us.

Rhaelin stepped in front of me, his body a shield. He moved forward first, placing his hand on top of the left curved blade jutting from the Severant. Metal bit deep, and his black blood started flowing as he applied more pressure. The runes flared in response.

He didn't wince or clean his palm. He pulled his hand away without looking at it, blood dripping onto stone. Instead, his gaze locked on mine and he stepped behind me. Close enough that the heat of him wrapped my back, and the tether steadied.

It was my turn.

The Severant drew me like a rip current. The closer I stepped, the stronger the pull. It wasn't just in my chest—

it was in my teeth, my eyes.

Lennan's voice rose in my head.

When it wakes, you'll want to hold your breath. Don't. Find the pulse between the strikes. Use it.

I set my palm to the twin blade.

I glanced over my shoulder. Rhaelin stood close behind, blood no longer dripping from his palm—one of the perks of immortality. His eyes burning into my back. He gave me nothing, no words, no command. Just a single nod of his head. With that, I pressed my hand against the opposite blade.

The cut was instant and searing. My blood spilled fast, red flowing down the metal. The device drank it greedily, the bowl at its base filling, the red light crawling to meet the glow already burning on Rhaelin's side.

Our halves answered each other. Each side of the Severant brightened when our blood met. The bond buckled, not wanting to go where the Severant was dragging it. I felt Rhaelin's body flex behind me like he would tear the device out of the floor if I asked.

"Breathe," I murmured, strained with the effort to defy the Severant's will.

He did. In, out—his rhythm, not the tower's. The Severant's light climbed higher, the crescent blades pulsing white, then red, as our blood soaked through. The taste of metal filled my mouth.

The council leaned in. Seraphine's smile widened. Cassira's eyes were bright. Merek muttered calculations. Orien never looked away.

The Severant's rumble grew. It found us.

The first tug was gentle, probing. The bond recoiled, pulling away from the heat. The device pursued, pulling harder. The line of light thickened, brightening like a star.

I felt it in my throat—where Rhaelin had bitten, where the skin hadn't fully healed. Pain flickered there, a slow warm leak down my neck.

I closed my eyes and breathed Rhaelin's pattern.

In four, out six. The Severant didn't care.

Another pull came, and I felt it in the center of me. The line of light snapped into focus. It wasn't a line at all. It was a braid. Three strands weaving and unweaving so fast it looked solid. One of them burned like Rhaelin—dark, steady. One of them burned like me—bright and restless. The third—small, quieter—was what Lennan had called the seam. The place bonds hide when they don't want to be found. Where they gather themselves when the world tries to tear them apart.

The device went for the seam.

Pain slid in—not the kind that screams. The kind that whispers. The kind that lets you think you can bear it, and then, inch by inch, walks inside your skin and asks for more.

My knees went soft. I set my feet wider and locked them. Rhaelin's hand found my back.

It brightened by the second. The braid between us grew thicker, brighter, until I could see it with my eyes closed. It pushed at my ribs. The council watched every movement.

Rhaelin's grip tightened. Every rune, every breath, every tremor that ran through his hand and into my own bones. The cut in my palm burned and then went numb.

The Severant drew a breath. The entire device began to flash white. And then it screamed.

The sound didn't come from the machine. It came from inside the bond, from the seam itself, like the braid had found a voice. It tore straight through me. My back bowed. My mouth opened and air left, but I didn't hear my own sound. Only the Severant's.

Rhaelin moved behind me—closer, his chest against my spine, holding me up without caging me. Every part of him said: *don't run, don't break, I am here.*

The scream slid through the chamber. For a breath's length, there was nothing. No pain. No sound. Only the bright line and his hands and my pulse.

Out six.

The Severant struck again. Sharper now, lower. It found the old pain in me and dragged it open—the places grief had carved, the places rage had filled with heat. My hands curled into fists. The room tilted.

I looked up and found Orien's gaze. She inclined her head the barest fraction. I couldn't tell what it meant.

Then, one last time. The Severant hitting the note it had been tuning for. The device lifted.

Pain opened its mouth.

I could feel my scream building in my chest, dragging claws all the way up. I could feel the seam come undone in the braid before us.

Rhaelin's lips brushed my ear. "I'm here," he said again, like a prayer, like a vow that had survived the blood and the ash and the years between. But I could feel his grasp on me slipping, his strength deteriorating.

I locked my knees. I set my palm harder on the blade. I fixed my eyes on the far wall so I wouldn't look at the council, wouldn't give them the satisfaction of my face.

The Severant took its breath.

And then it began to tear.

CHAPTER THIRTY-SIX

ZYRENNA

Pain.

Not the kind that makes you cry and then dulls. Not the kind that comes in a rush and fades. This was pain that set fire to nerves. Pain that unraveled me from the inside, deliberately and patiently.

This was the pain Lennan had warned me of. The kind that you don't walk away from, the kind that comes *for* you.

Every nerve in my body felt like it was being pulled, replacing blood with shards of glass. It felt like the air was carving me open from the inside. My scream turned hoarse too quickly, collapsing into a rasp that made me taste blood in my throat. The device did not relent. It wouldn't. It didn't need sound, it needed everything beneath it.

I clawed for my center, for anything that still belonged to me. But each strike stripped something else away, every limb began shaking so violently I couldn't keep control of them. My legs refused to hold.

The tether blazed. The bond that had once been a warmth beneath my skin turned into a noose that tightened with every pull. Each flare yanked a fresh scream out of me, no matter how hard I tried to keep silent. My throat tore until blood mixed with the sound.

Only a few feet separated Rhaelin and me now. He was still there, he was *always* there. But I could see his body begin to shake too. The Severant had its teeth in him as surely as it did me. His black blood streaked down his chin from where he'd bitten into his own lip to keep from roaring. His shoulders hunched, trembling as though even his immortal bones couldn't bear it.

I couldn't hold back. It felt like every bone in my body was snapping, then rebuilding, again and again. I screamed to the point where the look on Kalor's face resembled shock, like none of them had witnessed this level of agony before. "RHAE—" I couldn't finish the words, it was too painful.

He crawled over to me, somehow pinning me with his eyes—evidence that he was far stronger physically and mentally than I ever could have imagined. The light between us was a ball of blue and orange flame at this distance. He took my face in his hands, his face displaying desperation on every line, but still refused to look away from me.

"Ren, stay with me. Stay the fuck with me!" he muttered even in the most painful moment of it all. He tried to keep me alive. "I'm so sorry, I'm so sorry, I-" he choked on this last one, then began repeating the words in a whisper. The vast chamber and howling machine veiling everything from prying ears.

When I looked up, I noticed Orien leaving the room. Suddenly disoriented, I looked back at Rhaelin, reaching a hand up to his face and smiled. "I wouldn't take a second of anything back when it comes to you. I would choose you over and over," I said in barely a whisper, almost inaudible—lost beneath the Severant's lingering scream and the blood rushing.

The council watched from across the chamber, faces twisted in shock and calculation, but the deafening roar of the device and the vast stone hall swallowed our words whole. They saw the desperation. They didn't hear the truth.

"Absolutely fucking not." His voice broke, his hands trembling against my face. "Do not say that to me. Don't you dare." His forehead pressed to mine, breath ragged, words spilling between his teeth.

"You are not leaving me, Ren. Do you hear me? You will not *fucking* leave me. You promised me," his voice cracked, "I promised your sister. You do *not* get to go without me. I will be right behind you."

Alira's voice echoed in me, a ghost of hope and fear tangled as one. I couldn't leave her—the thought of breaking her like that nearly split me open.

I barely nodded my head in response. The obsidian walls stretched and warped, the runes blurring into streaks of blood-red light.

The Severant struck again.

My body convulsed—knees digging into the stone. My fingernails scraped the floor, blood streaking as if it were clawing for a way out.

And then Lennan's voice returned, a thread through the chaos:

The Third Breath. Collapse it inward. When you think there's nothing left, it's yours. Only yours.

I felt it then—the seam, the hidden braid intertwined with the tether. The thing that held us, formed us. And beneath it, I felt the edge. There was an end to this pain. It had a limit; it would break us both soon.

I turned my focus inward, dragging every scrap of energy I had left to the center of my chest. The pain wasn't pain anymore; it was everything. I envisioned the seam being pulled toward only me. Until I could feel nothing of Rhaelin except the echo of his heartbeat.

My lungs seized as I gathered it. Breath burned like fire down my throat. The Severant's claws raked against the inside of me, desperate to pry it free before I could. It was like trying to hold molten iron with bare hands. My vision flickered.

Right before I took the first inhale, I turned my head toward Rhaelin. His face was blood and desperation, fangs bared, eyes wild. Everything in him screamed to fight.

"NOW!"

At first, I saw confusion flicker between his eyebrows—frozen for half a heartbeat. Then his eyes changed. Fury ripped through them, bright and wild, the same fury I'd felt in the vineyard. He remembered my plea: *if you get even a second to fight, take it.*

And he did.

I saw the pain leaving him. The raw torment etched across his face unraveled, his body loosening like chains had fallen away. His eyes widened—not in relief, but in horror. Because we both knew where it had gone. Into me.

Rhaelin exploded forward like the weapon they all feared he was. His sword was in his hand before the nearest guard could blink. The first strike opened a throat; blood sprayed the stone. Steel struck. He moved like he'd been waiting years for permission.

I held the breath until my vision blackened, until the Severant's pull became teeth on bone. Then I let go, slow but ragged, my knees trembling against the floor. The machine screamed louder.

Second breath, in.

I drew it deep, deeper than my body wanted. The seam flickered where it entered into my chest, continuing to force it inward.

Rhaelin's boots struck stone, the hiss of steel and the grunt of a dying man filling the chamber. Another guard—he was taking them out first, silencing them before they could call for reinforcements. He was a shadow of motion at the edge of my vision—cutting, breaking, fury given form.

The Council roared around us, but the Severant drowned it all out.

I felt my body shutting down. Blood pooled around me, no longer knowing its source. Pain tore through me—twice—carried and doubled back, holding two breaking bodies inside one skin. My vision tunneled, the room tilted.

Third breath.

I pulled it in until my lungs screamed, until spots burst in my vision. I dragged it long, slower, slower, slower, my chest caving around it. I could feel it dying, folding in on itself, a star collapsing.

And then the exhale.

My scream would have been loud enough to wake gods— the kind of sound that shakes mountains, and burns through marrow.

It was not release. It was ruin. The seam collapsed, all light sucked to a single point. My body gave with it, falling, breaking, emptied.

The last thing I felt was his hands cradling my face, his voice a desperate, endless sound pouring into my skin. His green eyes were the last thing I saw before the light inside me went

out and the black swallowed everything.
No more pain.
No more sound.
Nothing.

CHAPTER THIRTY-SEVEN

RHAELIN

Her body went slack in my arms, heavy with a stillness that carved me hollow. The tether—the blazing thread that bound us—flickered once, a final, desperate convulsion, then died. Not dimmed, not quieted, but gone. Its absence ripped through me, a wound deeper than steel, tearing my chest open. The world narrowed to a high, keening silence, the chamber's sounds swallowed by the void where her pulse should have been.

I laid her down, as I had Thalia, Elias, my mother, my father. Slowly, as if time might turn backwards if I set her down with enough care. My fingers trembled as I smoothed her black hair from her face, brushing a streak of blood from her cheek, willing her to breathe again. Her skin was warm, but empty.

The pain hit first—white-hot, blinding, a silence that screamed—and behind it, the beast I'd chained for a century broke free, its hunger shaking my bones.

I stood, the weight of my rage filling the chamber like a gathering storm. My hand found the hilt of my sword, slick with blood from the two guards I'd already cut down, their bodies crumpled at my feet. Steel gleamed as I lifted it, my eyes burning with a fury that could raise empires. Two more guards stood at the door, their spears trembling. The council froze—Seraphine's cruel smile gone, Cassira's pulse racing in her throat. Orien long gone by then.

The entire chamber felt it: the hush. They had broken me. There was no restraint left to barter with.

"Ultimately," I said, voice low, each word cutting through the silence, "this all would have ended the same way, wouldn't it? We refuse the Severant, you attempt to kill us. We use the Severant, she lives, you attempt to kill her. We use the Severant, she dies—I slaughter you." My eyes swept the table, pinning each of them in place. "Violence was always the end."

The guards shifted, their spears wavering. I moved before their breath escaped, my sword flashing once, twice. Their necks opened, blood arcing as they collapsed, armor crashing against stone, louder than their silenced screams. Four bodies now lay before me, a testament to their ruin.

Kalor roared, leaping from his chair. His fangs bared.

I stepped closer, sword dripping, the tether's void a gaping wound in my chest.

We met in a crash of steel. He swung heavy and fast—rage lending him speed, a lifetime of privilege lending him sloppiness. My blade turned his, slipping inside his guard, carving across his chest. Armor split; black and crimson spilled. He staggered, disbelief etching his face. He lunged again, reckless. I let his blade graze my shoulder, pivoted, and slammed my elbow into his jaw. Bone cracked. He stumbled, but I pressed forward, my sword slicing a long line down his arm, blood pooling. It was not fight—it was torment. A taunt for the lives he'd cost me. It would be nothing to finish him now.

Seraphine was yelling, Cassira barking orders at no one.

I looked back at Kalor, but his gaze passed me, snagging on something over my shoulder—and dropped his sword.

A sound split the chamber, a high-pitched sound, and with it I turned.

The Severant was breaking.

Its runes cracked, sparks jumped and died. The blades shuddered, and then the machine split down its heart with a shriek.

I turned when movement came from the corner of my eye. A breath. Twice now, deeper. On the third, the tether roared back to life so violently my knees buckled. It was not gentle, it came in the form of a flood. Light slammed into me from that visible point where she was lying. I braced, lungs heaving on a laugh that was more shock.

Light opened under her skin. It ran through her like molten metal. The wounds at her throat glowed blue-white, refusing to break again.

Her eyes opened.

I'd memorized every shade they'd ever been. The color I had bled for. The color I had steadied with my hands. Now they were something else. Silver caught on permanent fire. Not mortal. Not vampire. Not anything the Houses could catalog and sell. Power sat in them like someone reborn.

The whole chamber bore witness. Smirks and indulgent smiles vanished. In a breath, they were glancing at one another—then bolting for the doors. All but Kalor.

Zyrenna rose slowly, still covered with blood—her blood—dark against her skin. Her hair shimmering like moonlight, alive with a permanent glow. She was herself, yet more—divine, unyielding. Her eyes met mine, her lips curving in a sure, radiant smile.

I mirrored it, a flicker of recognition. Not victory, not survival, but unity. The Severant, meant to tear us apart, had forged us instead. The tether was no longer a thread but a single current, night and moonlight fused. The histories spoke of bonds—rare and holy, gentle in their telling. But none spoke of this—of a bond that refused the will of the Spire, of the Veil, of fate itself.

She took a step toward me.

Pain lived in her—there was no pretending otherwise. It sat at the base of her throat, in her nightmares, in the way her breath cut short. But pain did not own her now. She moved like it had been demoted.

I reached for her; she reached back. Her fingers slid into mine, cold meeting heat, the tether humming like a pulse at my spine.

Her eyes cut past me to Kalor. He stood there in shock— unable to move.

Zyrenna squeezed my hand. She bent down and lifted my fallen sword. She set it in my other hand. The barest bow of her head, implying: *finish it.*

"Look at me," I said to Kalor.

He did. Because there are orders even monsters obey.

I released her hand and moved behind Kalor, his body locked in place. My left hand clamped hard around his jaw and dragged his head back.

"When the others join you," I said in his ear, voice steady, "remember who sent them."

Steel drew a clean line. Heat burst into my hands; his body crumpled. The thud against obsidian felt like something I'd been owed a lifetime.

For my mother. For my father. For Thalia. For Elias. For

every name the Houses had made nameless.

I let the sword fall. The ring of it traveled, touched every wall.

I turned back to Zyrenna.

Closer, until her heat erased everything else. I took her chin in my fingers and lifted. I had to see. I had to anchor on the silver blaze in her eyes, on the life I would not surrender to any throne. The tether bowed, as if this was something sacred. I felt her breath as if my lungs had learned her beat. A tremor rolled through the Spire. Torches flared like the tower itself had inhaled.

Without sound crossing the space, without opening her mouth, her voice slid clean into my mind.

Not a feeling, not a flare—a voice.

The reign they built dies in this room, Rhaelin.

I allowed her words to sink into me, allowed it to consume every nerve in my mind. I reached for the sound, for the heat of her mind brushing mine, the door that had always been half-open, but never enough.

When I found it, when I found her, the words poured into her mind.

Then I will put them on their knees for you. Every one of them. And I will make sure you are the last thing they see standing.

And far above, in the walls of the Spire, something old stirred awake.

Acknowledgements

First, I would like to thank my family. Their continuous support throughout this process has been unwavering.

To my mom: Your constant check-ins, full of questions and curiosity, fueled my excitement toward creating and allowed me to express my passion for what I was building. You made space for my dream long before it existed. I love you more than anything.

To my dad: For bringing me chocolate milk on those late nights and always telling me how proud you were. Those moments kept me going. *(Also, if you're reading this, please pretend you stopped at the title page — for both our sakes. I love you.)*

To my sister Kaylee: Thank you for providing my writing space and pushing me through the passion I developed for these characters and this story. I hope you loved this first book.

To my sister, Gabby: Thank you for taking the time to help me create this book I'm so incredibly proud of. This was born because of you! Your criticism, comments, and adjustments helped make it what it is. Thank you for pushing me to bring this story to life in Turks.

To my best friend, Tara. This story got it's soul because of you. Every late-night talk, every wild idea I threw your way in the beginning, every moment you listened, helped shape what this book became. The heart of this story, and the direction it will take in the next two, wouldn't exist without the space you gave me to be completely and unapologetically myself. You are my sunshine, and your excitement for this world has filled me with more gratitude than I will ever be able to express.

To Karissa—for all your endless support and graphic work throughout this process. You have been my hypewoman the entire way through and I cannot express my gratitude enough.

To the readers, to anyone who found their way into these pages, thank you. If even ten of you fall in love with these characters and this world the way I have, then every one of the hundreds of hours spent creating it was worth it. I cannot wait to do it all again, for you.

About the Author

J.G. Reese writes dark romance wrapped in the haunting beauty of fantasy—stories born from a lifelong fascination with love, power, and the parts of ourselves we try to hide. A devoted reader since childhood, J.G. grew up chasing the ache of stories that linger long after the last page. When she couldn't find enough books that blended the shadows of romance with the wonder of fantasy, she decided to write her own.

Outside of writing, J.G. is pursuing a career as a mental health therapist, exploring how love, grief, and trauma shape the human experience. That same curiosity for the mind and heart breathes life into every character and the world she's built.

Flamebound marks the beginning of the *Thrones of the Veil Trilogy*, with books two and three in the works. J.G. lives in New Jersey, where she enjoys late-night writing sessions, coffee-fueled edits, and dreams that her stories might touch the heart of just one person.

You can connect with me on:

🌐 https://www.jgreese.com

Subscribe to my newsletter:

✉ https://www.jgreese.com/newsletter